SPENCER'S COVE

What Reviewers Say About Missouri Vaun's Work

Take My Hand

"The chemistry between River and Clay is off the charts and their sex scenes were just plain hot!"—*Les Rêveur*

"The small town charms of *Take My Hand* evoke the heady perfume of pine needles and undergrowth, birdsong, and summer cocktails with friends."—*Omnivore Bibliosaur*

The Ground Beneath

"One of my favourite things about Missouri Vaun's writing is her ability to write the attraction between two women. Somehow she manages to get that twinkle in the stomach just right and she makes me feel it as if I am falling in love with my wife all over again." —*The Lesbian Review*

Crossing the Wide Forever

"*Crossing the Wide Forever* is a near-heroic love story set in an epic time, told with almost lyrical prose. Words on the page will carry the reader, along with the main characters, back into history and into adventure. It's a tale that's easy to read, with enchanting main characters, despicable villains, and supportive friendships, producing a fascinating account of passion and adventure." —*Lambda Literary Review*

All Things Rise

"The futuristic world that author Missouri Vaun has brought to life is as interesting as it is plausible. The sci-fi aspect, though, is not hard-core which makes for easy reading and understanding of the technology prevalent in the cloud cities. ...[T]he focus was really on the dynamics of the characters especially Cole, Ava and Audrey—whether they were interacting on the ground or above the clouds. From the first page to the last, the writing was just perfect."—*AoBibliosphere*

"Simply put, this book is easy to love. Everything about it makes for a wonderful read and re-read. I was able to go on a journey with these characters, an emotional, internal journey where I was able to take a look at the fact that while society and technology can change vastly until almost nothing remains the same, there are some fundamentals that never change, like hope, the raw emotion of human nature, and the far reaching search for the person who is able to soothe the fire in our souls with the love in theirs."—*Roses and Whimsy*

Birthright

"The author develops a world that has a medieval feeling, complete with monasteries and vassal farmers, while also being a place and time where a lesbian relationship is just as legitimate and open as a heterosexual one. This kept pleasantly surprising me throughout my reading of the book. The adventure part of the story was fun, including traveling across kingdoms, on "wind-ships" across deserts, and plenty of sword fighting. ...This book is worth reading for its fantasy world alone. In our world, where those in the LGBTQ communities still often face derision, prejudice, and danger for living and loving openly, being immersed in a world where the Queen can openly love another woman is a refreshing break from reality."
—Amanda Chapman, Librarian, Davisville Free Library (RI)

The Time Before Now

"[*The Time Before Now*] is just so good. Vaun's character work in this novel is flawless. She told a compelling story about a person so real you could just about reach out and touch her."—*The Lesbian Review*

Jane's World and the Case of the Mail Order Bride

"This is such a quirky, sweet novel with a cast of memorable characters. It has laugh out loud moments and will leave you feeling charmed."—*The Lesbian Review*

Love at Cooper's Creek

"Blown away…how have I not read a book by Missouri Vaun before. What a beautiful love story which, honestly, I wasn't ready to finish. Kate and Shaw's chemistry was instantaneous and as the reader I could feel it radiating off the page."—*Les Reveur*

"*Love at Cooper's Creek* is a gentle, warm hug of a book."—*The Lesbian Review*

Visit us at www.boldstrokesbooks.com

By the Author

All Things Rise

The Time Before Now

The Ground Beneath

Whiskey Sunrise

Valley of Fire

Death by Cocktail Straw

One More Reason to Leave Orlando

Smothered and Covered

Privacy Glass

Birthright

Crossing the Wide Forever

Love at Cooper's Creek

Take My Hand

Proxima Five

Spencer's Cove

Writing as Paige Braddock:

Jane's World: The Case of the Mail Order Bride

SPENCER'S COVE

by

Missouri Vaun

2019

CREDITS
EDITOR: CINDY CRESAP
PRODUCTION DESIGN: SUSAN RAMUNDO
COVER PHOTO BY MICHAEL RYAN
COVER DESIGN BY SHERI (HINDSIGHTGRAPHICS@GMAIL.COM)

Acknowledgments

Point Arena, California, is one of my favorite places. While this book is not technically set in Point Arena, my experiences there contributed heavily to the setting of this story. The photo on the cover, taken by Michael Ryan (an amazing nature photographer), is a shot of the coastline near Point Arena.

Rachel, my favorite local librarian, was incredibly helpful with research. Thank you!

I'd like to thank my beta readers, Jenny, D. Jackson Leigh, Vanessa, and Alena. And as always, thanks to the amazing crew at Bold Strokes Books, Rad, Sandy, Ruth, Paula, and my editor, Cindy.

The characters in this story came to me with vivid voices. I hope you enjoy their journey. Welcome to Spencer's Cove.

Dedication

To Evelyn, everything with you is magic.

CHAPTER ONE

Something pressed down on Foster, making it hard to breathe. It began to move. Points of intense pressure across her ribcage. The true horror came next, cat breath. She blinked. A sharp glare bounced off the hardwood floor from the uncovered window, bathing part of the sofa in sunlight. Daylight, unwelcome, and far too bright.

"Gah...stop breathing on me."

William Faulkner, twenty pounds of orange striped fur and feline girth, stood on her chest, his nose almost touching hers. A whiff of tuna arrived with every exhale.

"I'm up, I'm up."

Foster heaved the cat off as she rolled over. She'd fallen asleep on the couch, again. She rotated and sat up. Her faded flannel shirt was buttoned wrong and the collar was all askew. She rolled her shoulders and tilted her head from side to side; her neck popped and cracked. The side of her face tingled. The edge of the laptop had left a crease across her cheek. She rubbed the indentation with her fingers in an attempt to get the feeling to return. Foster was only thirty-five, but this morning she felt a hell of a lot older. The ergonomics of her grandma's hand-me-down sofa left a lot to be desired. A perpetual dent in the cushion where the springs had given out was clearly where her grandma sat each day to watch her *story*. She'd been a loyal follower of *Days of Our Lives* until her passing.

William Faulkner meowed loudly from the kitchen doorway. No doubt she'd forgotten to top off his bowl of kibble before falling asleep on her laptop.

"Stop yelling at me. I'm up, for cryin' out loud."

Just as she topped off his bowl, her cell phone buzzed on the counter, somewhere. Several days of story notes, magazines, and newspapers had to be shuffled before she found it. When she saw who was calling she considered not answering it, but she knew Rosalind would just keep hitting redial until Foster picked up. Rosalind King, her literary agent in New York City, had no respect for mornings, or those who were slow to rise.

Well, coffee was definitely in order to deal with whatever this conversation was going to be about.

"Hello, Rosalind." She put the phone on speaker and poured coffee beans into the grinder. She waited until she heard Rosalind's voice on the other end before turning it on. The grinder was so loud it might as well have been chewing metal.

"...are you finished?"

She'd missed the first half of whatever Rosalind had been saying, unable to hear it over the kitchen machinery.

"Sorry, I'm making coffee."

"You know that phone probably has a mute button."

"Really?" Foster pressed the cover down so that the grinder buzzed loudly again near the phone.

"It sounds like you're making coffee with a leaf blower."

Rosalind had a sense of humor. Foster always gave her points for that.

"How's the manuscript coming along?"

"I'm making progress." She basically said that every time Rosalind asked.

Foster had managed to write an entire paragraph the previous day, but almost as soon as she lifted her fingers off the keyboard had decided it was rubbish and deleted it. She'd been suffering from writer's block and was beginning to worry that it was never going to dissipate. Voicing the worry out loud would only make the whole situation more real, so she opted for denial and kept it to herself.

"I have a job for you."

"Dang it." Small mounds of ground coffee spilled on the counter, like potting soil from the garden.

"You haven't even heard what the job is yet."

"Sorry, I spilled the coffee grounds before I got them into the filter." She scooped them up with a spoon as best as she could and swept the rest into the sink, then dusted her palm across her boxer shorts.

"As I was saying, I have a job for you."

"You mean besides the job where I write books and you sell them to a publisher?" Foster took the phone off speaker and held it to her ear. She leaned against the counter's edge waiting for her morning brew to brew.

"Yes, see, that's the thing…when you don't actually write a book, then I can't sell it, and neither of us makes any money."

Foster pinched the bridge of her nose.

"Are you still there?"

"Yeah, I'm listening." She owed Rosalind. Most agents would probably have dropped an author who couldn't deliver, or at the very least, stopped calling them. Especially since she'd been unable to finish a new manuscript for almost three years.

"I got a call late yesterday from an attorney in San Francisco. She wants to hire you to ghostwrite a memoir for a client of hers. A woman named Abigail Spencer."

"That sounds like a terrible idea. I write mystery novels, thrillers. I've never written a memoir before—"

"She's offering to pay forty thousand dollars."

Foster had just taken a sip of coffee and almost choked. A coughing fit ensued.

"Are you okay? Should I call nine-one-one?" There wasn't even a hint of real concern.

"Forty thousand dollars?" Her voice cracked and she coughed again.

"I told her you'd take it." The rustle of shuffling papers came through the phone. "I emailed you the ticket info for the flight to San Francisco. You leave tomorrow morning."

"Rosalind, I don't know..."

"Foster, you need to be working, writing...I think this is a great opportunity to break out of your...well, whatever slump you're in." Rosalind paused. "Should I have turned it down?"

After taking a few seconds to do the math in her head, Foster confirmed that she really had no choice. Her bank account was on life support and she had a mortgage to pay, not to mention the monthly tab for cases of Fancy Feast that William Faulkner demanded. He required a full bowl of hard kibble with a serving of Fancy Feast on the side or things got ugly. He could literally scream meow for hours when he felt shortchanged for dinner.

"No, you did the right thing." She refilled her coffee cup. "I'll do it."

"Great. I'll send you the rest of the details. Call me in a week and let me know how things are going."

"Hey, Rosalind..."

"Yes?"

"Why me?"

"What?"

"Why did she want to hire me, specifically?"

"Apparently, this Abigail Spencer is a fan...and there's some sort of mystery about the family history." A second phone rang in the background. "Okay, well, I've gotta go. Call me in a week."

"Bye—" Rosalind had already clicked off.

Foster took several sips of her coffee. There had to be some catch to this. Forty thousand dollars was a crazy amount of money for a memoir that might not even be much of a story. Whoever this Abigail Spencer was she obviously had more money than sense. She pictured a matronly older lady, sipping tea daintily, surrounded by family albums, heirlooms, and several cats.

She topped off her coffee and went outside to get yesterday's mail. She was looking down as she shuffled envelopes of junk mail and didn't notice William Faulkner until it was too late. The way he looked at her through the window of the door, she knew he was standing partly on the washer, with one paw on the doorknob. She lunged for the door, sloshing her coffee, but a millisecond before she reached the handle she heard the unmistakable sound of the deadbolt handle flip, sliding the lock into the doorframe.

"No, no, no, nooooooo!" Foster banged on the door.

Unmoved by her threatening display, William Faulkner sniffed the air, stared at her for a moment, and then jumped down. He showed her his hind end as he leisurely strolled out of the laundry room into the living room. She stood at the window in her boxer shorts, barefoot, holding coffee and the mail as he calmly curled up in a sunny spot on the sofa.

"Damn you, William Faulkner," she said to no one.

Great. Now she'd have to walk down to her neighbor Patty's house to retrieve the spare key to get into her own house. She and Patty kept keys for each other in the event of pet care or other emergencies. Patty worked nights at the hospital, so with any luck she'd be home to give Foster the key. This was the second time William Faulkner had stepped on the deadbolt handle and locked her out. The last time she'd been fully dressed and wearing shoes, this time, she wasn't so lucky.

She dropped the mail on the steps in a haphazard pile and started down the street with her coffee. It was late morning, probably around eleven, so of course her neighbor, the elderly Mrs. Washington, was stooped over, tending her flower garden. Mrs. Washington stood and studied Foster. She looked at Foster as if she'd just seen the Lord himself walk by buck naked.

"Good morning, Mrs. Washington. Beautiful day, isn't it?" She tipped her coffee mug in Mrs. Washington's direction as if walking down the street half-dressed was the most normal thing in the world. As if grown women always wore plaid shirts and Sponge Bob Squarepants boxers when they strolled the neighborhood barefoot.

Mrs. Washington frowned and shook her head as Foster walked past where she stood in a large patch of bright yellow daffodils.

❖

Sunlight had not yet pierced the marine layer. A thick fog hid the horizon from view, the gray, damp cover like dense clouds riding the waves across the surface of the Pacific. By noon the fog would withdraw, and from this clifftop vantage, Abigail Spencer would have a breathtaking miles-long view of a rugged swath of the Northern California coastline. But not at this early hour. Before the warmth of the sun was allowed to reach the ground, everything would remain as it was now: cold, damp, and painted in myriad hues of gray.

Abby tightened the cashmere scarf around her neck and tucked it snuggly into the collar of her coat. A wisp of hair pulled loose and swept across her face in the steady breeze. She tugged her wool beanie down farther over her ears, taming the flyaway strands.

Her morning ritual since returning to Spencer's Cove was to ride along the cliffs, away from the lighthouse to the south, and then circle back to the house just as Cora had the teakettle boiling. Boots shifted beneath her. She leaned over and patted his neck. His coat was jet-black against the gray line of sea and fog. He stopped and turned so that Abby could face the ocean. Inhaling deeply awarded her the crisp scent of brine. Far below the high, dark cliff, a small strip of wet sand was slowly reclaimed by the returning tide. Swells grew as they rolled toward shore, crashed, and then withdrew as if the ocean also needed to draw a cleansing breath.

The idea of returning to her family's estate had been a withdrawal of sorts, but now she wondered if she'd made a mistake. The dreams had followed her anyway.

Focus on something positive. Don't go there.

Since her retreat home, the extensive library had become her comfort the past few weeks. She'd found solace in her return to literary friendships. She'd gone back to worlds she'd visited long ago, before leaving for college on the East Coast and then study abroad. Personal relationships came with a risk she wasn't sure she was ready to face again, or ever. She was alone but not lonely, so maybe this was her life. A solitary path. There were worse things.

Besides, she wasn't truly alone; she had the horses, and their care was almost a full-time job.

Cora was also with her. Cora had been taking care of the house since before her parents' deaths. She was the closest thing Abby had to family now, well, except for Gertrude Hampton, who managed the legal and financial affairs of the Spencer estate and was far too invested in Abby's lack of a romantic life.

The wind picked up and she shivered. Just thinking of holding a hot cup of tea between her chilled fingers was all it took for Boots to turn and head back toward the barn, as if he'd read her thoughts. Maybe he had.

The stable door was open as they approached, and Evan Bell, the new groundskeeper, stepped out to greet them, carrying a halter for Boots. It was still early so she hadn't expected to see anyone, but Evan seemed to have a similar habit of not sleeping in. Abby wondered if Evan suffered from bad dreams too. Evan had only been working on the property for a couple of weeks, too short a time for very many personal questions. Additionally, Evan was reserved. Abby might even have described her as aloof.

Evan was an imposing woman, taller than Abby by several inches, broad shouldered, with an athletic build. If she had to guess Evan's age she'd place her somewhere around forty, but of course she hadn't asked. Evan's brown hair was cut all one length, and it fell to the edge of her square jawline. Usually Evan wore a waxed cotton baseball cap that shadowed her dark eyes and kept her hair away from her face. This morning was no exception.

"Did you have a nice ride, Miss Spencer?" Evan swapped the bridle Boots was wearing while Abby removed the saddle.

"I wish you'd call me Abby." Miss Spencer sounded so formal, so distant, so old. She was just about to turn thirty and not ready to feel old.

"Yes, Miss Spencer—Abby." Evan turned Boots out in a separate paddock to cool down.

Abby took the saddle into the dark interior of the barn. She hadn't been sure about hiring Evan, but when George, the previous groundskeeper, had retired, Gertie had insisted. It was probably for the best. If Gertie hadn't jumped in and hired someone from out of the area it would likely have taken Abby forever to find someone. Especially since most of the locals believed the Spencer mansion was haunted. Maybe it was haunted, but if that was the case then the ghosts were friendly because the sprawling estate was the one place Abby felt most safe.

Abby leaned against the railing of the enclosure that abutted the barn. A brown mare stood in the grassy open area watching her. Her name was Journey's End. She'd arrived two days ago, rescued from an abusive situation by animal control. Her flight reflex was on high alert as she studied Abby, stomping her feet, ready to flee, with head up, and tail raised.

"Has Iain been here yet?" Iain Green was the salty old gentleman who helped Abby with the care of the horses. Evan was a skilled groundskeeper, but she seemed to have less experience with horses. Although she'd obviously ridden before and liked to brush Boots after Abby's regular early morning rides. There was simply too much maintenance for one person, so Iain's help with the equine residents of the estate had been a necessity.

"I haven't seen him this morning." Evan mirrored Abby's stance, resting her forearms on the top rail of the fence a few feet away.

She liked the fact that Evan seemed aware of her need for personal space. She never crowded Abby the way some well-intentioned people did, Cora included. Actually, Cora was the only person with whom Abby allowed any physical closeness. The occasional maternal hug was all she'd permit, even though, given the opportunity, Cora would gladly fuss over her like a mother hen.

Abby opened the gate and walked with slow, easy steps toward the mare. Halfway across the enclosure, Abby stopped. She focused on projecting calm. After a minute, the animal visibly relaxed, planted all four feet on the ground, and lowered her head.

"Everything is okay now. You're safe," she whispered. She stopped within a few feet of the mare and waited for Journey's End to come to her. With horses, the slower the better. Especially if they'd experienced any sort of trauma. It was impossible to know what this sweet animal had endured, but old scars marred her shoulders and her flank.

The horse brushed her velvet muzzle against Abby's jacket. Only then did she tenderly settle her palm on the mare's jaw.

"Hello there." She let her fingertips drift lightly down the mare's neck to her shoulder. "I'm going to call you Journey, because yours is just beginning. A new journey to a better life, okay?"

Journey snorted and shifted her stance.

"I'll see you later. You just rest now."

Journey trailed her halfway across the enclosure but stopped before she reached the fence where Evan was still standing.

"I don't think Iain's been able to get that close to her yet." Evan opened the gate for her. "You really have a special touch with horses."

"I sometimes think we see the world in the same way." Horses had only so much tolerance for stress—noise, trauma, overstimulation. She knew she had the same threshold, and when she reached that threshold she shut down too.

"Should I tell Iain to come find you when he gets here?"

"No, that's okay. I'll speak with him later. It's not urgent." She spoke over her shoulder as she walked toward the back entrance of the large house.

The kettle whistled in the kitchen. Abby shucked out of her jacket and tossed her scarf and gloves in a bundle onto the weathered bench along the entryway at the back of the house. She swept her fingers through her hair to fluff it a little after removing the wool knit hat. It crackled with static from the change in air temperature. The golden glow of the lit fire in the kitchen created an oasis of warmth that contrasted sharply with the cool blue gray stone floor of the entryway.

"Did you and Mr. Bright Boots have a pleasant jaunt?" Cora Taylor, chief cook and house matron, turned and smiled. She was nearly sixty, but her accent still carried a hint of her childhood in Ireland.

"We did, thank you for asking. It's pretty chilly so we didn't go far." When Abby had first seen Boots she'd felt compelled to name him Bright Boots. Bright because of the sparkle in his eyes and Boots because of the two white stockings on his front feet. But now she mostly called him Boots for short.

"Here, warm your hands." Cora set a cup of steaming tea in front of Abby.

She added a dash of cream and then cradled the warm mug with both hands.

"Something smells good."

"Muffins with blueberries."

"Yum."

"My thoughts exactly." Cora set the pan on the stove and served a few of the muffins onto a plate in the center of the table. Then she joined Abby, slathering a healthy dose of butter on the warm bread before taking a bite. "Now, tell me, what are your plans for the day?"

Abby was reluctant to share that she had very few.

"That reminds me, Ms. Hampton left a message for you late yesterday. I forgot to let you know, but it seems we're to have a visitor." Cora grinned cheerfully over her tea, her round and rosy cheeks bookending her mischievous smile.

"What?" Abby's stomach clenched, and tension crept up the back of her neck. The last thing she wanted to deal with was a guest in the house.

Evan needed to make a phone call, and she was late making it. Abby had returned later than usual from her morning ride, and Evan had wanted to be sure of her return before leaving. She'd put Boots in a stall with fresh hay, and made sure Abby was in the house before she climbed in her truck and headed into town.

A secure call was only possible from a public landline, and Spencer's Cove had just one pay phone. It was located on the corner, near the library. The location was a bit public for Evan's preference, but there was no other option.

The breeze was chilly in the open-air phone booth. This wasn't the sort of booth Superman could have changed clothes in. There was no lower half and no door, only a three-sided clear plexiglass box. She cradled the receiver against her shoulder as she zipped the front of her jacket, turned up the collar, and scanned the street for onlookers.

"You're late." A woman's voice, not much more than a husky whisper through the phone.

She didn't recognize the voice, although there was something familiar that tickled Evan's ear. It was hard to even hear her over the coastal breeze winging its way past the phone booth.

"I don't control her schedule." Evan wasn't that late anyway.

"Are there any signs of transition?" Another whispered question.

"No." That wasn't entirely true. Evan had seen things she'd describe as shadows, hints, but not conclusive signs. Nothing she felt like sharing.

"Why are you still there?"

"What?" The question caught her off guard.

"Why would you still be there if you didn't feel that there was a reason to stay?"

Was this woman challenging her?

"I report what I see." She wasn't about to let this woman, whoever she was, bait her into revealing something she wasn't ready to reveal.

Evan had been in this one-phone-booth town, literally at what felt like the edge of the earth, for two weeks, and she'd not seen enough to report with certainty that they had a legitimate target. Unless this woman knew something Evan didn't, in which case she should share those details.

"I'll relay your status update to the Council."

"I—" But she'd already hung up. The dial tone drilled annoyingly into her ear.

Evan replaced the receiver and let out a long, slow breath. She stood still, head down, hands in her jacket pockets, waiting for her pulse to slow. She was pissed. Pissed off and tired of getting jerked around by some nameless, faceless whispered voice on the phone. She was the one in the field. She was the one taking all the chances, not the Council. The elders never put themselves on the line to retrieve a candidate. And she shouldn't even be here. This wasn't what she'd signed up for or what she'd trained for.

Jacqueline was dead.

She reminded herself that if not directly, then indirectly, it was her fault. Security for the ceremony had been her responsibility and she'd failed. Jacqueline had died in an uncontrolled tumble from the altar before the ritual was complete. The collapse had been catastrophic, and Evan had been badly injured in her attempt to save Jacqueline.

Because of her failure, she'd been kicked to the curb by Leath Dane. Put out to pasture, literally, by Leath, the new Council head.

Leath didn't like her. That was clear. Ever since, scratch that, their conflict had begun long before Jacqueline's death. Leath's failed seduction had caused a rift beyond repair between them. Declining the offer only made her more of a target for Leath's petty, bullying tactics.

The minute Leath had been in any position of power she'd exiled Evan to the West Coast, the lost coast.

This was nothing more than a babysitting assignment. All she was required to do was observe and report, and it was bullshit.

"Fuck."

She strode across the street to get a to-go coffee before heading back to the Spencer estate. The breakfast crowd was sparse. A couple of older men wearing well-seasoned caps sat in a booth next to the wall. Several young men in hoodies, probably surfers, were seated at a four-top near the front window. It was Evan's nature to canvas any room she entered, to catalog details about who, what, and any potential risks. In Jacqueline's service she'd done this for years. It was a hard habit to break.

"You can take a seat anywhere you like." A pretty waitress behind the counter spoke to her as she approached.

The woman was probably in her mid-thirties, warm brown skin, dreamy dark eyes, and a sexy braided bob of black hair, adorned with several gold braid cuffs. A scooped neck, faded blue T-shirt emblazoned with the restaurant's name hugged the contours of her yoga-fit curves. Skinny jeans and black Converse low tops rounded out the ensemble. *Wow, gorgeous.*

"I was hoping to get a coffee."

"Sure." The waitress reached for a paper cup near the coffee pot. "Do you need room for cream?"

"That depends on how good the coffee is."

Evan couldn't help flirting a little. The woman would either be annoyed, or maybe she wouldn't even notice. Evan wondered for a fleeting moment what it was like to have a normal life, a girlfriend, maybe even a dog.

"I make the coffee." The waitress matched Evan's direct gaze and smiled.

"I'm sure it's good then. No need to leave room for cream." Evan fished in her pocket for cash.

"To go?"

Evan had to think for a minute. It was very tempting to sit at the counter, sip coffee, and enjoy the view, but she needed to get back.

"Yeah, to go."

"Are you sure you don't want to sit and drink it here?"

Was the waitress flirting? Evan tried to read her nametag quickly so that it wouldn't seem as if she was staring at her breasts, which were nice, but the glare from the overhead light made it impossible.

"Maybe another time." And she meant it. She'd come back when her time was her own and maybe even sit and eat a meal. Evan left way too much cash on the counter for a small coffee and smiled.

"Okay, another time then."

Evan backed toward the door, and the waitress made no secret of watching her leave. The coffee was good. She smiled as she sipped. She had to stow the to-go cup in the holder and use both hands as she steered slowly along the scenic, winding two-lane road back to the Spencer place. She mulled the past couple of weeks over in her head trying to figure out why everything felt so screwed up. Although, to figure that out she'd have to rewind further than two weeks. Details from the day Jacqueline died kept cycling through her head, especially at night. Something wasn't right. Something didn't make sense. Evan couldn't put her finger on why everything was off; she just knew that it was.

Evan had only done fieldwork a few times when she was much younger, before she'd been promoted to Jacqueline's security detail. She'd forgotten what it was like to be out in the real world, surrounded by those who knew nothing of the otherness that had been her reality since she was a child, taken in and sheltered by the elders, groomed to serve them. She loved Jacqueline like the mother she never knew. She'd been happy to serve as her bodyguard.

Did sentinels usually like their candidate as much as she liked Abby? She didn't think she was supposed to have any sort of feeling about a candidate one way or the other. Evan tried her best to remain neutral, but there was something about Abby, an unguarded innocence that triggered every protective urge she possessed. If she were honest, there had been things she should have reported to the Council, but she'd kept those details to herself. And she wasn't sure just yet why.

Sometimes the truth of a thing revealed itself over time. So she'd wait. And in the meantime, trust her gut.

CHAPTER TWO

The Atlanta airport was a small city unto itself, complete with a train running every three minutes between terminals. Foster was anxious to get to her gate, having left barely enough time for the enormous line at the main security checkpoint.

Looking the way Foster looked made TSA an adventure, and not always a pleasant one. She was tall, with hardly any hips to speak of. Lanky was her mother's description. Plus, she usually wore jeans and a blazer of some sort, which hid her small breasts from view. This seemed to always cause gender confusion for TSA agents.

She'd done her best to pick a line that not only moved quickly, but where the agent operating the metal detector looked as if they'd be able to discern which gender she was. Inevitably, the guys always picked the blue icon on the scanner screen, so that she'd have to go back through once they realized their mistake. Today her choices had been a woman who looked like she'd formerly been a member of the Soviet weightlifting team and a woman who looked like she'd been a top pledge candidate for a sorority at the University of Georgia, or maybe a cheerleader. At any rate, neither option seemed great.

In the end, the choice was made for her because *Helga* waved Foster toward the sorority girl's line. Pensive and in sock feet, Foster stepped through the scanner only to be held back for further inspection.

"Would you prefer a private room?" Expertly applied eyeliner highlighted her blue eyes as the agent looked up at Foster. The nametag over the breast pocket of her pressed TSA uniform read Heather.

"No, I'm fine here."

Heather ran her palms along Foster's arms, down her ribs, then stepped a little closer and reached around to slide searching fingers up her back. This seemed more intimate than usual, right? Foster scanned the surrounding travelers, but no one seemed to be paying any attention. Now Heather was kneeling in front of her sweeping her hands slowly up the inside of Foster's leg toward her crotch. She slowed her sweep as she ran her palm across Foster's zipper. When she looked down, Heather winked.

It had been weeks, months maybe, since Foster had been on a date. This far too public intimate contact with Heather made her cheeks flame hotly.

Heather stood and smiled. "You have a nice flight." Her southern drawl was laced with flirtation.

"Uh, thank you...I mean, I will." Foster was flustered. She fumbled with her shoes, her belt, her laptop, and then dropped one wingtip shoe as she angled for a bench to reassemble herself.

Foster tried to regain her composure while she rode the train to terminal B. She reached for the overhead handlebar as the train sped toward its next stop. Had she forgotten anything? Traveling wasn't really her thing. She didn't do it often enough to have a good system in place. She'd made arrangements with Gloria to take care of William Faulkner. Gloria was the epitome of crazy cat sitters, more able to deal with pets than people. She drove Foster crazy with her long pet sitting diary notes and Ziploc bags of collected cat hair, but William Faulkner loved Gloria more than air, so Foster put up with Gloria's OCD behavior for his benefit.

She wasn't sure how long this writing trip would take. Two weeks was her hope, but it would all depend on how much research was involved.

The gate area was crowded. No one seemed to understand the concept of a line. Foster wasn't in the mood to jockey for a position so she leaned against the wall across from the gate and waited. The attorney who'd hired her had purchased a first-class ticket to San Francisco. Having never flown first class before, she was looking forward to discovering what that felt like. The speaker overhead crackled as the Delta service staff announced the first call for boarding.

Foster took a deep breath. This was it. What had she gotten herself into?

❖

Evan sank into the overstuffed armchair in the small sitting room of the cottage. The grounds job included free room and board in the cottage near the lighthouse. This had been the home of the lightkeeper originally. But no one manned the lighthouse these days, or in recent decades, and the structure would need some upgrades to be safe for visitors if it was ever turned it into an historic site for tourists.

Too bad, because in Evan's opinion, lighthouses were unique, something to be protected, experienced. She'd thought of climbing to the top when she'd first moved into the cottage, but the spiral stairs seemed unstable.

Cora always invited Evan to eat in the main house, but Evan was trying hard to keep her distance. She brought meals back to the cottage and ate alone. It was better to have some emotional detachment from the candidate, the target, so that she could remain objective. Losing objectivity could be bad, for both of them.

If this assignment ended up being the real deal, then she was supposed to report her findings and hand Abby over to the Council of Elders. She wouldn't be required to do any heavy lifting for the actual ceremony, although her assistance might be required for transport. A true positive would need to be taken back to the East Coast for the ritual of transmutation.

Thinking of Abby as nothing more than a candidate didn't settle well in her stomach. Evan had every intention of handling this case by the book so that she could get back to her old life, but something nagged at the back of her brain. Something sinister was at play here; she felt it but couldn't yet give it a name.

Evan rolled her shoulder and flexed her arm. She'd been injured in the platform collapse that had caused Jacqueline's death. No one had anticipated the accident, which was almost impossible to imagine given the fact that eleven elders with various gifts of sight were present. Evan kept replaying the day over and over, and every time, she came to the same conclusion. The accident was not an accident. Some other power had been present at the time of Jacqueline's death. It was hard to believe she was the only person who'd sensed it.

She rotated her shoulder again slowly. She'd balked at the idea of playing groundskeeper, but as it had turned out, the daily physical labor was strengthening her shoulder. In another couple of weeks, she might even be back to full strength. She brushed her fingertips over the tattoo on her forearm. The symbol meant nothing now unless she was returned to her former status.

A seagull hung in the air just outside the window, balanced on some updraft as if it were a winged hovercraft. Evan chewed the blueberry muffin slowly as she watched from her seat by the window. She'd never spent any time in this part of California and had to admit that the landscape was stunning, ruggedly wild and beautiful. If someone wanted to hide, this would be a good place to do it.

❖

The flight seemed shorter than the allotted time, probably because Foster was nervous. This whole excursion had all the earmarks of a bad idea: air turbulence, crowded terminals, and surly flight attendants, yes, even in first class.

One of the biggest perks of becoming a writer was that she got to work at home, alone. People tended to annoy her. What with their noise and chattiness and general neediness.

The drive from the airport took about a half hour. Atlanta had at least fifty thoroughfares named Peachtree, which could be confusing at times, but San Francisco was an infuriating web of one-way streets. It took several passes to figure out how to maneuver to where she needed to be, and then parking was another challenge to conquer. Finally, she stood on the curb facing a narrow Victorian looking building. A bronze plaque next to the mahogany door read *Gertrude Hampton, Attorney at Law*.

The ancient floorboards creaked when Foster stepped through the door. A wisp of a girl sat at the reception desk in the foyer. She was pale and rail thin with a nose ring.

"May I help you?"

"Um, yes, I'm here to see Gertrude Hampton."

"Do you have an appointment?"

"Yes, I'm Foster Owen."

"Please take a seat." She slipped past Foster and down a hallway lined with doors toward the end of the hall.

Foster tried unsuccessfully to get a glimpse of who was on the other side of the last door. While she waited she busied herself by examining several photos of turn-of-the-century San Francisco hanging in the waiting area.

"Ms. Hampton will see you now. Please follow me." She stopped just before they reached the door. "Would you care for water or coffee?"

"Coffee would be great." The time difference was catching up with Foster. She'd missed her afternoon caffeine break.

"Do you take cream or sugar?"

"Just cream, thanks."

She held the door open for Foster to step past.

A hazy cloud of smoke filled the dark paneled office. Wait, not smoke, vapor, and it smelled like...strawberries. A stout woman who bore a strong resemblance to Helga from the TSA crew in

Atlanta stood and extended her hand to Foster. She was wearing a dark gray skirt suit with a white collared shirt underneath. Her gray hair was cropped short all over her head, offset with large blue-jeweled earrings.

"Sorry for the strawberry haze." Gertrude Hampton wiggled an e-cig in her hand. "They tell me this contraption will help me quit smoking. So far all it's done is make me crave pie." She set the device on her desk and waved to a chair on the other side. "Please, take a seat."

"Thank you." Foster had only just sat down when the receptionist returned with coffee. She smiled and nodded as she gratefully accepted the beverage.

As she sampled the coffee, Gertrude studied her from across the desk. She sucked on the e-cig, and it gurgled like when a kid tries to get the last bit of soda pop with a straw.

"Hmm, I thought you'd be…" Gertrude didn't finish the statement.

"A guy? Yeah, I get that a lot. Foster isn't exactly a traditional feminine name."

"Plus, you've got that whole scruffy writer look with the jacket and the unkempt, devil-may-care hair…does your generation have something against combs?"

Foster chafed a bit at the critique.

"This jacket is vintage." She felt the sudden need to defend her fashion choices, if not her hairstyle.

"Thrift stores…ugh…they smell worse than my great-aunt's attic on a rainy day."

Foster held the lapel up to her nose and sniffed just to be sure. She thought the jacket smelled good. She'd had it dry-cleaned more than once. Sitting across from Gertrude Hampton's disapproval, she was transported back to her grandma's kitchen where she'd received a dressing-down for wanting to wear one of her brother Frank's suits to her senior prom. That night had ended in disaster, and this meeting seemed to be headed in the same direction.

"Listen, Ms. Hampton, not to seem overly sensitive here, but I figure you hired me for my writing skills, not my wardrobe." Foster shifted in her chair, setting the half empty coffee cup on the edge of the large oak desk. "If your intention is to insult me into saying no to this assignment then you're gonna have to try a little harder."

Gertrude laughed, a genuine, deep down in your belly sort of laugh.

"Don't get your boxers in a bunch. On the contrary, Foster Owen, I'm starting to like you. I think you might just be the perfect choice for this project." She set the e-cig aside and leaned forward, resting her elbows on the desk. "First things first, call me Gertie."

Foster settled back in her chair and finished off the coffee.

"Listen, you should know that this memoir project was my idea." Gertie's intense gaze bored into her.

"Meaning?"

"Meaning Abigail may be reluctant at first, but don't let that discourage you."

Great. The subject of the memoir didn't even want the story to be written. Her intuition that this whole jaunt was a bad idea couldn't have been more on point.

"If Abigail doesn't want to do this project then why do it?" Foster figured it would save everyone a lot of trouble if she asked the obvious, painful question now.

"Because it'll be good for her."

Deciding what was good for someone else, whether they liked it or not, had a familiar ring. Her mother followed the same school of thought. Foster had a twinge of empathy for Abigail Spencer.

"The Spencer estate is about a two- or three-hour drive north from here, depending on how often you stop to sightsee…and traffic." Gertie shuffled some papers around on her desk as if she was looking for something she'd misplaced. She handed a manila folder to Foster. "This is a bit of history to get you started, along with the address and phone number for the Spencer place. Cell service will be spotty along the coast as you head north."

Foster frowned. Gertie had clearly decided the memoir project was moving forward, with or without Abigail's endorsement. Foster would get paid either way, according to the contract she'd received from her agent. She might as well play this out for the sake of her mortgage.

"Is this the area they call the lost coast?" Foster absently thumbed through the contents of the folder, not really focusing on any one thing.

"No, that's farther north, but the northern part of Mendocino County is pretty rural. It might as well be lost." Gertie leaned back in her high-backed leather chair. "I think you should leave now so that you arrive before dark."

"Why, what happens when it gets dark?"

"When it's dark it's harder to find the driveway." Gertie cocked an eyebrow as if Foster had just asked something truly crazy.

"Oh, I see."

Gertie stood, an obvious signal that the meeting was over. She extended her hand to Foster.

"Call me if you have any trouble or..." Her words trailed off.

"Or?"

"Or if you need anything."

"Thank you. I'm sure I'll be fine." She nodded to Gertie and let herself out.

Once on the sidewalk she realized she'd forgotten to find out any details about this mysterious Abigail Spencer, except for the fact that this project wasn't her idea. Oh well, she'd meet the woman soon enough. As she turned toward where she'd left her rental car, the chilled, damp San Francisco breeze cut through her shirt. She held the front of her jacket closed. It was June, but damn near cold despite the bright sunlit cloudless sky.

She'd heeded Mark Twain's famous observation about wintry summers in San Francisco but now was doubting she'd packed enough sweaters to survive her two-week stay along the blustery Pacific coast.

It took several moments of sitting in the sunbaked warmth of her rental car to chase away the chill. A few minutes later, she entered the Spencer estate address in her phone and hit go.

"Proceed to the route."

Why did Siri always say that? The whole point of using GPS was that she had no idea where *the route* was, except that it was north. A few missed turns, rerouted along one-way streets, and finally Foster spotted the red-orange struts of the Golden Gate Bridge rising above the treetops of the Presidio. The far end of the bridge was completely hidden in the dense marine layer. She followed traffic as if they'd all decided to drive off the edge of the earth together. As the road rose from the fog, a tunnel painted with a rainbow was visible just ahead. Like a sixteen-year-old on her first road trip, Foster honked the horn as she drove through. She couldn't stop the smile that followed.

CHAPTER THREE

The phone in the study rang and Abby reached for it. Cell service wasn't great on the property so Abby rarely used her personal phone. The landline in the house was more reliable. She sank back into the chaise and dropped the book she'd been reading into her lap.

"Hello?"

"Hi, Abigail."

"Hello, Gertie."

"I met with Foster Owen."

Abby let Gertie's statement hang in the air for a minute.

"I still don't think this is a good idea. I thought I asked you to cancel this project." Abby pressed two fingers to her temple where she felt a headache beginning.

She'd voiced her concerns, but Gertie was stubborn and Abby had sort of been good-naturedly bullied into considering the idea. Even after all these years, Abby sometimes thought Gertie didn't really *get* her. Gertie had her perception of who Abby was, and that perception fit neatly into the prearranged box Gertie had for Abby. But Abby wasn't who Gertie thought she was. She struggled to be seen, by Gertie and perhaps everyone else.

"Just give the project a chance. After a couple of days, if you see no merit in capturing the Spencer family history, then we abort the whole thing."

"You say that, but I don't believe you."

"Abigail…"

"Are you simply trying to force me to interact with someone?" The process of researching a memoir would no doubt be intimate, and Abby was already dreading every minute of forced closeness.

"I thought you were a fan of Foster Owen. Now you can meet in person."

"Are you trying to set me up with Foster Owen?" Despite her best efforts, the pitch of her voice went up. Why hadn't she guessed this from the beginning? Gertie was so concerned that Abby would end up old and alone that she was forever trying to set Abby up. Every single time, regardless of the contrived interaction, all Gertie's attempts had ended without success.

Gertie failed to understand that the primary goal in seeking a fortress of solitude was to actually have solitude.

Anxiety began to knot in her stomach. Sure, she was a fan of Foster's books, but she certainly didn't want to meet her in person or have her stay here. It was far too stressful to have a complete stranger in the house for one night, let alone two nights. A week was unimaginable. Her head began to throb.

"Please call her and ask her not to come."

"She's already on the road…left the office about an hour ago." The gurgle of Gertie's e-cig came through the phone, and then she exhaled as she spoke. "By the way, with a name like that I expected Foster to be a man. Did you know Foster was a woman?"

"Yes, I knew Foster was a woman." Which made Gertie's attempt to set her up even more curious. Gertie's other targeted attempts at romantic meddling had been with men. Abby had never really dated anyone of either gender, so how would Gertie know her preferences?

Of course she knew Foster was a woman. She made a point of knowing who authors were, or at least trying to know them through their books and blogs. Although, Foster didn't have a blog. From what Abby had been able to discern, Foster seemed to exist in a world apart from social media or the internet. The fact that Foster guarded her privacy so carefully made Abby even more curious about her.

"Abigail?"

"Yes?"

"Just give it a chance, okay? I worry about you up there all by yourself. Sometimes meeting our heroes is a good thing."

"She's not my hero." Abby pinched the bridge of her nose and squeezed her eyes shut. "I have to go. I don't feel well."

"Just try to relax, Abby." Gertie's voice softened. She knew Gertie meant well, but sometimes she had the maternal instincts of a stone. "I made a promise to look out for you, and that's exactly what I'm trying to do."

Whether I like it or not. Abby sighed.

"I know." She'd try her best to be gracious.

"Okay, now don't stress yourself out about this."

The absolute least helpful thing to say to someone with social anxiety.

"I have to go." Abby desperately wanted to get off the phone.

"Call me later and let me know how it's going."

"Okay." The headache was now climbing the back of her neck, knotting all the muscles as it passed.

She settled the phone back in the cradle and headed for her room. The heavy curtains, when drawn, cast the room in blissful darkness. If she lay down for a while, maybe she could ward off the worst of the headache; maybe she wouldn't have to deal with Foster's arrival until the morning. She curled into a fetal position and used a second pillow to cover her head. Even the sliver of light seeping along the edge of the drapes was too much.

The distant sound of the crashing surf filtered into her head as the migraine gained strength, like a storm, like a monster from the deep. The noise inside her head began to crescendo, as if she was standing in the middle of an airport terminal in the midst of a thousand aggravated passengers. Noise, voices, words.

The headaches were getting worse.

She tried to redirect her thoughts by counting slowly as if she were meditating...one, two, three...one, two, three...but the cacophony of indecipherable voices grew louder. She tried again to redirect her mind, to imagine something calming that would help her relax. If she didn't relax, the tension in her neck and shoulders would build, making the headache worse, which in turn created more tension, which made the headache even more nauseating. The cycle was vicious even when she tried to stave off a migraine in its earliest moments.

Abby visualized the sea, undulating soft waves, a light breeze. She imagined the sensation of floating on the surface for a moment and then letting herself sink, deeper and deeper. Sunlight filtered through the ocean like twilight; shifting patterns of sunlight moved across the water's surface above her.

Was she in bed or was she underwater?

Suddenly, Abby couldn't breathe. She fought through the murkiness to the surface. Gasping, she sat up. She was in bed, in her room, her hair damply plastered to her cheek. The sensation of drowning had been so real.

Something was happening to her. The headaches were getting worse and striking more often, but they weren't nearly as disconcerting as the dreams. She'd not been sleeping well, was almost afraid to go to sleep, and had been reading till all hours of the night to stay awake, to hide from the dreams. But the headaches wouldn't allow her to read. She had no choice but to give in to the darkness. And then inevitably night would come, and with it, the dreams and the wild things. And rooms...dim, smoky, candlelit rooms populated with shadow figures. A strong sense of foreboding washed over her.

Abby dropped back to the pillow, curled up again, clenched the second pillow to her chest, and waited for the throbbing pain to subside.

❖

Evan shifted into reverse and angled the truck toward the nearest enclosure. She climbed into the bed of the truck and used a pitchfork to toss fresh hay over the fence, careful not to overextend her injured shoulder. Journey watched intently from across the pen. Evan knew she wouldn't get anywhere near the truck. The only person she'd let get within touching distance was Abby.

Abby had an eerie way with these large, skittish animals, possibly a signal that Abby had some special gift, but not conclusive. Evan needed other signs for confirmation. Come to think of it, where was Abby?

It was unusual that she hadn't been out to see the other horses today. She usually checked on all of the horses twice a day. Abby had only briefly been with Journey first thing that morning, but Evan hadn't seen her since.

After Evan unloaded the rest of the hay, she decided to check at the house. She knocked at the rear entrance, near the kitchen, but no one answered.

"Hello?" She stuck her head through the door. When no one responded she stepped into the entry and waited, listening. Nothing. "Hello?" She said it louder.

"Hullo," Cora called back. The click of heels on the stone floor signaled her approach before Cora appeared at the end of the hallway.

"Hi, Cora. I haven't seen Abby. She's usually down with the horses by this time."

"She's not at the barn?"

Evan's pulse quickened just a little.

"No, she hasn't been there since her morning ride."

"Maybe she's in the library. Shall we have a look?"

Evan looked down. Her boots were muddy.

"I should wait here."

"Quite right." Cora noticed her muck-covered boots too. "Let me just check then and I'll be right back."

Evan sat on the bench along the wall and waited. The house was quiet. The distant click of Cora's steps was the only sound, except for the very loud ticking of a clock somewhere in the kitchen. The scent of something savory hung in the air, and it reminded Evan that she'd skipped lunch. The late morning coffee and muffin had obviously curbed her appetite.

After a few minutes, she caught a glimpse of Cora at the far end of the hallway, just before she started to climb the grand staircase to the second floor. Maybe Evan should have shucked her boots and followed Cora. What if something was wrong?

She dismissed the thought. This place was secluded and she'd seen no suspicious activity and no strange visitors.

❖

Abby wasn't sure of the time when she heard a soft knock at the door.

"Come in." Her throat was dry so her words faltered.

"Abby, honey, are you all right?" Cora stood at the door, probably unable to see very well inside the lightless room.

"Just a headache."

"Do you want me to bring you something?"

"Maybe some hot tea."

"Isn't that writer from Atlanta supposed to arrive this evening?"

Abby could tell that Cora was unsure of what to do about their impending houseguest.

"Yes, but I can't see her tonight. Can you get her settled and then tomorrow we can ask her to leave?"

"Is it another migraine, dear?" Cora ignored the last part of Abby's request.

"Yes." Abby's response was muffled by the pillow.

"I'll bring you some hot tea and some soup." She didn't know Cora was so near until Cora gently stroked her forehead. "You feel hot. Let me get you a cool cloth."

After a minute, Cora returned and laid the damp cloth on Abby's forehead. The cool compress felt soothing.

"Thank you."

"You just rest. I'll take care of your guest. Don't even give it a thought."

Abby nodded. The light from the hallway caused her to squint as she looked up. "Thank you, Cora."

The door clicked softly and the room returned to midnight. Knowing that she was off the hook for now, that she didn't have to meet Foster, made some of the tension in her shoulders begin to ease. She rolled onto her side, exhaled slowly, and shifted the compress to cover the dull throb at her temple.

❖

"I'm sorry I kept you waiting."

Evan stood up as Cora approached, a look of concern on her face.

"I'm afraid Abby has one of her terrible headaches." Cora smoothed the front of her dress with both hands. "They seem to be happening more often."

"Headaches?"

"Yes, terrible, horrible headaches. They make her quite ill. She'll likely not leave her room the rest of the day."

"Okay, I'll find Iain. He and I can see to the horses. I hope she feels well again soon." Evan reached for the door. Abby was in the house and safe. Severe headaches could be a sign, but still not conclusive. She had to be sure, and in order to be sure, she'd have to wait.

"Did you get any lunch?"

Evan held the door open and looked back at Cora. Lunch sounded good.

"Actually, I haven't had a chance to eat yet."

"Take those off and come in the kitchen. I'll make you a sandwich." Cora pointed at Evan's boots. "Does ham and cheese sound good? I could even grill it for a moment." Cora was already in the kitchen.

"That would be great." Evan worked her boots off and then tried to keep from getting muddy residue from the floor near the entry on her socks.

"Just take a seat." Cora lit the forward gas eye of the stove and reached for a cast iron skillet. "When you see Iain, would you ask him to stop by the house before he leaves? I have something for him."

"Sure." Evan didn't usually, or ever, eat in the kitchen. Partly to guard personal space but mostly because she was so inept at small talk.

Now she was thinking this had been a mistake and was anxious to escape, but the smell of the grilled sandwich rooted her to the chair. She'd make quick work of the food and be gone. Cora served the toasted sandwich, cut from corner to corner, and then took the seat across from her.

"Please don't feel as if you have to wait with me while I eat." Evan didn't really want an audience. "I'm sure you've got other things to do."

"Oh, not at all. It's nice to sit for a minute. I swear I've climbed those stairs a hundred times today." Cora got up and filled the teakettle. "Come to think of it, a spot of tea would perk me up. Would you care for a cup?"

Evan shook her head. "Thanks, but I'm good with water."

"So, how do you think the horses are coming along?" Cora sat back down while she waited for the kettle to boil.

Evan shook her head again and swallowed so that she wasn't talking with food in her mouth. "I wouldn't really know. I'm not that experienced with horses."

"I see." Cora seemed to consider this as if she weren't sure she believed Evan. "Abby has such a way with them, don't you think?"

Evan nodded. She took another huge bite.

"If she'd only allow herself the same comfort with people."

"Does she keep to herself?"

"I'm afraid so." Cora brightened for a moment. "Maybe you could coax her out for dinner or a movie sometime."

Evan's stomach lurched. Was Cora trying to fix them up? No, there was no way. Cora was just suggesting they should be friends.

"I'm afraid I don't get out much at night either." Spending more time with Abby wasn't going to happen. She needed to shut that notion down right away.

"What is up with you young people? In my day we lived for a fun outing at the movie house." Cora smiled as she filled her teacup.

"Just busy I guess."

"Too busy for fun is too busy in my book."

Evan finished the last bite and put the plate in the sink. "Thank you for the late lunch. I really appreciate it."

"Anytime." Cora followed her with her eyes as she padded to the door in sock feet. "Will you not forget my message to Iain?"

"I won't forget." She smiled thinly.

She sank to the bench and tugged on her boots. The mud had hardened, making them stiff. She had to fight with them to get them on.

As she strode across the grounds in search of Iain, she looked up. The sky was clear and blue. A fog bank had parked itself at sea, along the horizon, but where the sunlight hit the sea it was deep blue. Evan paused to take in the view.

Abby avoided people. She filed that detail away.

CHAPTER FOUR

Gertie had failed to mention that there was an entire town named after the Spencer family. Actually, it was more like a village than an actual town. Foster slowed as she drove north along Main Street. Spencer's Cove looked like any rural, one-drugstore kind of community. Although, Spencer's Cove seemed to have more than its share of surfers. Vintage vans with roof rack mounted surfboards were parked along Main Street in front of Cove Coffee & Tackle. That combination made Foster smile.

There was a sign for the pier along a westward side street off Main. A couple of scruffy looking guys who could easily have just come back from a year at sea sat on a bench under the eaves of the hardware store. They made no bones about studying Foster unabashedly as she drove slowly past. This looked like the sort of place that didn't get lots of out-of-town visitors. Spencer's Cove didn't strike Foster as a hot spot for tourism.

The drive up the Pacific Coast Highway had been breathtaking and remote. At times the road climbed to a dizzying height above the crashing surf. In some spots, there weren't even guardrails. In other places, cattle crossed the two-lane road at their leisure and Foster had to wait for them. Gertie hadn't been kidding when she said this area might as well be lost. She'd rented an economy car with hardly any horsepower. If she'd known the drive would be so spectacular she'd have upgraded to something a bit sportier, maybe even a convertible. Although, it was a bit chilly to have the top down. Her thin southern blood wasn't properly acclimated for this sort of Pacific Northwest climate.

Foster was glad she'd stopped for gas before breaking away from the freeway for coastal Highway 1 because she hadn't passed any service stations along the winding route north. Spencer's Cove had been the first sign of life she'd seen in more than forty minutes. At one point she'd wondered if she was on the wrong road or had missed a turn somewhere along the way.

Spencer's Cove consisted of one central road. Clustered along the two-lane blacktop were a tiny movie house with a vintage marquis, a drugstore, organic grocery, the coffee shop, and city hall of which half the building was the local library. The entire town was only about five blocks long with a one-story public school as the main street turned west. Past the school was a church and a very spooky looking cemetery.

She reached for her phone to see if she was getting close to her destination. The sun was sitting on the western edge of the glassy Pacific like a big orange marble. Gertie's words about finding the Spencer place before dark echoed in her head. This looked like the sort of community where the sidewalks rolled up early so she didn't relish having to seek someone out for directions in the dark.

The destination is on your left. Her phone spoke from where she'd tossed it on the passenger seat.

"Yeah, but where?" Foster said to no one. She leaned forward trying to look for a hidden driveway.

The destination is on your left. Arrived.

She rounded a curve, and just as she passed a rock wall, she saw the open iron gate. Foster checked the rearview mirror before throwing the car in reverse to correct her approach into the driveway. When she turned in and was on the other side of the stone wall, she got her first glimpse of the Spencer estate. This place was a house the same way Windsor Castle was a house. Yes, people probably lived in it, but this was no normal house. This place was like Downton Abbey's American twin.

"Jesus H. Christmas Cakes." Foster sat for a minute, letting the car idle as she took in the view of the enormous dwelling. The sprawling, multistory residence was a mixture of stone, brick, and timbers. It looked like something built in the 1800s at least.

Had Gertie mentioned this was practically a castle and she'd just missed that detail? It made sense though. Who else could afford to pay forty thousand dollars for something that might turn out to be nothing more than a glorified family holiday letter? The sort of holiday letter her cousin Janice liked to send to brag about all the trips she'd taken in the last twelve months and how her two children were brilliant and gifted and were winning awards for all kinds of activities that Foster couldn't care less about.

Well, she couldn't just sit in the driveway all night. The sun was setting. She'd barely parked and hadn't even gotten out of the car when a menacing looking dual-axel Ford truck pulled up behind her in the large circular drive in front of the main entrance. The truck had wide off-road tires that had kicked mud all up both sides. A very intense woman wearing a baseball cap got out and approached just as Foster climbed out.

"Can I help you with something?" The woman seemed unfriendly.

"I'm here to see Abigail Spencer."

"I doubt that."

Yes, definitely unfriendly.

Foster pulled up to her full height and tried her best to look unintimidated by the slightly taller, aggressively butch ranch hand. The woman had a classic, all-American square jaw and the shoulders of a collegiate rower. She was wearing jeans, mud covered boots and a well-worn Carhartt jacket. Usually, in this sort of confrontational situation, the best defense was to turn on the Southern charm. A well-delivered Southern accent could disarm any number of tense encounters, especially with non-southerners who, upon hearing a thick Southern accent, automatically assumed two things: dumb and friendly. Foster figured it was worth a try.

"I don't believe we've met." She extended her hand. "I'm Foster Owen."

The woman looked down at her open palm as if she was visiting from some foreign culture where shaking hands was considered taboo. After what seemed like forever, the woman pulled off her leather work glove and shook Foster's hand. It was the sort of overly firm handshake that let Foster know she'd just as soon kick her ass as make nice.

"I'm Evan Bell, the groundskeeper."

"Nice to meet you." She didn't really mean it. "Maybe I'll just go knock and see if Ms. Spencer is in." She tipped her head toward the door.

"I'll walk with you." Evan's escort didn't really sound optional.

"Since you work here maybe you should lead the way." Foster wasn't about to try to out alpha Evan at the moment. She was jetlagged and out of her element. Better to simply roll over and show her soft underbelly.

Evan pushed the enormous mahogany door open. Foster followed on Evan's heels into an entryway with a stone tile floor. In less than thirty seconds, a rotund older woman scurried in their direction. Her heels clicked rapidly on the stone as she crossed the open room past the foyer.

"You must be Foster Owen." The woman smiled warmly as she approached. Foster instantly felt more at ease. "I'm Cora Taylor, chief cook and bottle washer here at Spencer House." Cora took Foster's hand between hers and shook it. "I was beginning to worry that you'd gotten lost."

"I probably took longer than necessary to make the drive. It was far too scenic a route to rush."

"Indeed…indeed." Cora finally released her hand.

To say the drive from San Francisco had been scenic was like saying Homer's *Odyssey* was a poem. *The Odyssey* was epic, and so was the Pacific Coast Highway.

From Bodega Bay heading north, the two-lane road wove from rocky cliffs with plummeting seaside drop-offs to shadowed stands of redwoods. Microclimate shifts of fifteen degrees modulated between sun and shade. The shadowy curves were carpeted with ferns, thick at the base of the redwoods.

Wild lupine, foxglove, and yarrow, punctuated with the vibrant orange of California poppies, clung to the cliff edges between the ocean and the blacktop. At one point she'd driven through a grove of eucalyptus. The smell of menthol invaded the car's open windows, cool like camphor, bright and cleansing.

California's Highway 1 was a bizarre convergence of forest, rocky cliffs, and the vast blue-green of the Pacific. The end result was a breathtaking drive that felt like you'd wandered into a painted movie set, a landscape that couldn't possibly be real, except that it was.

"Well now, you must be starved. I have dinner enough for a crowd. Evan, would you like to join us?" Cora looked at Evan expectantly.

Please say no.

Beside her, Evan shifted and adjusted her cap lower over her eyes.

"Thank you, Cora, but I have other plans."

"All right then, it'll just be Foster and me for my homemade lasagna." Cora shadowed Evan to the front door.

"Miss Spencer won't be joining you?" Evan seemed surprised, maybe even concerned.

"I'm afraid not. She's still down with that terrible headache." Cora turned to Foster apologetically. "She had to retire to her room a few hours ago. We probably won't see her until tomorrow."

Damn. The mysterious Abigail Spencer would remain a mystery for one more day. It was just as well. Foster was tired and after a meal would no doubt be ready to turn in early. She was in the wrong time zone. It was well past the dinner hour in Georgia.

"Evan, before you take your leave maybe you could help Ms. Owen with her bags. You do have bags, don't you?" Evan paused on the threshold as Cora turned to Foster.

"I just have the one bag. I can manage." There was no way she was gonna let Butchy McButch tote her luggage for her.

"Are you sure?" Cora pressed her.

"Yep, I'm sure. But thanks for offering." She followed Evan out the door to claim her luggage from the car.

Her economy-sized rental was hilariously dwarfed by Evan's truck. She smiled and gave a half-hearted wave to Evan as she pulled away. She shouldered her leather briefcase and then popped the trunk for her suitcase. Cora fidgeted in the doorway until Foster returned with her bag, a faded blue Samsonite that had belonged to her grandma. She was fairly certain her grandma had only ever used it once, on a vacation to Disney World in Orlando when Foster was a kid. Her grandma wasn't big on travel or vacations, or fun, for that matter.

"Let's get you settled into your room and then you can join me in the kitchen for dinner." Cora glanced over her shoulder as she led Foster up the grand staircase.

The house looked like something from a classic movie. The wide staircase curved gradually as it rose to the second floor. The wood, darkened from age, had a scarlet carpet runner up the center. Foster tried to notice details without tripping on the stairs as she followed Cora. Portraits were stacked all along the staircase. Serious looking individuals painted in dark tones, thickly rendered in oil. She wondered if any of them were acquainted with her grandma because they had a similar expression of disapproval on their faces. Foster knew it well. Her grandma had mastered it and passed it down to her mother. Owen women had a gift for making you feel loved and barely tolerated at the same time.

She nearly bumped into Cora who'd stopped at a door along the upstairs hallway. Foster had been distracted by a particularly spooky looking sculpture. The hallway was full of them. This one looked like some fabled creature, half man and half horse. The next one looked like a bighorn sheep emerging from a rock. There were others, but she couldn't make out the details of them in the low wattage lighting.

"This room should suit you. There's a bathroom just across the hall." Cora swiveled with her arm outstretched. "I left clean towels at the foot of the bed. I'll give you a minute to settle in then just come down to the kitchen when you're ready."

"Um…where is the kitchen exactly?"

"Oh, yes, you haven't had the tour." Cora rested her hands on her hips. "At the bottom of the staircase, then left. You can't miss it."

"Got it." She stepped past Cora into the lushly decorated room. "I won't be long."

"Good. I'll just go set the table for us."

Foster leaned back through the door to say thank you, but Cora was already halfway down the stairs. She closed the door and surveyed the large room. There were deep red tapestries hanging on the wall on either side of a very substantial four-poster bed piled with pillows. The bed faced a fireplace with an ornate wood mantel carved with what looked like Celtic patterns. She set her suitcase at the foot of the bed and rotated in the room. A dressing table and oval mirror were opposite the hearth. On either side of the dressing table were tall windows facing west. The heavy drapes were open so that the last bit of the sun's orange glow lit the edge of the earth, the Pacific horizon.

A proper writing desk was the only thing the elegant room lacked. But surely a house like this must have a beautiful study or possibly even a library lined with books. Maybe she'd get a chance to investigate after dinner.

It was getting dark when Evan parked the truck in front of the cottage. She took off her boots just inside the front door and stomped to the fridge for a beer. Who the hell was Foster Owen? And why hadn't Cora mentioned her earlier during her late lunch? Having one more person to navigate would only make keeping things quiet more difficult.

She'd have taken Cora up on her offer of lasagna in order to find out a little more about Abby, but not with Foster as an audience.

She hated chitchat, and she certainly wasn't in the mood to make small talk with Clark Kent's nerdy younger sister.

Evan sank into her new favorite armchair by the window and took a long draw of beer. It felt cool on her throat, but she had the immediate thought that this beer would taste so much better with a burger, or even pizza.

She put on shoes that hadn't spent all day tromping around on soggy ground, grabbed her keys and her jacket. Foster's rental car was still parked in front of the main house as she left. The tiny Toyota inspired a frown. Who was Foster Owen and why was she here? Was she an old college friend? That seemed doubtful because she'd referred to Abby as Ms. Spencer. Was it possible she didn't even know Abby? And if that was the case then Evan was exponentially more annoyed by her presence.

It turned out that the taqueria on the far end of town was the least crowded spot for food. She revised her craving. Beer also tasted good with Mexican food. Yeah, tacos and beer sounded just about perfect.

Evan was reaching for the door when the waitress who'd served her coffee that morning surprised her by stepping out. She held the door with one hand and a brown paper bag with the other.

"Hi." The woman blocked the door for a moment before letting it swish closed behind her.

"Hi." Evan was regretting she'd stayed at home for that first beer. If she'd been fifteen minutes faster maybe she'd have ended up with a dinner date.

"Are you working at the Spencer place?"

Evan was flattered that the woman had obviously asked around about her, possibly someone at the feed store knew who she was. The coffee shop was probably the social hub of Spencer's Cove. The hardware store and the feed store were her main stops in town, and the Spencer estate had an account at both places.

"Yeah, I'm Evan." She didn't really want to broadcast personal details, but if they stayed on a first-name only basis what would be the harm?

"I'm Jaiden. My friends call me Jai." Jai held out her hand and Evan accepted it, keeping contact for a little longer than was necessary.

Yes, Jai was definitely flirting. The direct and lingering eye contact, the tilt of her oval face as she tossed her hair. She was still wearing the snug fitting T-shirt from the café, signaling she'd probably just gotten off work.

"It looks like you already have dinner, or I'd have asked you to join me for a beer." Evan was fishing to find out who the to-go bag of food was for.

"Maybe another time." Jai smiled teasingly.

Evan couldn't help smiling too because Jai had used her earlier brush-off line. She watched the tempting sway of Jai's hips as she walked toward the car. She looked back at Evan and smiled one more time before she opened the passenger door and climbed in. The driver was nothing more than a shadowed outline, which gave away no details. Evan shook her head as she turned and entered the restaurant. It was just as well that she'd missed Jai. It wasn't like she was on holiday; she had a fucking job to do, a job she wasn't feeling particularly good about at the moment.

Foster was anxious to explore the Spencer residence, but good manners dictated that she tamp down her enthusiasm a bit. At least until someone offered her a tour. The first order of business was to sample Cora's lasagna. She left the room and followed the grand staircase back down to the first floor in search of the kitchen. She needn't have worried about finding it. The delicious aroma was an easy guide to follow.

"Well, now…just have a seat. Would you care for water?" Cora served a healthy portion of lasagna onto a plate.

"Yes, water would be great." Maybe it was the air travel, but Foster was feeling very thirsty. She sat down, and after a minute, Cora joined her.

She was trying to guess Cora's age but couldn't. She was probably in her early sixties, and she had a very pleasing Irish accent. Her round and rosy cheeks kept wrinkles to a minimum. Age didn't really matter, but as a writer, Foster always wondered about names and the eras they likely came from. She kept a running list of interesting names for future story use.

"Have you worked here at the Spencer place for very long?"

"Oh, let me see… Goodness me, I think it's been twenty years now." Cora looked away as if she were picturing something in her head. "Hard to believe it's been that long, but yes, a little over twenty years."

"So, you must know a lot about the family history then?" Foster figured she might as well ask a few questions over dinner. Maybe Cora would say something that would give her a clue of where to begin this Spencer family history project.

"Some I know, some of it might be more folklore than fact." Cora chewed thoughtfully.

Hmm, folklore? That sounded promising.

"Folklore, huh?"

"Oh, yes…and I'm not giving away any family secrets here. Everyone knows the story."

"Everyone except me."

"Well, everyone in Spencer's Cove." Cora smiled.

"Can you tell me then?"

"The story goes that in the mid eighteen hundreds there was a shipwreck in the cove. This was before the lighthouse, mind you, or about the time the lighthouse was being built. It was an opium ship from the Far East. When some men from the town finally got through the rough water to the ship, they found not a soul on board except one young girl, floating in a lifeboat, the captain's daughter."

Cora took another bite. Foster chewed slowly and waited for her to continue. Maybe this would make an interesting book after all. It sounded as if there was some sort of mystery to be solved, her favorite sort of story to research. Even if the memoir was a bust, which, given what Gertie said about Abigail's lack of interest in the project, might be the case, she could still craft a convincing work of fiction on the bones of an actual historical event. She was encouraged.

"This young woman ended up being taken in by one of the founding families, and when she came of age she married Thomas Spencer. He was the one who built this house…as the story goes, in the hopes of having lots of children."

"And did they? Have lots of children?"

"No, only one son." Cora paused, as if she were pulling some fact from some recess of her brain that she rarely accessed. "Funny thing about all the Spencer families. In each generation only one son was born…until Abigail. And she has no children, so she'll be the end of the line. The last Spencer." A sad expression passed over Cora's face.

What were the odds that in every generation since the mid 1800s only one child was born in the Spencer line and that child was always male? That seemed to defy the odds.

"So, Abigail's great-grandfather was Thomas Spencer?"

"Her third great-grandfather was Thomas Spencer."

"Oh, right." Foster hadn't quite done the math correctly. "Maybe I'll get a chance to meet Ms. Spencer tomorrow."

"I hope so." Cora took a sip of her tea. "She's a bit…shy."

Cora nearly whispered the detail as if shyness was a disfiguring and contagious condition.

"Oh, I didn't know." Foster tried to remain serious, but it was hard not to smile.

"She's spent too much time by herself in my opinion."

"Well, maybe she'll help me with some research of the family history."

"I hope so."

CHAPTER FIVE

Abby blinked, but the darkness didn't recede. She sat at the edge of the bed and tilted her head from side to side in an attempt to ease the tense muscles in her neck. When she tugged the thick drapes aside, moonlight flooded the room. The sky was clear and so was her head, finally. She wondered how many hours had passed. She'd left her cell phone in the library so she couldn't check the time.

Cora had brought soup and tea to her room, but she'd been unable to eat more than a few spoonfuls without feeling nauseous. Food was what she needed more than a clock.

A few coals on the hearth in the kitchen still glowed. She stirred them and added one stick of wood. It wasn't so chilly that it was necessary to build a fire, but a small flame would be pleasant while she ate. Watching the fire would be soothing. The kettle was still fairly full so she lit the gas eye and set the water to boil. There was a good chance that she'd find some leftovers in the refrigerator, and if not, she'd make toast or something simple and go back to bed.

Abby was staring into the glow of the fridge when she heard a noise and turned.

Foster stopped dead in her tracks when she saw the woman standing in the kitchen. Like some ethereal creature frozen in place, the woman was cast in a ghostly glow from the light of the open refrigerator. Maybe she was a ghost because surely this old mansion had a few.

"I'm sorry, I didn't know anyone else was up." Foster wondered if she should leave. The woman didn't exactly look interested in sharing the space. "I'll just…I'll go…"

"Are you Foster Owen?" The woman let the door go and it closed with a soft whoosh.

"Yes."

The small bulb under the stove vent hood was the only illumination in the room besides the fireplace. The woman took a few steps toward Foster. She was beautiful. That was Foster's first thought, and she considered pinching herself to make sure she was awake, but if she were awake then that would probably seem weird.

"I'm Abby Spencer."

"You mean, as in, Abigail Spencer?" This was not who she'd pictured at all. "It's nice to meet you." Foster extended her hand, but rather than accept it, Abigail hugged herself and took a step back.

"Only Gertie calls me Abigail."

Okay, Abigail Spencer was not surrounded by cats and she certainly wasn't old. What had Cora said? That she was shy. That seemed obvious. Foster guessed her age to be thirty, maybe. Her skin was fair. She had blond hair that fell past her shoulders, not curly, but not straight either. It framed her face in subtle silky waves. Her fingers were tapered and delicate. The T-shirt she was wearing looked like a favorite, washed and worn until it had reached maximum softness. The scooped neck cotton shirt hugged her girlish frame from the waist up. Plaid flannel pajama pants finished off the sleepwear ensemble.

"You can call me Abby."

Foster's hand still hung in midair while she inventoried Abby's appealing features. Feeling awkward now, she swept her fingers through her hair. Meeting Abby, she had the eeriest sensation of déjà vu, as if they'd met before, but that was impossible. She couldn't imagine forgetting someone like Abby.

"I'm sorry, did you say something?" She could've sworn she heard something, someone. Maybe more of an echo than a voice.

"Um, no…" Abby tilted her head and regarded Foster as if she'd just shared some secret, or as if she was surprised by the question.

Weird. She would have sworn Abby said something. Foster cleared her throat and shifted weight from one foot to the other. It had not been her intention to make Abby uncomfortable, and even as she thought it, she wasn't sure she had. If it was possible, Abby seemed simultaneously shy and intimidating, aloof and alluring. Not knowing what else to do, Foster smiled.

Abby wanted to ask Foster a million questions just to hear her talk. The cadence of her speech, the smooth drawl of her Southern accent, made Abby want to curl up by the fire in the library and have Foster read aloud for hours. She wasn't sure she'd ever been around someone with such a pleasing voice.

There was something unexpected about Foster, some ineffable quality that she probably had no conscious awareness of, but Abby assumed a lot of women responded to. Foster had a gentleness about her that, despite Abby's usual anxiety, put her at ease. The expression on Foster's face was guileless, open, and the thick dark frames of her vintage-looking glasses drew attention to her soft brown eyes.

From the stove, the kettle whistled, breaking the silence. Abby walked around the large rectangular table in the center of the room to the stove. She felt Foster's eyes on her as she set the teakettle off the burner. The most tantalizing shiver slithered up her spine. She turned to see that Foster was indeed watching her, wide-eyed, and without one hint of reserve. Abby had caught her staring. And after a moment, Foster averted her gaze.

Foster hadn't said she wanted tea, but Abby made them each a cup of chamomile anyway.

Foster was much cuter in person than in her author photos. In those pictures she looked so serious. In person, she gave off a more whimsical air. She was tall, with angular broad shoulders beneath a white cotton crew neck T-shirt. She had a slender face with a strong jaw and a patrician nose, capped with tousled short dark brown hair. She was barefoot, with faded jeans cuffed just enough that they still brushed the stone floor.

This was not at all how Abby imagined they'd meet. In fact, several hours earlier even the idea of meeting Foster had caused such anxiety that it had probably contributed to the migraine. But now here they were, facing each other in the dimly lit kitchen.

Foster watched Abby glide across the room. She held the steaming cup out for Foster to take it. Had Foster said she wanted tea? She didn't think so. Unlike almost every lesbian on the planet, she rarely drank tea, but she had the distinct feeling that whatever Abby offered she would gladly take, even herbal tea.

"Thank you." Foster accepted the mug, and when she did, their fingers overlapped. Neither of them moved. Foster looked down at their joined hands. Her arm tingled as a warm vibration traveled up her forearm, inside the sleeve of her T-shirt, past her shoulder, and then nested in the small hairs at the back of her neck. This whole encounter felt so…strange.

Abby blinked, as if in slow motion, and Foster was struck by her long lashes and how blue her eyes were.

Foster realized she was still touching Abby's hand and pulled the mug away, breaking contact. The release almost caused her to sway on her feet. Instinctively, she reached for the nearest solid object, a chair.

"Well, good night then." Abby seemed suddenly uncomfortable, as if she couldn't leave the room quickly enough.

"Good night." She rotated to watch Abby's retreat and then slumped into the chair she'd been holding on to. The entire encounter was surreal. She wondered if in the morning she'd wake to realize it had all just been a lovely dream.

The midnight snack she'd been in search of now forgotten, she watched the low flame of the fire, and sipped the tea.

Abby's heart still raced when she finally made it back to her room and closed the door. She leaned against it for a moment and took a few deep breaths, cradling the warm cup of tea against her chest.

She was not prepared to see Foster. She certainly was *not* prepared for Foster to see *her*, especially in her pajamas. The kitchen was such an intimate place in the middle of the night. Abby couldn't even shake Foster's hand. But their fingers had touched despite her efforts to avoid physical contact. She held her hand up and examined it as if she expected to find some mark or scar from their connection.

Foster absolutely had to leave.

She would find Cora first thing in the morning and ask her to deliver the news. Abby was certain that Foster had lots of other things she'd rather be doing. Ending the project would give Foster the opportunity to do something else, anything else.

Abby shimmied under the covers, careful not to slosh her tea. She sank back against the deep feather pillow, held the mug with both hands, and sipped. Since she'd slept all afternoon she wasn't feeling tired. She reached for a book among the haphazard stack on her bedside table. She wanted to read something familiar, something that wouldn't engage her mind too completely because she already knew how the story ended. Rereading a favorite novel would quiet her mind and help her relax, but not so much that she'd sleep, or dream.

As she opened the book, she visualized Foster, somewhere in the house. Had she returned to the guest room or remained in the kitchen? Abby now realized she wouldn't be able to relax until she knew where Foster was. The thought of a stranger roaming the house at night was too unsettling. She tugged a light dressing gown over her T-shirt and pajama pants. The hallway was dark as she walked in the direction of the guest room at the top of the stairs.

When she arrived the door was closed, but a golden glow was visible along the bottom edge of the door where it didn't quite meet the floor. She saw a shadow beneath the door. Foster was in the room. For a second, Abby considered knocking; she wasn't sure why. She hugged herself and looked back through the darkness toward her room. When she again faced forward Foster was standing in the open doorway looking at her.

"Hi." Foster held onto the door's edge with one hand as she casually leaned against the doorframe with her opposite shoulder.

"Hi. How did you know…"

"I heard you knock."

Only Abby was sure she hadn't. She'd only thought of knocking.

"I'm sorry I disturbed you."

"You didn't, I mean, you aren't." Foster released the door and sank her hand in the pocket of her jeans. "I guess you can't sleep either? I'm sort of a homebody, and when I travel I have a hard time settling down."

"Is there something you need?" Abby wasn't sure what to offer, but until tomorrow Foster was her guest and she should at least try to be a gracious host.

"I should have brought a book with me. Reading helps quiet my brain."

"We have a library. You could select something from our collection."

"Our collection?"

"Well, not all of the volumes are mine. The library spans several generations…books collected by my grandfather and parents…" Why was she sharing personal details with Foster? It was as if she couldn't stop herself.

"If it wouldn't be an imposition I'd love to borrow a book for the night."

"It's this way." Abby descended the stairs to the first floor without really waiting to see if Foster was keeping up.

After traveling halfway through the hallway to the right of the staircase, she checked over her shoulder. Foster was trailing her, but was moving much slower, sightseeing along the way. Abby reached for the lightswitch closest to where she was standing. Foster blinked at the sudden overhead glare.

"Sorry, there's just so much to look at here." Foster smiled and quickened her pace.

The library was at the far end of the first floor. Abby stood in the center of the room and watched Foster slowly peruse the shelves. Abby lifted a book she'd left on the chaise earlier and flipped through the pages, just to have a distraction.

"I have to confess that you aren't who I expected you to be." Foster was across the room watching her.

There it was again, that whiskey smooth drawl. The soothing cadence was such a pleasant surprise. She took a deep breath and tried to settle. When she didn't respond, Foster continued.

"I thought you'd be older." A slow smile spread across her face.

"Really?"

"I also pictured lots of cats."

"There's one tabby cat living in the barn."

"Only one, huh?"

They stood silently for a moment looking at each other. Foster's gaze was direct but not invasive.

"I suppose I had an unfair advantage because I've seen your photo on the jackets of your books." She looked away, feeling exposed. She hadn't meant to blurt out that she'd read Foster's books. Foster would no doubt think she was a silly fan girl.

"I never liked that photo the publisher used. The marketing people thought it made me look serious…like a serious writer. But I think it just makes it look like someone stomped on my foot and I'm trying not to cry about it."

"It's not that bad."

"See? You said *not that bad*…which means you noticed it too."

Abby couldn't help smiling. Foster had graciously shifted the conversation away from her fandom and put Abby at ease.

"The photographer was trying to make me look sophisticated, and in the end, I kinda just look like an elitist ass." Foster ran her fingertip over the spines of the books nearest her. "I mean, I write mystery novels. That's not exactly Pulitzer material."

"I like your books. That's why Gertie hired you."

"So, this whole thing was Gertie's idea, not yours?"

Abby nodded. Did acknowledging the truth make Foster wish she hadn't come? She was rethinking her impulse to send Foster away immediately. There was something magnetic about Foster. Maybe Gertie was right. Maybe she should get out of her comfort zone a little. She could always call the project off if she became uncomfortable with the situation.

"How do you write such convincing stories?" Abby hugged the book she'd been holding against her chest.

"I find actual crime stories and then embellish. Truth always makes the most convincing fiction." Foster smiled. "There I go, giving away trade secrets."

"Your secrets are safe with me." That sounded far more flirtatious than she'd meant for it to, and she was fairly sure she'd made both of them blush. Foster was definitely blushing.

"Well, I should choose something to read and let you get back to sleep." Foster turned abruptly and pulled a couple of books from the shelf.

They didn't talk as they climbed the stairs back to the second level.

"This is my stop." Foster smiled shyly as she tipped her head in the direction of the guest room.

"Good night."

"Good night." Foster gave a little wave as she closed the bedroom door.

Abby fairly glided back to her room, feeling uncharacteristically lightened by her second late-night encounter with Foster. She pulled the comforter up to her chin and sank into the soft, down-filled pillow. The room was dark except for the soft moonlight from the partially open drapes. Sleep crept up on her and she let it come. Knowing Foster was just down the hall awake and reading filled her with an unusual sense of calm.

CHAPTER SIX

The sound of crickets dragged Foster from sleep. She squinted into the dimly lit room. It took a minute for her foggy brain to realize her cell phone was ringing. But who would call at such an unholy hour? She stumbled toward her laptop bag. The screen lit up with the caller ID and Foster frowned.

"Hello, Gloria." Her cat sitter had no working concept of time zones.

This wasn't the first time she'd called Foster at an unreasonable hour. Once when she'd been in Amsterdam, Gloria had called in the middle of the night just to let her know that everything was okay.

"Foster, I'm calling because there's this wooden board game on your coffee table with marbles and one of them is missing? Have you lost any…marbles?"

Foster glanced at her phone. One bar. The signal wasn't great, and Foster wondered if she was catching only part of what Gloria was saying. Every few words the line dropped for a split second.

"Sorry, I'm not sure I caught that last part…I thought you asked if I'd lost my marbles." Which was a fair question under normal circumstances.

"Marbles…are you missing marbles from the game on the coffee table?"

"Gloria, that game is solitaire. There's supposed to be one empty spot on the board."

"Are you sure? Because I worry that William Faulkner may have swallowed one."

There was no way her cat would eat a marble unless it was tuna flavored and even then, it was a long shot.

"Yes, I'm sure. The point of the game is to jump the marbles until only one is left. That's why there's one empty space."

"Well, I think I should put this in a cabinet just to be safe."

Foster heard a shuffling sound on the other end of the phone.

"If you're worried, why not just put the marbles in a Ziploc bag—" Too late. The sound of marbles cascading off metal pots in her kitchen cabinet pinged loudly through the phone.

"Oh, dear…yes, maybe a Ziploc bag is a good idea." More shuffling as Gloria no doubt balanced her phone against her shoulder. "I should go deal with this."

"Yeah, sounds like it."

"Everything is fine here. You just enjoy your trip."

"Thank you, Gloria. I'll try."

Gloria clicked off. It wouldn't do any good to give Gloria a hard time. She was annoying, but harmless. And William Faulkner loved Gloria. A couple of times, Foster had tried to test out other pet sitters, but William Faulkner had practically revolted as only a twenty-pound cat can. He'd scream at her for hours when she returned home and he just looked, for lack of a better description, frazzled.

Foster rubbed her face with her hands to chase away a bit more sleep. She tugged the heavy drapes apart. It was early and there was no sun to speak of. A dense marine layer hovered at the edge of the grounds where the cliff dropped off. She'd arrived so late the previous evening that a stroll around the estate hadn't been possible, but she was anxious to explore a little.

Sleep had been fitful. She'd had the strangest series of dreams. Presently, she couldn't quite recall them entirely except that they were unsettling. Dark figures just outside the realm of recognition, ominous, but not advancing. And then a dream about drowning. She'd been underwater, the light dancing across the surface in undulating patterns. Maybe the sound of the ocean waves had conjured that one.

A dark shape moving through the fog caught her eye. She reached for her glasses. There was a rider on a horse ambling from the cliff's edge toward the barn. Foster decided to investigate. She tugged on jeans and rummaged in her Samsonite for the sweater she'd packed.

Foster needed coffee, but curiosity about the horse and rider drew her outside. She exited through the door nearest the kitchen rather than the front door. The barn was behind the house, and that seemed to be the direction the rider was headed.

She sank her hands in her pockets and kept her arms tightly against her sides against the chill in the air. The tall, brownish grass was soaked with dew; the toes of her brown wingtips darkened from the moisture as she crossed the ground between the manor and the barn. A woman dismounted, and as she got closer she saw that the woman was Abby. For some reason it surprised her that Abby rode a horse, but why should it? Everything else about this place was like a scene from a gothic romance novel. In that context, Abby on horseback made total sense.

An older fellow took the reins from Abby. He was round in the middle and his face was weathered like he'd spent years at sea, or maybe years by the sea. He nodded to Abby. She turned toward the house without looking up. Abby studied the ground. She seemed to be intently thinking of something and practically bumped into Foster, who spoke just before they made contact.

"Sorry, I didn't mean to surprise you." Foster sidestepped.

Abby looked up with one leather glove off and the other only partially removed.

"I saw the horse coming out of the fog, and curiosity got the better of me." It was clear that Abby wasn't happy to see her, or possibly she was bothered by something else that had nothing to do with Foster. Either way, the easiness between them from the previous night was gone.

Abby held both gloves in one hand and tugged the knit cap off. Loose strands of hair blew across her face, and she swept her fingers over her hair to smooth it. She was wearing form-fitting riding pants and knee-high black boots along with a jacket and scarf. Foster wondered if Abby had any idea how gorgeous she was. Abby had an easy grace that defied her age. She made casual riding togs look elegant.

Abby was wearing what would pass for winter gear in the Deep South, but it was June. Shouldn't it be a lot warmer? This Pacific climate was a puzzle. Foster knew she was staring and reminded herself this arrangement between them was purely professional. She'd been hired by Gertie to write a memoir and nothing more. She looked away as she shifted her weight from one foot to the other and then, despite every effort to appear impervious to the chill in the air, she shivered.

"You're cold."

"I suppose I should have packed a heavier sweater." Foster hugged herself, tucking her hands under her armpits for warmth.

"Let's go inside. Cora will have breakfast ready soon." Abby started walking and Foster had to take quick steps to catch up. "Do you drink coffee?"

Does the earth circle the sun?

"Yes, I drink coffee." Foster quickly stepped past Abby and held the door for her.

The sound of clinking dishware came from the kitchen. Foster waited in the entryway while Abby shrugged out of her jacket and hung it, along with the scarf, on a peg near the door. Abby seemed to prefer a bubble of open personal space at all times and Foster tried to honor that. She'd noticed it the previous night in the library. At all times, even climbing the stairs, Abby kept her just beyond arm's reach, a cushion of air between them. Foster wasn't sure exactly how she knew that Abby needed space, but she did.

"Good morning," Cora cheerfully greeted them from the stove. "I've made some biscuits. And I have coffee in case Ms. Owen prefers it. Abby and I are tea drinkers you see."

"Please, call me Foster." Cora would likely provide a wealth of random facts if Foster got a chance to sit down and interview her properly. Her tale about the shipwreck the previous evening had been intriguing.

Her glasses had fogged up the second they'd stepped into the warmth of the cozy kitchen. She wiped at them with her sweater and held them away from her face as she waited for the glass to adjust to the room temperature.

"You two sit and eat. I'm going to run a cup of tea out to Iain in the barn." Cora set a plate of biscuits on the table next to a serving tray of butter, fruit jam, and honey. "Oh, maybe I should take him one of these as well." She reached over and scooped up a biscuit with a cloth napkin.

Abby smiled, as if there was some inside joke afoot.

"What's funny?"

Abby waited until Cora was out the door before responding. "I think Cora has designs on Mr. Green."

"Was he the man who took your horse just now?"

"Yes, Iain Green. He's a local farrier and he's been helping me with the horses."

"How many horses do you have?" Foster added cream to her coffee and stirred slowly. She couldn't seem to take her eyes off Abby, whose cheeks were pink from the chilly morning air.

"At the moment, five, including Boots. Boots is really the only one I ride regularly. The others are in recovery."

"Recovery?"

"We take in horses that have suffered trauma, neglect, or abuse." Abby put butter on a biscuit and allowed it to melt. "I have the acreage and the time, and…"

"And?"

"Nothing." Abby seemed suddenly shy.

Foster wondered if she'd been about to say money. Foster didn't know much about horses, but she figured they were expensive.

"I always ride first thing in the morning. Before the fog lifts."

"So, it does get sunny in California at some point?" She was beginning to think every postcard she'd ever seen was a lie.

"Usually by noon."

"I'm not really a morning person. I'm only up now because it's nearly ten o'clock in Atlanta and my phone woke me up." Foster ate half a biscuit in two bites. It was delicious. Cora was a good cook, that was evident.

Abby watched Foster as she studied the old dresser along the far wall of the kitchen. Teacups with various patterns hung across the front of it, and the shelves were lined with vintage dishware. The antique cabinet had belonged to her great-great-grandmother. After a minute, Foster looked back, and Abby turned her focus to refilling her tea.

Foster was an adorable soft butch. Her hair was charmingly tousled from sleep, and she had on a well-worn blue crew neck sweater over a white T-shirt. The sweater looked like a hand-me-down from a bygone era. Foster adjusted her glasses and smiled.

Abby had never dated a woman before, but if she ever did, she decided that Foster would be her type. She had an alluring innocence that made Abby want to scoop her up, cradle her head against her chest, and run her fingers through Foster's hair. But that would be a terrible idea. Abby knew that getting close to someone she was attracted to, physical contact, was never a good idea.

But was separation what she really wanted? Not really, but she'd decided a long time ago it was safer for others if she kept to herself. Ever since that fateful kiss when she was a teen, she'd been afraid to let anyone get close. Richard, the boy, had recovered fully from the—accident—but things were never the same after that with the other kids in town. And then it had happened again with Elissa, in college. Abby took a deep breath and sighed.

"Is everything okay?" Foster had a look of concern on her face.

"Yes, sorry." She'd let her mind wander to dark places. She fidgeted in her chair and smiled.

"Can I ask you a few questions?"

Abby was reminded that Foster was here to write a memoir. This wasn't a casual breakfast with a friend. This whole thing had been arranged by Gertie. She'd meant to ask Foster to leave, but now they were sitting here having tea and biscuits as if they were becoming fast friends. Maybe she should allow Foster to stay for another day. It seemed rude to send her away after only one night in California after traveling from Georgia.

"What sort of questions?"

"Well, I was thinking I'd drive into Spencer's Cove later and visit the library." Foster sipped her coffee. "It doesn't seem like you have Wi–Fi here and my cell service is so spotty that I can't really use my phone as a hotspot."

"No, sorry, we don't have Wi–Fi."

"It's okay. I need to visit the library anyway to start research for the book." She reached for another biscuit and applied jam as she talked. "Cora mentioned a shipwreck yesterday, and I just wondered how much you knew about it."

"Not much really." That wasn't entirely true. She held her tea with both hands and sipped. "It's probably more folklore than fact."

"Funny, that's the same thing Cora said."

"Really?"

"So, you've never checked into the story?"

"No, not really." The truth was, she had been curious, but her father had sort of shut down her pursuit of details. She was much younger then and let it go. Now she wondered why he'd done that.

"Do you by chance have any journals or personal papers from any of your grandparents? If you did, that'd be a good place to start."

"What are you looking for?"

"Specifics. You know, names, dates."

"There are some things in my grandfather's old desk in the study. I could—" What was she doing? She'd forgotten for a moment not to trust Foster. She cleared her throat. "I'm sorry, um, will you excuse me." Abby stood, scraping the wooden chair loudly across the stones of the tile floor. "Please enjoy your coffee."

She fled the kitchen and climbed the steps hurriedly to her room as if she feared Foster would give chase. She'd felt backed into a corner by their conversation and didn't know how else to escape. Once in her room she crossed to the bathroom sink and splashed cold water on her face. She needed to calm down. A warm soak in the tub would help her relax and refocus. She sank to the side of the tub with her face in her hands and let the water run.

CHAPTER SEVEN

Foster stared at the empty chair across from her. Abby had practically rushed from the room without preamble and without warning. Had she done something to upset Abby? She replayed the conversation in her head, but nothing stood out. She stared at the empty seat, with a half-eaten biscuit midair, when she heard the back door close.

"Oh, hello there. You're all by yourself then?" Cora seemed as surprised as Foster.

"Yes, um, Abby had somewhere to be." Foster wasn't sure what else to say.

"Well, I'll just sit for a minute and keep you company then." Cora poured herself a cup of tea and reached for a biscuit. "I'm needing a second cup of tea anyway."

Foster found Cora to be pleasant company, but Abby's abrupt exit was still bothering her. She'd thought if she lingered for another cup of coffee that Abby might return to join them, but she didn't. Finally, Foster excused herself to shower and change. She was anxious to see what she could sleuth out at the library about the origins of Spencer's Cove. Even if Abby chose not to participate in the research, her curiosity about the shipwreck was piqued.

By ten past ten she was parked along Main Street near the front of the Spencer's Cove public library. It was a small, square building. Red brick rose halfway up the front. The rest of the building was constructed of weathered gray wood. The thought had occurred to Foster that most of the structures were wooden because of earthquakes, but that was just a hypothesis.

The library seemed empty except for a woman at the checkout desk. She was probably in her late forties and was the antithesis of the sexy librarian fantasy. Not that Foster cared, but if she'd been cute that would have only made the research more fun. The woman looked up as Foster approached the desk. Her shaggy brown hair was dangerously close to a mullet. She wore large round glasses that looked like they were a holdover from the eighties and possibly had not been properly cleaned since then. Fingerprint smudges on glasses bothered Foster to no end. The woman was wearing a flannel shirt, two sizes too large, baggy jeans, and Crocs. Foster liked Crocs about as much as socks with sandals. No one should wear them, ever.

"Hello." Foster spoke first. Trying for her best friendly Southerner routine.

"Can I help you?" The woman's question had an insincere ring to it.

"Yeah, I'm trying to find some information about a shipwreck..." She angled her head to read the woman's nametag. Dena Alvarez. "...Dena."

"I'm afraid you'll need to be a bit more specific." Dena was surly, her demeanor completely flat. She had clearly not attended charm school, in fact, if there was a charm school in the area Dena had never even driven by it. "If you know the date and the name of the ship and perhaps its captain, where it came from, and where it was headed, then perhaps I could help you."

Foster opened her mouth, but before she could formulate a response, Dena cut her off.

"Ships had to register from port to port even during that era, so there would certainly be records."

"Actually, I believe it was a shipwreck that happened here. Probably in the 1850s." Foster took an educated guess at the date.

"Hmm, the *Equus*."

"As in, the Latin word for horse?" That seemed like an odd coincidence given Abby's interest in horses.

"Equus is a genus of mammals in the family Equidae, which includes horses."

Foster bristled at the librarian smackdown but was determined not to let Dena get to her. If she was the only librarian in town then Foster needed her help, at least initially.

"Yes, I guess that's the wreck I'm looking for."

"The *Equus* sank near Lighthouse Point in the summer of 1850." Dena turned to scribble something on a scrap of paper. "Luckily, California was hopping at that time because the gold rush was in full swing. A number of newspapers covered the wreck. Check this source."

Dena handed the paper to Foster. On it, was a URL for the library at the University of Southern California's list of historical newspapers by region. Jackpot.

"Thank you." Despite her grumpy, "I'd rather chew barbed wire than smile" demeanor, Dena had just given her a great launch point for her research.

It didn't take long to find two stories about the *Equus*. One from the *Bombay Times* and the other from the *Alta California*, the first daily newspaper in California. The first issue was published from San Francisco on Thursday, January 4 in 1849, and the paper had some connection to Mark Twain. He was a literary hero of Foster's so she made a note to return to that lead at a later date.

According to the story in the *Alta California*, the *Equus* was a V-hulled ship built by the Gardner Brothers of Baltimore. A cross-reference told her that V-hulled ships were built for speed and often used for the opium or slave trade. That last detail tingled uncomfortably in her gut. She scrolled down.

The headline read *Shipwreck and loss of life*. The brig *Equus* had sailed from Boston to India and then departed China on the sixteenth of June. The ship was lost on the reef about sixty miles above Fort Ross on the twenty-sixth. A point of origin from China meant this ship was probably carrying opium or other goods from

Asia. Master E. H. Howe had been at the helm, and only his daughter had survived. Now Foster was really intrigued.

❖

Abby couldn't stop thinking about the questions Foster had asked during breakfast. The house was quiet when she came back down after her bath, even Cora wasn't about. She assumed Foster had embarked on her research trip to the library. Abby decided to pay a visit to her grandfather's old roll top desk and do a little research of her own.

The study was a small room adjacent to the library. Most days the door remained closed and Abby rarely went in. There were items in that room that had not been used in years. Cora dusted the room, but she put things back in their place. The small study was lined with bookshelves, and there were random stacks of books that had probably been where they were since her father had read them. A well-loved, well-worn upholstered chair sat in one corner, with a small ottoman in front of it. A floor lamp, an antique radio from the 1920s with wooden sides, an old camera on a nearby shelf, and her grandfather's desk along the opposite wall. The entire space looked like a collection of things from the *Antiques Roadshow*.

The room offered a sense of comfort and sadness at the same time. Comfort from objects loved by persons who at one time were close to her, and sadness because every object in the room reminded her of the loss of those connections.

She traced the groove of the roll top with her fingertip before she lifted it. Expecting it to be stiff, she gave it more force than was required. The top retracted like an accordion fan, slipping up and over to reveal her grandfather's writing instruments. Two glass jars of ink, one almost empty, a blotter, and random sheets of loose-leaf paper were on top of the main desk surface. Slots above the surface were filled with folded notes and envelopes. She pulled one of the envelopes free and realized right away it had been sent from her father back in the 1960s. The postmark was from Chicago, so he'd no doubt sent the letter during his study there at Northwestern. She stowed the letter with the intention to come back and read it later.

What she was really looking for was the journal she'd thought of earlier during her conversation with Foster. She'd seen it once, a long time ago, in the drawer of this desk. She drew the drawer out slowly. There it was, just where she remembered it.

Abby didn't have a lot of memories of her grandfather, as he'd died when she was a child, but she remembered her father saying once that his father had been too distracted by history. Her father never wanted to dwell in the past; he was always about moving forward. Abby had always held this belief that certain aspects of the past made people who they were. Not that people were predestined to be who they were, but maybe at least their past, their heritage, foreshadowed who they might become.

Sometimes Abby felt as if she'd been born in the wrong era. She'd have felt much more at home had she come into the world a hundred and fifty years earlier. This feeling made her an ill fit with her very modern parents. It was also one of the reasons that she'd never put Wi-Fi in the house, or cable TV. She wanted to hold at bay the twenty-four-hour news cycle and create a place where one could still seek and find quiet spaces.

She lifted the journal from the drawer and closed it, and then settled into the overstuffed chair across the room. The pages of the journal were stiff from age and dried ink. The variation in the opacity of the ink made it obvious that the words had been written with a quill of some sort. Abby marveled at how much of the density of the ink on the page had been preserved. But enough with the tactile details, she began to focus on the words. She returned to the beginning, then sank back into the high-backed chair and read.

Research at the library made the hours pass quickly. The discovery of Howe's daughter made Foster's brain light up with other questions. She wondered if it was unusual for a captain to bring his daughter along. A secondary search revealed that while it wasn't common practice, it also wasn't unheard of, if the girl was preteen. For a little while, Foster got utterly sidetracked following related threads about women at sea before she was able to tear herself away and return to her original search.

Sometimes that happened. She'd come across some tantalizing tidbit doing research for something else and she'd have to follow the wormhole to see where it might lead. Foster could waste hours getting lost in subsequent searches. During her recent bout of writer's block, the tendency to lose herself for hours by following a line of investigation had only gotten worse.

Who was this Howe fellow, the captain? She started a search for E. H. Howe of Boston and fairly quickly found a connection between Howe and the Salem witch trials. That was unexpected. One of his ancestors, Mercy Howe, had been accused of witchcraft and hanged. What had she been accused of?

Sidetracked again, Foster couldn't help herself.

In 1692, the Massachusetts Bay Colony had executed fourteen women, five men, and two dogs for witchcraft. Innocents were hanged, while some, believed to be guilty, actually escaped. From recorded accounts it seemed that in the darkness, at the edge of the wilderness, the sacred and the occult had collided. Several unfortunate citizens were caught up in the carnage.

Fascinating, but she was unable to find a direct reference to Mercy Howe's acts of witchery. She sank back in the chair. There was definitely a story here, somewhere. A story behind the so-called facts. Hunger pangs caused her to check her watch. She'd been scrolling through entries for two hours. It was almost twelve and the biscuits had worn off. She copied the links and emailed them to herself so that she could easily find her place after lunch.

Her cell phone rang just as she was stowing her laptop. Gloria again. How much trouble could one oversized feline cause?

"Hello, Gloria."

"I think William Faulkner has escaped." Gloria sounded panicked. "I can't find him anywhere."

"Did you check my car?"

"William Faulkner can drive?"

Yeah, about as often as he eats marbles.

"No, Gloria, he can't drive." Foster held the phone against her shoulder as she slid her notes into her bag. "If he gets into the garage he sometimes likes to climb into the back seat of the car."

When she looked up, Dena was glaring at her, arms across her chest.

"There he is! I found him." Gloria was out of breath from hustling to the garage. The garage was attached to the kitchen, but there were a few steps involved. "Everything's okay. Don't you worry."

"Thanks, Gloria. I've gotta go." She clicked off.

"This is a library, not some snooty café where everyone is permanently attached to their cell phones. The policy is clearly marked." Dena pointed to a sign near the main entrance with a big red circle and a horizontal line drawn across a very rudimentary drawing of a cell phone.

"Got it." Foster was hungry and not in the mood to argue.

She amused herself for a few seconds imagining introducing Dena and Gloria. That would be a floorshow for sure. Foster and Dena were still the only people in the library. She wondered if it was safe to take a chance and ask Dena for a recommendation after the whole cell phone incident. She waited a few minutes to give Dena time to calm down.

"Hi, sorry to bother you, but could you point me in the direction of a good spot for lunch?"

Dena pointed toward the window. Foster partially turned to look over her shoulder.

"That direction?" When she'd asked Dena to point, she hadn't meant it literally.

"Uneda Eat."

"Yeah, I do need to eat, but—"

"No, Uneda Eat. Uneda, with a U. It's across the street." Dena pointed again.

"Oh." She started for the door. "Thanks."

Once outside, she could see that the vintage sign had at one time read Uneda Meats, but the "M" and the "S" were now missing. She checked for traffic and then strolled across the street. Abby had been right about the sun. It was breaking through the clouds and warming the sea scented air. In another half hour she wouldn't need her thrift store jacket with the suede elbow patches. She'd brought two suit jackets. Foster felt pretty sure that this one, with the suede elbow patches, raised her IQ a few points. At least that was her theory, although Dena was clearly not impressed.

CHAPTER EIGHT

A bby stood quietly in the center of the grassy enclosure, giving Sasha time to adjust to her presence. She'd spent more than an hour looking through her grandfather's journal and could have stayed there for another hour. One repeated note puzzled her, that he was seeking mercy. Mercy from what or from whom? The entries were unclear. And she'd have to wait to sort them out because she needed to be out with the horses for now. She took another step closer to Sasha and then held her position.

Sasha was a nine-year-old Arabian cross chocolate bay. She'd been found after a stormy night in someone's pasture. Someone who didn't own a horse. It had taken three hours for the local veterinarian, Abby, and Iain to herd Sasha into a trailer. By the time they got her back to the barn, Sasha was shivering and frightened.

There were rope burns all around her feet. The vet and Iain both believed the scars most likely meant that Sasha had been the victim of an illegal Mexican Charreada rope tripping contest. Money was bet on which cowboy could throw a rope around a young horse's feet at full speed and slam them to the ground. These horrible events usually ended with the horse suffering broken legs, dislocated shoulders, and then death. Sasha had obviously survived by fighting her way out.

Sasha edged closer. The muscles in her shoulder twitched. She was probably deciding whether to stay or flee. Abby assumed a relaxed stance with her hands at her sides. Sasha took a few more steps in her direction.

It's okay, girl. You're safe now. No one is going to hurt you again. Abby sensed Sasha's uncertain fear as if it were her own. Her heart ached.

Sasha snorted and dipped her head. It took a few more minutes before she completely closed the space between them. Abby didn't reach for her immediately. She allowed Sasha to stand very close and nibble grass. After a while, Sasha rubbed her muzzle against Abby, gauging her scent. When she did finally place her palm on Sasha's neck, she jerked her head up, eyes wide, black pools of distress.

"Easy, Sasha. You're safe." This time Abby spoke aloud, but barely more than a whisper. She kept light contact with her hand as Sasha shifted her weight from foot to foot.

She stayed with Sasha for about twenty minutes before she turned toward the gate where Iain was leaning against the railing.

"That was good." He was talking to Abby, but he was watching Sasha move slowly back toward the far side of the fenced enclosure.

"She's getting better. I only had to wait a half hour or so before she came to me."

"You're so good with these animals." Iain turned toward her so that only one arm rested on the top rail. "It's as if you can read their minds and you know exactly what they need."

"I suppose I'm just a good listener." His earnest compliment made her feel shy.

"I dare say it's a bit more than that." He smiled.

It was true. Something else happened when she was with animals. They had a way of understanding each other that she couldn't explain. She felt what they felt, and she was fairly sure the same was true in reverse. Sometimes all she had to do was think something and animals seemed to respond. Abby spent more time with horses now, but when she was younger she'd had similar experiences with dogs and cats, sometimes even birds and rabbits.

"How are we for supplies?" Abby walked beside Iain toward the barn.

"We could use another few bags of feed."

Mostly, horses just ate grass or hay, but since they were nursing a few of their residents back to full health, they were supplementing their grass diet with corn and oats, boosted with additional nutrients. "I'll see if Evan can pick some up later." Evan seemed to make trips to town every day. Abby wasn't sure why and hadn't asked. Evan kept to herself which suited Abby.

She left Iain and walked toward a second enclosure where Journey was leisurely grazing. She rested her chin on her arms as she leaned against the fence rail. Abby was just about to return to the house to find lunch when a sharp pain caused her to double over. It was almost as if a sharp object had been driven through her abdomen. She dropped to the ground in a heap, gasping for air.

Foster crumpled into a ball on the floor. She'd reached for a book on an upper shelf, and it thumped loudly in the quiet space as she dropped it. She hugged herself and pulled her knees to her chest as she lay on her side on the floor between high library shelves crammed with books. Air rushed from her lungs as if she'd been punched in the stomach. This was nothing like a menstrual cramp. And besides, she was nowhere near her cycle. This was the sort of intense pain that caused someone to dial 9-1-1.

After a moment, the pain subsided. She sat up, with her back resting against the nearest shelf. She swept her hand across her forehead, which was damp with perspiration. What just happened? Was she having appendicitis? The sharp pain came out of nowhere and receded just as quickly as it had arrived. She'd only just returned to the library after getting a bite to eat. Had the lunch been bad? She'd had soup and a half sandwich, pretty tame by lunch standards.

Foster tilted her head back, closed her eyes, and waited. Before she got to her feet she wanted to make sure the pain was gone for sure.

"Is everything all right back here?"

Good thing there wasn't an actual emergency because it had taken Dena a good seven minutes to respond.

"I thought I heard something fall." Dena stood at the end of the aisle with her hands on her hips.

"I dropped a book." Foster still hadn't gotten to her feet.

"Why are you on the floor?" A question asked without an ounce of genuine concern.

"I got dizzy for a moment." Not really true, but Foster didn't feel like going into detail about the truth with such an unsympathetic listener.

Maybe she should get another cup of coffee. She almost laughed. She'd had stomach pains and had almost passed out, so of course her elixir of choice was coffee. Maybe not the smartest choice, but what could she do? Coffee was her go-to drink for almost any ailment: headaches, stress, writer's block, and the common cold.

The weathered sign for Cove Coffee and Tackle squeaked in the breeze, calling her forward. Fresh air, a walk, and caffeine was never a bad thing. She packed up her laptop, shouldered her leather bag, and waved to Dena as she left. Dena didn't wave back, big surprise. She'd downloaded enough material to keep her busy for a couple of hours. She could camp out in the coffee shop and read. That would probably be a friendlier environment to hang out in anyway.

Evan saw Abby crumple to the ground. She scanned the area quickly. Iain was in the barn, and no one else had been around to witness the event. She rushed to where Abby had fallen. Abby was in a fetal position on the ground. The earth beneath where she lay looked charred. Jagged dark lines extended out from the darkened spot like singed lightning.

The transmutation had begun, and luckily for everyone, Abby had grounded herself. The question was, did she understand what was happening or had she acted intuitively? Abby's eyes fluttered.

"Abby?" Evan knelt down.

Abby looked at her, confusion, possibly fear, in her eyes.

She doesn't know. And Evan wasn't really authorized to inform her.

"I'm okay." Abby tried to sit up.

Evan started to reach for Abby, but she held her hand up. Abby clearly didn't want Evan to touch her, so she must have some sense of her potential ability to affect others.

"I'm fine, thank you." Abby slowly stood, using the fence railing to stabilize.

"Are you sure you're okay? Let me get the ATV so I can give you a ride up to the house."

Abby shook her head. It was only about a hundred yards from the barn to the house. She started walking without looking at the ground. Evan wondered if Abby had even noticed the blackened, singed grass. She seemed visibly shaken and not entirely stable on her feet.

Abby was several feet away when she looked back.

"Iain said we need a few bags of feed. Would you mind driving the truck into town to pick some up?"

"I'd be happy to. There are some other things I need anyway." Evan needed to report this incident as soon as possible.

"Do you mind if I ride with you?"

"Not at all." She'd prefer to go alone, but how could she refuse?

"Thank you. I'll come find you in a little while." Abby smiled and started again toward the house.

Evan lingered, looking down at the dark pattern on the ground where Abby had fallen. She'd never seen a marking this large before. The power surge must have been huge to leave such a pattern. The headaches, the intuition with the animals, the social anxiety, Abby's raw magnetism, her penetrating gaze, and now this. The evidence seemed to be multiplying.

She'd never seen anything like this before. Her flesh tingled, not from the cool sea breeze, but from the knowledge of what was coming.

CHAPTER NINE

Abby retreated to her room. She kicked off her muddy boots and slipped under the covers fully clothed. What was happening to her? She'd had anxiety before, even brief panic attacks, but she was beginning to feel truly afraid.

Was she having some sort of mental break? Was she delusional?

If she tried to explain what she'd been experiencing surely someone would suggest she be admitted to a mental health facility. Maybe she should be. The headaches, the dreams...the dreams that seemed too real, almost as if they were a glimpse into some parallel world, or possibly a glimpse into the past or future, but not necessarily hers.

She squeezed her eyes shut and pulled a pillow over her head. The darkness soothed her. Her breathing slowed. The event, whatever it was, had exhausted her. Sleep seeped in from the edges of the pillow and pulled her under.

Her body tingled.

Without opening her eyes, she licked her lips. They tasted of salt. Wind whipped across her face, laden with sea spray. She opened her eyes and reached for something to hold on to. Her footing felt unstable as the plank flooring under her feet shifted sharply. Somehow, Abby was at sea. She looked down at clothing foreign to her: a long dress, ankle-high shoes buttoned up the sides. All around her was chaos. Men shouted above the wind, sails tore and tumbled, and the loud crack of timbers breaking apart pierced the air. Suddenly, her vision was filled by a bearded man. He grabbed her and shoved her into a cabin behind where she'd been standing. Once inside she stood dumbly beside him as he rummaged with urgency through a drawer in a cabinet affixed to the wall.

"Swallow this!" The roar of the sea and wind were so loud that he practically had to shout to be heard.

He held something in his hand, but before she could take it from him the floor lurched sharply and they both tumbled. He crawled toward her keeping one hand balled into a fist.

"Open your mouth."

Somehow, Abby knew this man was her father, or the father of whomever this vision belonged to.

"Open your mouth!"

Abby did as she was told. The substance was gritty and bitter as she tried to swallow it. From his vest pocket he pulled an amulet. It took three attempts because of the rocking of the ship to place the gold chain over her head. Instinctively, she covered the jewel with her hand.

"Hold this talisman tightly. Do not let go." He pressed his lips to her forehead. "I love you, Mercy."

"Daddy—" The mixture on her tongue choked her words.

"You are my daughter, you are the love of my life…and you… will live." He kissed her again.

He got to his feet and with faltering steps exited the cabin into the fray on deck. Abby held the amulet up so that she could see it. It was a stone of aquamarine inside an ornate gold setting that looked like sculpted, braided rope. The cabin floor tilted violently. She closed her fist around the stone as she was tossed hard against the sideboard.

A small shaving mirror fell to the floor nearby, along with other sundries from her father's desk. The reflection that stared back at Abby was not hers. There was definitely a familial resemblance, blue eyes, blond hair, and tapered jawline. The reflection could easily have belonged to a younger cousin. As Abby stared at the girl's image, the reflected face spoke. It wasn't Abby's voice, but she heard the young girl speak inside her head. She repeated the phrase.

"Abby, you are the one."

The ship rocked ferociously, tossing Abby back. A rushing sound flooded her ears.

Abby jolted awake. Her heart was racing.

The pillow fell to the floor as she sat up in bed. She ran her tongue over her lips and tasted salt. When she held her hand up to examine it, the indentation of the braided rope that bordered the amulet was visible in her palm. Mercy, her grandfather had been seeking Mercy, the girl from her vision. A shiver ran up her arm.

Foster laced her fingers together, stretched her arms over her head, and arched her back. She'd been scrolling through pages on her laptop for a few hours without standing up. Cove Coffee and Tackle had Wi-Fi and refills. She'd gotten a chance to follow various threads while a very attractive barista named Jai kept her caffeinated. The coffee shop was a pleasant alternative locale for research, and it was only a block away from the library.

Her online sleuthing had revealed that Abby's great-great-great-grandmother, the young girl who'd been the sole survivor aboard the *Equus*, was named Mercy.

Mercy Howe, the younger, had been named after an ancestor put to death for witchcraft. For some reason, this discovery surprised Foster. She'd figured someone of that era, in the 1800s, would have been a bit more superstitious. Mercy had been rescued and eventually married Thomas Spencer. She wondered how much of this family history Abby already knew. It sure would make her job easier if Abby considered sharing.

"Do you need another refill?" Jai paused next to her chair with the carafe.

"No, thank you. If I drink any more coffee I might just float away." Foster shut her laptop. "Do you guys really sell bait and tackle in addition to coffee?"

Jai smiled. "Not really, thank goodness. You can get a fishing license here, and sunscreen, but not bait. Live bait and baked goods don't mix well. Can you imagine?" She looked up as if she were about to perform improv. "I'd like a container of live crickets, oh, and one of those raspberry scones...thanks."

"Yeah, not appetizing for sure." Foster laughed. "So, Cove Coffee and Tackle in name only. Good to know."

"I love your accent." Jai rested her free hand on her hip and gave Foster her full attention. "Are you from Texas?"

"No, Georgia."

This was the third time since arriving in California that she'd been asked this question. It seemed that Texas was the only southern state Californians were familiar with, maybe because it was geographically the closest. As anyone from the South would confirm, a Texas accent and a Georgia accent were absolutely not the same. It was possibly offensive to even suggest that they were, but Foster was gonna let this slide, given Jai's long list of otherwise pleasant traits.

"We don't get new people here that often and now we have two. And you couldn't be more different from one another."

"Oh, really? Who else is new besides me?"

"Her name is Evan. She works at the Spencer place." Jai reached for Foster's empty coffee cup.

"You don't say? I just assumed she was a local."

"Oh, so you know each other?" Jai seemed surprised.

"We only just met. I'm doing some research about the Spencer family."

Jai's eyes brightened and she sat in the empty chair across from Foster. She rested the coffee carafe on the edge of the table.

"What sort of research?"

Foster was surprised anyone would be interested, especially someone who lived in Spencer's Cove. She figured the residents knew more about the founding family's origins than she did.

"It's not that exciting, really, just a memoir project." Foster tried to downplay what she'd discovered so far.

"I love history." Jai rested her chin on her hand as if she were settling in for a long chat.

"Yeah, so do I."

The bell over the door chimed. Jai reluctantly stood to return to the counter.

"Come back some time and let me know what you find out."

"Sure." Foster started packing up her laptop and dog-eared notebook.

It was late afternoon. The wind had picked up again, but it wasn't nearly as chilly as it had been earlier. Probably because the marine layer was still camped out at sea. Foster thought she'd stroll down to the pier for a look before returning to her rental car.

The pier area was pretty quiet. There was some sort of large machinery, probably a boat wench, and there were white and red floatation rings hanging along the rail with the word *Rescue* stenciled in black letters on them. A faded sign at the end of the fifty-foot pier warned about strong surf and tsunamis. Foster leaned against the railing at the end of the pier and studied the churning water. To the left was a narrow strip of rocky beach. There were some fairly thick lengths of driftwood piled at the edge of the cliff. Probably successive tides had washed the dead trees backward against the steep incline. To the right were cliffs, with no approach to sea level. In the distance to the north, she could just barely see the top of the old lighthouse located at the edge of the Spencer property.

The *Equus* had hit a jagged reef somewhere between this point and the lighthouse. Foster tried to imagine the scene. A stormy night, a mostly uncharted coastline, a native Pomo Indian watching the floating castle sink from the top of the cliff. His had been the only eyewitness account, except for Mercy Howe, the captain's daughter. Ironic that Mercy, with the unlucky namesake, was the only member of the crew to survive.

Foster was anxious to spend some time with Abby and find out how much of the story she knew, or what, if any, additional details Abby could provide.

She held the front of her jacket together with one hand and walked up the gradual rise from the pier toward where she'd left her car.

CHAPTER TEN

The feed store and the hardware store were part of the same building, owned by a local family. Between the two shops, brimming with inventory, almost anything a person needed could be purchased. Evan left the store to pull the truck around back for the bags of feed they'd purchased, and Abby had wandered into the clothing department. Levi's, Carhartt, and a few other outdoor brands hung on round racks. A pile fleece lined Levi's jacket caught her eye, and she thought of Foster shivering in the early morning chill.

Abby held up a men's medium. That looked like the right size. She carried it up front and paid for it. Evan was pulling along the side of the building just as she stepped out onto the sidewalk.

"You bought a jacket? Nice." Evan looked over, then faced forward and put the truck in drive.

Abby hadn't gotten a bag for the purchase; she folded the jacket across her lap.

"It's for Foster." Abby wasn't sure why, but revealing the garment was a gift made her cheeks warm.

"Oh."

Was Evan bothered by the jacket? Abby was sure she'd imagined it.

As they turned north on Main Street to drive back to the estate, Foster stood on the side of the road next to her rental car, as if she'd conjured her.

"Will you pull over?" Abby lowered her window as Evan eased the giant truck alongside Foster's parked car.

"Hi." Foster smiled.

"Hi."

"I'm really glad to see you. The car is dead."

"Dead?"

Evan leaned on the steering wheel to listen, but she let Abby do all the talking.

"I'm not used to these damn keyless cars. I think I must have left the ignition on when I got back in to raise the windows." Foster sank her hands in her pockets. "At any rate, it's deader than a door nail. I was just about to walk to the café and try to call someone when I saw your truck."

"I can give you a jump." Evan spoke for the first time. She threw the truck in park and climbed out. She rummaged in the tool compartment in the bed of the truck, just behind the cabin. "Or maybe not."

"No cables?" Foster leaned against the edge of the truck bed.

"I must have left them in the barn. I had to recharge the battery in the ATV the other day." Evan frowned.

"We'll give you a ride home and come back later for your car." Abby opened her door for Foster to climb in.

"Let me get my bag." Foster leaned in through the passenger side door and returned with a laptop bag.

Abby scooted across the bench seat to make room for her. Evan seemed annoyed, but she wasn't sure why. It wasn't as if Foster had stranded herself on purpose.

"That's a nice jacket." Foster's elbow was on the windowsill, but the truck picked up speed, and after a few seconds the cool air caused her to raise the window.

"Oh, I bought this for you." Abby's cheeks felt warm again as she handed the garment to Foster.

"For me?"

"Yes, you seemed…well, you seemed cold this morning. I thought you might need something warmer." Abby smiled thinly and averted her gaze. For some reason she couldn't look at Foster.

Foster's soft brown eyes made her feel things, and feeling things would only be dangerous for Foster.

"Wow, thank you, that's very generous." Foster sounded genuinely pleased with the gift.

That made Abby happy. Her mood brightened and she forgot for a moment the frightening vision of the ship at sea.

❖

Evan felt like a chaperone on a first date, and she wasn't happy about it.

She needed to relay the details of this afternoon's event to the Council, but she couldn't very well get away to make that call with Abby inviting herself along on afternoon errands. And now she had Foster to contend with too. Well, she'd drive them home and then come back to town to phone the East Coast. It would be late, but the Council did much of its business at night anyway.

"Hey, would you mind stopping there for a minute?" Foster pointed toward a graveyard just ahead. "I just wanted to check for some names."

"We should get back to the house. I'm sure Abby has things to do." Evan tried to deflect Foster's request.

"It's okay. I don't mind stopping," Abby said before Evan had a chance to craft a better excuse not to stop.

Evan begrudgingly turned in. An iron gate hung askew, some of its hinges having rusted through, severing its connection to the stone arch over the entrance. This was an ancient cemetery by western standards. As they climbed out of the truck, Evan saw some of the dates went back to the 1830s.

The fog was starting to roll in, creating a spooky, nearly twilight scene. Evan felt as if she'd stumbled into an old black-and-white horror film. This was the perfect setting for some sinister thing to transpire. She zipped the front of her jacket and shoved her hands in her pockets. Foster and Abby were walking away from the truck in the opposite direction. She had no choice but to follow them.

Being in a cemetery was a terrible idea, but Evan hadn't been able to deflect the excursion. This was an especially bad idea because Evan had no idea where Abby was in her transition. The dead carried much to the grave. Graveyards were charged with emotion—unsaid things, unfinished lives, unrequited love.

Evan checked over her shoulder. Was the sky darkening or was that only her imagination?

"What exactly are you looking for?" Evan was careful to walk between the graves and not on top of them.

"I'm looking for the headstone of...there it is." Foster stopped beside a small headstone with the outline of a ship in relief inset into the top of it. "Mercy Howe Spencer."

"Mercy..." Abby turned away, looking off, as if she was putting something together in her head.

"Hey, are you okay?" Evan thought Abby looked pale.

Abby wasn't looking at Mercy's grave, but at the headstones opposite Mercy's. It only took a second for Evan to realize Abby was looking at her parents' joint headstone. Foster was such an asshole for suggesting they come here.

"Oh, Abby, I'm so sorry...I was so in my own head with the research that I didn't stop to think..." Foster didn't finish the thought. She stepped around the nearest grave and reached for Abby's hand.

Evan was too slow to stop her.

Foster grasped Abby's wrist to offer comfort, a very normal thing to do under any other similar circumstances. But the moment they made skin to skin contact a deafening crack struck down from above. A boom, as if the sound barrier had been breached, and an arc of intense light encircled Foster and Abby for only a second before it rippled outward, knocking Evan to the ground. Charged particles hung in the air around Foster and Abby like fireflies before the particles broke apart and sifted to the ground like stardust. Foster was still holding Abby's hand but had dropped to one knee as if she were about to propose.

What the fuck?

Evan scrambled to her feet. It was as if Foster and Abby were frozen in time and space. Black birds flocked toward the cemetery and began to circle above where they stood, hundreds of birds, so many birds that they darkened the already twilight sky. Evan felt the beating of their frenzied wings in her chest. The wind had increased and the fog thickened to the point that Evan could no longer see her truck parked only thirty feet away.

What just happened? Was that an uncontrolled binding? She'd never witnessed one before; she'd only heard stories about them. As far as she knew, there hadn't been a binding like this in more than a century, maybe longer than that. She wracked her memory for the details. Either way, they needed to seek cover.

Evan approached, but neither Abby nor Foster noticed her presence. It was as if they were lost in some trance.

"Abby!" Evan shouted above the wind and the mad, swirling avian swarm overhead. "Foster!" She didn't dare touch them until the trance was broken.

The first thing Foster noticed was silence, absolute silence. She was standing facing Abby. She looked down at their joined hands. Something had happened when she'd touched Abby, and now they were in some other place. Foster rotated, while she maintained contact with Abby, but she couldn't get her bearings. They seemed to be in some dark space with no horizon, no edge, no above, and no below, and yet, they were obviously standing on some sort of firm surface.

"Don't let go." Abby spoke for the first time. She sounded afraid. She regarded Foster with wide eyes.

"I won't." For some reason, Foster wasn't afraid, and maybe she should've been. "What happened? Where are we?"

"I don't know." Abby looked around. "When I touch people… things happen."

"What sort of things?"

"It's hard to explain."

"I'd say this…right now…is hard to explain." Foster motioned with her free hand. "Has this happened before?"

"No. This is something different."

It was so strange. They were surrounded by darkness and there was no discernible light source, and yet, Foster could see Abby so clearly. It was as if there was some sort of soft spotlight shining directly on Abby from above, some heavenly glow, while Foster's position seemed to be in partial shadow. Abby looked up and the light enhanced the blue of her eyes to a brilliant hue.

"Did you hear that?" Foster cocked her head.

"Hear what?"

"I could swear I just heard someone call my name." Faintly at first, then louder.

What was that other sound? The wind, and something else. Her ability to focus was returning. Had she passed out? No, she was kneeling. She was still holding Abby's hand and Abby was looking down at her. She tried to let go but couldn't.

"Foster! Get up!"

She turned her head as if in slow motion. It was almost as if she were drunk. She was lightheaded. She blinked several times to clear her vision. Evan was shouting at her over a torrential windstorm, but she couldn't feel it. She and Abby were in some sort of protective bubble, although she could see that Evan was straining against howling gusts. Evan's hat had blown off, and her hair whipped around her face. She leaned forward in an attempt to remain upright.

Foster stood up. She shook her head. Abby was in some sort of trance.

"Abby? Abby, can you hear me?" Foster lightly touched Abby's face.

The instant she made contact, Abby's gaze regained focus. Foster felt Abby's penetrating gaze pierce her chest like a spear. Abby held her with her eyes for a few seconds, then looked down at their joined hands. The instant she released Foster's hand, whatever had protected them from the raging storm evaporated and Abby faltered. Foster managed to catch her just before she slumped to the ground.

"Abby!" Foster cradled Abby in her arms. She was out cold.

"We need to get out of here!" Evan knelt across from her.

Evan hoisted Abby out of Foster's arms and fought the headwind back toward the truck. Foster salvaged Evan's hat from where it had been pinned against a gravestone. Once in the truck, she pulled Abby against her shoulder and held her. Evan shifted the truck into reverse so quickly that the huge off-road tires threw gravel. Raindrops the size of silver dollars had started to pelt the windshield. The storm was vicious and had come out of nowhere.

"Where are you going?" Foster realized they were headed toward the Spencer estate. "Abby needs a doctor. We should go back to town."

"A doctor can't fix this."

"What do you mean? What the hell happened back there?" For some reason, Foster had only just become aware that Evan didn't seem shocked by what had transpired. "Who are you?"

Evan glanced over with a dark expression but didn't answer.

A large branch dropped across the road, and Evan swerved to miss it. Abby's head lolled to one side. Foster shifted and pulled Abby partially into her lap to stabilize her as Evan fought to keep the truck on the narrow, winding road.

She didn't want to relinquish Abby when they arrived at the house, but she didn't think she could carry Abby by herself. She held the door for Evan. They escaped into the house. The wind drove sharp raindrops against the door as Foster braced her shoulder and used all her weight to close it.

"What the hell is going on?" Foster initially hadn't felt fear, but the longer it took for Abby to wake up the more anxiety crept up her spine to lodge itself at the base of her occipital ridge. She rubbed the hair at the back of her head briskly to get rid of the pins and needles.

Once again, Evan didn't answer. She started up the stairs with Abby in her arms.

"Get candles from the kitchen." Evan yelled to Foster without looking back.

"Candles?" Foster was still following Evan up the stairs.

"Candles! We need five candles, rosemary oil, and salt." Evan glanced back, and Foster could see by her expression that she was deadly serious. "Lots of salt."

"Okay, okay…" Foster turned back toward the kitchen.

"And don't forget matches!" Evan called after her.

Foster rummaged in every single cabinet before she found rosemary oil in the pantry. She had a one-pound canister of Morton's salt under one arm and a box of tea candles when she realized she'd forgotten matches. She jogged back to the kitchen and searched drawers until she found them.

The lights flickered out just as she reached the door of Abby's bedroom. The wind outside was making some rather otherworldly sounds. To say it was howling would have been an understatement. Foster strained to see what was outside the darkened window at the end of the hallway when Evan shouted.

"Hurry!"

Foster rushed into the room. Evan had moved all the furniture and the sectional rug to create a large open space. Abby was lying, still unconscious, on the bed, which had been shoved against the wall.

"Quick, give me the salt." Evan took the canister.

Foster watched, dumbfounded, as Evan began to create a shape on the hardwood floor with lines of salt. It was hard to see exactly what it was in the darkened room until it was almost complete. Foster had seen enough horror movies to recognize the shape right away.

"Hey, wait a minute. That's a pentagram! I'm not gonna stand by while you work some dark spell here…I'm Southern Baptist you know, and I—"

"Shut up, Foster, and hand me the candles. We're running out of time." Evan scowled at her as she held out her hand for the box of candles. She took three and handed the box back to Foster. "I put a drop of oil at each corner. Now place a candle at each point and light it."

Foster worked to light the candles, burning the tip of her finger once. While she struggled to keep them lit, Evan carried Abby from the bed and laid her in the center of the pattern she'd drawn on the floor. Abby was as limp as a rag doll.

"By the dark and the light, let the unforeseen see nothing."

Evan made a motion with her hand for Foster to repeat the words. "By the dark and the light, let the unforeseen see nothing."

"By the dark and the light, let the unforeseen see nothing. Lift away this darkness that hides the light." Again, Evan nodded for Foster to join her.

She mimicked Evan, sitting cross-legged on the opposite side of Abby, just beyond the pentagram's edge.

"By the dark and the light, let the unforeseen see nothing. Lift away this darkness that hides the light." Foster murmured the words in unison with Evan.

"You have to mean it." Evan frowned at her.

"By the dark and the light, let the unforeseen see nothing. Lift away this darkness that hides the light." If this helped Abby in any way, then Foster did mean it. She glared back at Evan and spoke louder. Outside, the wind continued its frenzy. Rain pelted the roof and the windows. "By the dark and the light, let the unforeseen see nothing. Lift away this darkness that hides the light."

Foster wasn't sure how many times they repeated the words when finally, Abby began to stir. The candles had burned almost to the floor.

"Don't." Foster was about to reach for Abby, but Evan held up her hand to stop her. "Give her a minute."

Abby blinked, then looked from side to side. She slowly rose to a seated position as the candle nearest Foster went out.

"Foster?" Abby sounded weak.

"I'm here." She nodded in Evan's direction. "And so is Evan."

"I feel...I feel so strange." Abby rested her palm on her forehead.

For a brief instant, Foster could have sworn that Abby's head had a glowing aura around it, but as quickly as it had appeared, it faded. Abby looked down at the five-pointed star on the floor around her and then glanced from Evan back to Foster.

"What is this?"

"A protection spell." Evan got to her feet. She offered her hand to Abby.

"I don't think that's a good idea." Abby looked at Evan's hand as if it were a threat of some kind.

"It will be okay now." Evan sounded so sure. "Take my hand."

Abby wasn't convinced she could trust what Evan was saying. She was about to refuse again, but Evan stubbornly insisted. Abby closed her eyes as she reached for Evan's hand, preparing for the worst. Strong fingers closed around hers and nothing happened. She opened one eye, half afraid to look, and then the other.

Once on her feet, she didn't release Evan's hand right away. She stared at their clasped hands in disbelief. Ever since she was a teen, physical contact had been dangerous.

"How is this possible?" Abby looked up at Evan.

"I think you'll feel something different when you touch Foster." Evan tipped her head in Foster's direction.

Abby rotated and took Foster's hand between hers. The strangest sensation traveled up her arm, almost like a low voltage electrical current. But it didn't hurt. It wasn't unpleasant, in fact, the almost imperceptible vibration was soothing.

Foster looked down at their joined hands and then back at Abby's face. Foster looked spooked, as if she'd just seen a ghost. Abby glanced up as the overhead light came back to life.

"Can someone please tell me what the hell is going on?" Foster didn't sound angry, maybe just a little on edge.

"Not now." Evan started toward the door. "I will try to explain later. At the moment, I need to drive into town."

"Right now? After what just happened?"

"Yes, right now." Evan was halfway to the door but turned back, invading Foster's personal space. "You…You do not leave Abby's side for one minute. Not one. Do you hear me?"

"Yes, I hear you. But—"

"Do not leave her alone."

"Okay, okay. Calm down." Foster held up her palms in surrender.

"If you knew what I know, you would not be calm either."

That sounded ominous. Abby hugged herself as Evan strode to the door and was gone. She and Foster stood around for a moment as if neither one of them was sure what to do next. Out of nowhere, Abby realized she was starving. She'd had hardly any appetite for days, and right now, all she wanted to do was raid the kitchen.

"Have you had dinner?" That seemed like a ridiculously mundane question, given the circumstances.

"No, and I'm kinda hungry." Foster rested her hand over her stomach. "It seems weird to say that, but it's true."

"Me too. Let's find something to eat." Abby took Foster's hand and tugged her along toward the kitchen.

She'd taken Foster's hand so casually, as if she held hands with people all the time. This was all new territory for Abby, and she felt oddly liberated, from what, or for what purpose, she had no idea.

CHAPTER ELEVEN

Main Street was deserted when Evan parked and crossed the street to the pay phone.

"Report," the same woman as before whispered on the other end of the phone.

Evan wasn't sure how the protectorates who worked in the field dealt with this cloak-and-dagger crap. It felt like being strung along. She was doing her part, calling in, but she wasn't getting any satisfactory information from the other end of the line. Was this how it usually worked? Was this her life now, to be forever in the dark?

"There's been an event."

"Conclusive?"

Evan hesitated for a few seconds. The tiny hairs at the back of her neck were on alert. What was she sensing? She couldn't be sure.

"Well?" An insistent, impatient, whisper.

"Yes, conclusive."

The line went dead and Evan immediately regretted sharing her conclusion.

Fuck this.

Evan dialed the number again. No one answered.

Was the Council going to dispatch a retrieval team for Abby? And if so, when? She'd expected some sort of ETA once she gave them a positive ID. The fucking clock was ticking, and something about this didn't feel right. No, it didn't feel right at all.

Evan had an eerie sense of déjà vu. She'd suffered a similar sense of unease the night of the ritual for Jacqueline, but Jacqueline had dismissed Evan's concerns. In the end, Evan had been right to raise warning flags. She should have been more insistent. Jacqueline wasn't well. If only Evan had been more forceful about postponing the ceremony. If, if, if. Every time she closed her eyes she saw the platform give way; she saw Jacqueline fall to her death. Like some brutal loop inside her head, she'd walk through every step leading up to the accident. What had she missed? That question haunted her.

She'd been sidelined for her failure, but at the same time, this was a second chance to do things right. She fished in her pocket for a handful of change and dialed a different number.

"Hello?" Lisel sounded sleepy. It was three hours later on the East Coast.

"Sorry if I woke you."

"Evan?" There was a rustling sound. "What time is it? What's wrong?"

Lisel had been part of her security team the night everything went to hell. Lisel was the closest thing to a sister Evan had and she'd trust Lisel with her life.

"I think I'm in trouble." Evan wasn't known for her willingness to ask for help, but she was in the dark, literally and figuratively. She didn't want Abby to suffer because she was too arrogant to call and ask for assistance.

"What do you need?" Just like that, Lisel had her back, without hesitation, without reservation.

"Is there anyone we can trust on the West Coast? Someone local?"

"Is the candidate a positive?"

Evan hesitated, unsure of how much to share. She didn't want to put Lisel in danger by breaking protocol and divulging information meant only for the Council of Elders.

"Something is happening that I've never before... And after what happened to Jaqueline..."

"That wasn't your fault. Evan, listen to me—"

"It was my fault." Evan swallowed the lump in her throat. She coughed, but she was sure she hadn't fooled Lisel.

"Don't take any chances. I'm going to reach out to someone I know in LA. What's the number where you are? Give me a few hours."

"Do you have a pen?"

Evan gave Lisel the number for the pay phone. She didn't know what was going on with the Council, but she'd failed to trust her gut the night of Jaqueline's death, and she wasn't taking chances this time. If she was wrong she was wrong and she'd deal with the fallout from her breach in protocol later, when she knew Abby was no longer in danger.

Evan crossed the street to her pickup promising herself that this time everything would be different.

Abby was feeling great appreciation for Cora's thoughtfulness. Cora had the night off but left dinner in a casserole dish on the stove. It was still warm to the touch when they arrived in the kitchen. She reached for dishes and served Foster and then herself. It was some sort of chicken and rice casserole with carrots and mushrooms. Was this dish exceptionally good, or was she simply famished? It was hard to know. Abby finished the first serving and went back for seconds.

"Would you like more?" She glanced over her shoulder from the stove.

"No, I'm good." Foster had barely eaten half of what Abby had heaped onto her plate.

"Why am I so hungry?" Abby didn't really expect an answer. She was musing out loud, to no one in particular. She felt so strange. Was she having some sort of out-of-body experience?

"You seem…different." Foster looked a little pale.

"Are you okay?" Abby stopped eating, fork midair.

"I'm okay, but are *you* okay?" Foster swept her fingers through her hair. "I mean, that thing in the graveyard…and right now there's a pentagram drawn in salt on the floor in your bedroom…and… Evan bullied me into doing some chanting thing, for God only knows what purpose…and…" The words tumbled out. "…and, no, I'm not okay."

Abby settled her fork at the edge of her plate. She was just about to offer some reassurance but stopped herself. Someone was coming. How did she know that?

The back door near the kitchen opened and closed. A moment later, Evan presented herself at the end of the table. No one spoke.

"Would you like something to eat?" Abby finally broke the awkward silence.

"Yeah, food isn't a bad idea." Evan shrugged out of her jacket. Abby handed her a serving of Cora's casserole.

"Where did you go?" Foster had pushed her plate aside without finishing it.

"I had to make a phone call." Evan took three huge forkfuls.

"We have phones in the house." Abby was confused.

"I had to make the call from a public phone, in town, so that it couldn't be traced back here."

"Well, if someone did trace a call to Spencer's Cove it wouldn't take much detective work to end up here—"

"Thank you for that newsflash." Evan glared at Foster.

"Listen, I don't know who you really are, but you need to start sharing…and I mean, right now." Foster turned in her chair and jabbed a finger in the air in Evan's direction. "Who are you?"

"Evan is the groundskeeper." Abby felt as if she'd missed the first act of a play.

"If she's a gardener then I'm the Pope." Foster snorted.

The muscle in Evan's jaw tightened.

"The all-American jock here just happens to show up two weeks ago. And did you notice how she didn't seem surprised by the lightshow in the cemetery?" Foster paused. "And, oh yeah, there was that whole protection spell thing upstairs. So, as someone who is concerned for Abby's safety, I'm asking again…who the hell are you?"

Evan scowled at Foster. She'd inhaled half the serving on her plate while hardly looking up, but now she'd stopped eating and frowned at Foster. Evan slowly, deliberately, wiped her mouth with a cloth napkin. She pushed aside her half-eaten food and leaned forward on her elbows at the edge of the table.

"I'm a lieutenant. A member of the protectorate."

"What's the protectorate?" Foster pressed Evan for more.

Abby sat in shocked silence, looking back and forth between Foster and Evan.

"We provide security and protection for the Council of Elders." Evan was so calm, as if she was completely unaware that what she was saying sounded insane. She rolled up the sleeves of her shirt to reveal tattoos on her forearms. When she pressed her forearms together the two halves combined to create a single image.

"Is that a triquetra?" Abby recognized the design, a trinity knot. It was a symbol used in ancient times by the Celts.

"You know your pagan symbols." Evan quirked an eyebrow as if she hadn't expected her to know a trinity symbol from an Eastern Orthodox cross. "Anyway, the elders used to go by Coven of Elders, but coven is such a loaded word these days. So they abandoned that nomenclature a couple hundred years ago."

"Wait a minute." Abby's pulse increased. "Are you saying coven, as in, witches?"

Evan didn't answer her, but the look on her face told Abby yes.

"I feel like I just stumbled into a bad episode of *Charmed*." Foster folded her arms across her chest. "There's more to this story, and I need to hear it." She sounded like she was cross-examining a witness in a capital case.

"I came here to verify a candidate."

"Verify a candidate for whom?" Foster's interrogation continued.

"I already told you, the Council of Elders."

"And once you verify the candidate, who I assume is Abby…" Foster swung her arm in Abby's direction. "Then what?"

"Should that candidate turn out to be a true positive, then I was to alert the Council of the need for an extraction."

"You'd take Abby somewhere against her will?"

"No, it's not like that…I'd planned to inform her about the ritual." Evan was becoming agitated. "Listen, it's not safe for a candidate to transition without the support and oversight of an elder witch, preferably more than one."

"I'll bet." Foster leaned back in her chair and crossed her arms. "I don't like it."

"There's nothing for you to like or not like. This isn't open for negotiation."

"Who are you to tell us—"

"Hey, there is no *us*." Evan was definitely getting angry. "You just got here, Jethro. You have no idea what's really going on."

"I'm a candidate?" They'd been talking over Abby as if she wasn't even in the room. She swallowed a lump rising in her throat from the anxiety that had been oddly missing until about three minutes ago.

"Not any longer." Evan's tone softened as she turned to Abby. "I've never seen anything like what I saw today. The transmutation has already begun. You're no longer a candidate, you're the real thing."

"You're saying…you're saying Abby is a witch?" Foster took a deep breath to calm down.

"And you're a keeper…I think." Evan looked at Foster. "Unfortunately." She murmured the last comment so that Abby wasn't sure Foster heard it.

"A keeper… Yeah, that's what my Mama used to say." Foster laughed at her own joke. "Wait…what?"

"There are certain people, through history, that are bound to witches. They are called soul keepers, because they are…well…the keeper of souls. Specifically, the soul of the witch they are bound to. They become their bonded witch's tether to this world." Evan took a sip of water, never breaking eye contact with Foster.

"As opposed to what? Now you're telling me there's another world?" Foster scowled at Evan.

"More of an alternative reality…it's difficult to explain…"

"Okay, we'll come back to that." Foster pinched the bridge of her nose, pushing her glasses up on her forehead. "About the other part. You're saying I'm Abby's keeper? We just met...I only just arrived like a day ago."

"It has nothing to do with time. That event in the graveyard..."

"Yeah?"

"I can't be completely certain, because I've never witnessed one in person, but I believe that was a binding."

"Stop talking, both of you." Abby covered her face, then dropped her hands, and shook her head. "You can't be serious." She looked at Evan.

"I'm deadly serious."

Abby couldn't listen any longer. The anxiety was becoming tension, and the tension was climbing the back of her neck. Her head was beginning to throb.

"I can't talk about this any longer." She gave each of them a fleeting glance before she left the room.

She climbed the stairs and collapsed on her bed just as the raging noise of the storm inside her head began to crescendo.

CHAPTER TWELVE

F oster drank several gulps of water, never taking her eyes off Evan. They sat staring at each other across the table.

"You should stay with her tonight." Evan's words sounded like a command.

"I'm in the house—"

"In her room." Evan shifted, leaning back in her chair.

"Look, I don't take kindly to getting bullied and bossed around by some jock gardener I'm not even sure I trust."

Evan ignored the jab.

"If you *are* her keeper, and I'm pretty sure you are, then you can't leave her alone. Especially not right now."

"Why? What's happening to her? What did you call it…a transmutation?"

"Abby is experiencing an alchemical transmutation. Basically, the energy she is about to inherit is transforming her from a raw state to a higher state of being."

"I still don't know what that means."

"Abby turns thirty in two days. At nine o'clock p.m., on her birthday, she will inherit the powers that will make her a witch. Think of it as an ascension. She's been having symptoms for weeks, probably months…headaches, dreams, visions, paranormal episodes, and now, big electrical surges."

"Wait, why such a specific time?"

"Because according to birth records, Abby was born at nine p.m."

"I just don't know if I believe all of this." Foster couldn't explain what happened in the cemetery, but even still, that didn't equate to Abby being a witch.

"The truth is the truth whether you believe it or not." Evan scraped remnants of food into the compost bin on the counter and put her dish in the sink. She turned and leaned against the edge of the counter, facing Foster. "You either work with me on this or you don't. But you can't stop what's happening, and I'm not going to allow your disbelief to put Abby in harm's way."

"Who did you call? When you left earlier, who did you call?"

"I told you. I've been making regular reports to the Council on the East Coast."

"So, now they're going to come out here and help Abby through this?"

Evan hesitated.

The hesitation bothered Foster. What was Evan not saying?

"What aren't you telling me?"

"Nothing." Evan sank her hands in her pockets. "Yes, the Council will be here to help."

Evan's response didn't instill confidence. Something nagged at Foster.

"But you're not confident about that." It wasn't a question. She could read the doubt in Evan's expression.

"I'm not usually in the field, so what do I know?"

Evan was obviously holding something back.

"Look, if we're in this…if I'm in this with you…and you care at all about Abby, then you owe it to both of us to be honest." Foster tempered her frustration. A confrontational tactic was just going to make Evan angry again.

"Something doesn't feel right." Evan exhaled and studied the floor before looking back up. "I did call the Council tonight, but I also called a friend for some backup. I want us to be prepared for whatever is coming."

Foster covered her face with her hands for a minute and then swept her fingers briskly through her hair a couple of times. This was a lot of information and she needed time to thread it all together. Evan was being honest so it was her turn to share.

"I did uncover a connection between Abby and Mercy Howe, who was hanged for witchcraft in Salem in the 1600s." Foster ran her fingertip across a divot in the wooden tabletop, not making eye contact with Evan. "And Abby's great-great-grandmother was also named Mercy. That seemed like an odd coincidence."

"And every heir since Mercy has been male, until now."

Foster looked up, meeting Evan's intense gaze. She felt as if they were coming to some sort of understanding, some sort of truce. Maybe they were, for Abby's sake.

"Mercy's line was missing, dormant, until now. The bloodline branches off in multiple directions. There are others in the field, like me, investigating candidates. Looking for signs, looking for positives... But clearly, Abby is the one." Evan looked at the clock near the stove. "It's getting late, and you really shouldn't leave her alone. I'll stay in the house tonight too. I think the room next to hers has a bed."

"What are you afraid of?" For the first time, Foster realized that Evan wasn't just being an angry jerk. She was worried, possibly scared.

"Any time this much power is endowed, someone wants to take it for themselves."

"You think someone might try to hurt Abby?"

"It's possible." Evan crossed her arms over her chest. "I'd rather be prepared for the worst than get surprised by it."

Foster nodded. She actually agreed with that approach.

"I'll sleep in the chair in Abby's room. Wake me if anything happens."

Foster stood and took a few steps toward the door before Evan spoke.

"Hey, Foster..."

"Yeah?"

"I'm on your side. In case you had any doubts about that."

Foster nodded, even though she still had her doubts. "Good night, Evan."

The house was quiet and mostly dark, except for a lit sconce partway down the hall, as she made her way to Abby's room. The almost life-sized sculpture of a majestic buck cast a long dark shadow across her path. All the sculptures along this hallway gained an ominous presence in the low light.

Her head was spinning from all that Evan had said. Sleep would likely elude her as she replayed the day's events. She'd stopped by the guest room first and changed into a T-shirt more comfortable for lounging. She also brought a book with her, one of the volumes she'd borrowed the first night, a collection of poems by Keats. When she reached Abby's room, she sensed that something wasn't right. The lights were off, but there was enough ambient light from the lamp in the hall that she could just make out the outline of Abby beneath the covers. She wasn't sure how she knew something was wrong, she just did, almost like a sixth sense. She knew as clearly as if Abby had spoken to her from across the room.

"Abby?" Foster set the book on the bedside table. She walked to the side of the four-poster bed. Abby's eyes were closed, but she wasn't asleep. Energy radiated off her. "Abby?" Foster whispered her name again.

When Abby didn't respond, Foster climbed onto the bed, letting one foot keep contact with the floor. She didn't want to crawl into bed with Abby without an invitation and was acutely aware that she'd probably already crossed some boundary of intimacy just by touching Abby while she was asleep.

When she put her hand on Abby's shoulder, an undulating pulse of electricity traveled up her arm. The sensation was oddly similar to an experience she'd had at church camp one summer when one of the do-it-yourself deacons had accidentally crossed wires on the hot water heater so that if you were in the shower and stood on the drain and under the spray at the same time while holding the handle, you'd get a low-level electrical charge. This sensation was very similar, noticeable, but not painful. However, Abby's furrowed brow told her that she might be in pain.

"Abby?" Foster spoke a little louder.

Abby moaned softly and pressed her fingers to her temple. She drew her knees up to her chest under the covers and rolled away from Foster.

Instinctively, Foster moved all the way onto the bed and spooned against Abby's back. Abby rocked against her. Foster encircled Abby with her arms and squeezed.

"I'm here, Abby. What can I do to help?" More electrical current vibrated off Abby. Foster could feel it, and the muscles in her arms twitched, but she held on.

To her surprise, Abby rolled toward her, wedged her head under Foster's chin, and her face against Foster's neck. Abby's lips brushed against Foster's skin, sending shivers down her spine.

"I'm here, Abby. I'm here."

This was too much. Everything was too much. Abby had retreated to her room, her sanctuary, only moments before the headache overwhelmed her like a tsunami. But something was different this time. She wasn't alone in the dark place. She sensed a presence. Someone held her. In the strange, otherworldly murkiness of the dreamscape, it took her a moment to realize that someone was Foster. She couldn't see Foster's face, but she knew with certainty that Foster was there and that the physical contact between them was keeping her from getting lost. Foster was grounding her, a lifeline, a way back.

As before, she heard voices. A growing hum of many voices, like the loud murmur of an airport terminal. Around the edges of the ethereal landscape, dark figures gathered, not menacing necessarily as they undulated along the horizon of her view. One tall, slender, obviously female shape separated from the mass of swaying figures and slowly approached. The woman was only visible in silhouette until she drew closer. Aside from the vision with Mercy on the ship, this was the only time someone had presented themselves clearly to Abby in one of her painful visions.

Other smoky, ghostly shapes hung along the margins of her vision, and the headache was still there, thundering in the background like an approaching storm. Abby squinted and tried to focus on the advancing figure.

"Hello, Abby." Some of the woman's features were unclear. It was hard to tell anything about her clothing, except that she wore some kind of black draped clothing, which only made her pale, narrow, elegant face more ghostlike. Did she have long dark hair or was it something else that swirled in slow motion around her face? Abby felt no movement in the air around them.

"Do you know me?"

The woman's words sent goose bumps up her arm.

Abby shook her head. Obviously, the woman could see her also, because she'd called her by name.

"You will know me soon." The woman was taller than Abby by a few inches. She pressed into Abby's personal space. "I am coming for you."

"Who are you?" This woman was menacing, and Abby was suddenly afraid. Instinctively, she squeezed Foster's hand, reassuring herself that Foster's presence was still with her, even though she couldn't see her.

"Your keeper cannot save you from this." The woman held Abby's face in her hands. Her fingers were icy and seemed to lengthen around Abby's throat like tentacles. "I will see you soon." She kissed Abby's forehead.

Abby tried to speak but couldn't. She tried to free herself, but the tentacles had morphed into something else, an ever-expanding tangle of tree limbs or roots covering her face. She couldn't breathe. She was being pulled under. She felt Foster's fingers slipping away. And then she heard a faint sound pierce the murmur of noise.

"Abby."

Her name, faint, but distinct.

"Abby."

She closed her eyes and focused on the sound of her name.

"Abby." This time louder.

She concentrated on Foster's voice.

"Abby, wake up."

When she opened her eyes, she was in Foster's arms, in her room. It was dark, probably late. Foster brushed strands of damp hair away from her face.

"Abby, are you okay?" Concern was evident in Foster's question.

"It was a dream." Abby faltered, her throat was dry. It was more than a dream, but she wasn't sure exactly how to explain.

"Apparently a bad one."

Foster reached for a glass of water on the bedside table and handed it to Abby. She tilted her head up to take a few sips and then dropped back to the pillow. The headache was receding. Like distant footsteps, the pounding was beginning to ebb.

And then she remembered.

Foster had been there, with her, in the dream. Foster had been her way back.

She met Foster's gaze. The moon, from the window, was a speck of white in her dark eyes. Abby became acutely aware of their bodies pressed together, of Foster's arms holding her protectively, of the warmth of Foster's skin, the pulse near her exposed collarbone, and her lips, slightly parted, as if she were about to speak.

Abby angled her head up just enough to kiss Foster. At first tentatively, not much more than a brush of light contact. She waited to gauge Foster's reaction, which seemed to be surprise. She'd only ever kissed one woman before, in college, with catastrophic fallout. Not that Elissa had minded the kiss, but the static discharge that resulted from the physical contact had thrown Elissa across the room and scared Abby. Scared her so terribly that she hadn't acted on a physical attraction with anyone since. But this was somehow different. She'd just kissed Foster and there'd been no *event*. No electrical storm, except the one snaking through her nervous system. She wanted Foster, badly.

She kissed Foster again, and this time Foster kissed her back. As Foster invaded her senses, she forgot to be afraid.

Abby was under the covers, while Foster was on top. Their bodies were pressed together, but the covering was an unwanted barrier. She tugged at the comforter without breaking the kiss, trying to indicate that Foster should join her.

Foster fumbled with the covers, but finally managed to shimmy underneath. Abby snuggled against Foster's shoulder, in her arms. She tilted her face up. With eyes closed, she brushed her face against Foster's cheek. Foster's skin was soft, warm, and smelled of something sweet, vanilla perhaps. Abby rotated her body so that their legs became entwined, Foster's thigh was between her legs, and she shifted against it. Her skin was on fire. She had the strongest urge to rid herself of her clothing and make love to Foster. Only, she'd never been with anyone like that and didn't know where to begin.

Her eyes were still closed, but she felt Foster's lips press against hers. She opened up to Foster. Their tongues danced lightly as Foster tightened her embrace. Foster's mouth was hot against hers, and Foster's hands began to roam under the hem of her T-shirt and up. Foster's hand grazed the outside curve of her breast, and she exhaled sharply against Foster's mouth. Their closeness was causing the most exquisite pain deep inside, a need to be touched, to be loved, to be possessed.

"Abby." Foster whispered her name in the darkness.

She blinked and pulled back, as if hearing her name had broken some trance she'd been in.

"Abby, you're so beautiful." Foster feathered kisses along her neck as she teased Abby's nipple under her shirt.

Abby covered Foster's hand with hers. She didn't necessarily want this to stop, or did she? Her head was in conflict with every other cell in her body at the moment. Her head was reminding her that less than forty-eight hours ago she'd wanted Foster to leave. Now she wanted nothing in the world more desperately than Foster in her bed. Was this change of heart because of what had happened in the graveyard? There was an intensity to Foster that she couldn't ignore, or was the intensity hers and Foster only its focus? It was impossible to know. Everything was getting all jumbled up as Foster shifted her thigh more firmly against her sex. She tightened her legs around Foster's and rocked against her.

❖

Evan stayed in the kitchen for a while after Foster left. She needed a few minutes to think. Foster was smart. She'd asked all the same questions that Evan would ask if the situation was reversed. The only problem was Evan didn't have all the answers. In truth, she was unsettled and she couldn't put her finger on exactly why.

After staring into space for about a half hour, she trudged upstairs.

She wanted to check on Foster and Abby before retiring to the adjoining room. The bedroom door was ajar, but the lights were off, so she knocked lightly. A rustling of covers signaled they weren't asleep. Once again, she felt like a chaperone, which was *not* the role she wanted to play. She was a little older than Abby, but she and Foster were about the same age.

"Sorry, didn't mean to wake you." She spoke from outside the door.

"It's okay. Is something wrong?" Foster asked.

"No, nothing like that. I was just checking in. Sorry I bothered you."

"It's no problem." Abby sounded like she meant it. "Sleep well, Evan."

"You too."

Evan settled into the room next door. As she took off her shirt, she realized she liked Abby, really liked her. Because Abby was a candidate, she'd tried to keep some distance between them, but Abby had stolen past her defenses. Maybe that was one of Abby's gifts, breaching defenses. She'd watched Abby do it repeatedly with the horses she sheltered.

Abby had a sweetness about her that was hard to resist. Obviously, Foster was having a hard time resisting. She didn't really know what she'd interrupted, but it wasn't hard to imagine the sexual tension building between Foster and Abby. Transitioning was like going through adolescence again, but worse. Abby's desire for sex would only increase, and transmutation would whip her hormones into a frenzy, kicking her libido into overdrive.

I hope Foster can handle it.

She couldn't help smiling as she sank farther under the covers. Foster seemed capable enough, for one of those nerdy bookish types. Foster didn't seem completely inept anyway, so that was good news.

Evan had no idea what it felt like to be a keeper. She'd known a few, but not well enough to ask personal questions about their connection to their bonded witch. Not all witches became sexually involved with their keepers, but some did, and the connection between them when you were around them was palpable.

Evan wondered what that felt like. A deep, soul connection with another person. She'd like to find out…someday.

Foster was frustrated by the interruption. Although it wasn't Evan's fault. How could she have known? Even Foster hadn't anticipated this and she'd known she was attracted to Abby from the first moment she saw her. Abby's wounded, soulful blue eyes, her remote shyness, her unspoken cry to be saved, all of it was like a drug for Foster. Abby was Foster's type six ways to Sunday. Yeah, in every way possible. And she might have been able to tamp down her attraction if Abby hadn't kissed her, but that first tentative kiss had stoked a flame Foster had been tossing water on since she'd arrived.

Evan's interruption had ruined the moment.

Abby kissed Foster on the cheek and rolled away from her, facing the wall. Foster wasn't going to be so easily dismissed. She scooted close, spooned against Abby's back, and draped her arm around Abby's waist.

"Are you okay?" Abby's abrupt shift away from her was almost painful.

"I'm fine. I...I shouldn't have let things go so far."

"Things didn't get very far." Not nearly far enough, from Foster's perspective. Nothing more than a sweet taste of possibility.

Abby rolled over in Foster's arms. The expression on her face was so serious that Foster felt bad for making light of things. She really wasn't taking any of this lightly.

"I hardly know you, Foster, but I want to do things with you." Abby hesitated. "Things I've never done with anyone."

Was Abby saying she'd never had sex with someone before? That seemed highly unlikely.

"I'm not sure what you're saying." Better to ask than assume, or guess.

Abby looked away for a moment, as if she was embarrassed by what she'd revealed. When she turned back, Foster could see the wet path of a tear on her cheek catch the moonlight from the window. Abby wiped it away with her hand.

"Foster, I've never been with anyone like this before. I don't know what's happening, but before, when I've been close to someone I'm attracted to...things happened, people got hurt."

"Hurt how?"

Abby sighed and covered her face with her hands.

"The last time I kissed a woman was in college. We were in a park, under a tree. It was dusk, and we'd been lying on a blanket talking for hours."

"That sounds terrible." Foster was trying to lighten the mood by making a joke.

"It's not funny." Abby uncovered her eyes and looked at Foster. "When we kissed there was a flash of light and an electrical surge, and Elissa was thrown several feet away."

"I'm sorry, I didn't mean to joke at your expense."

"Elissa assumed that we'd been struck by lightning and I didn't correct her." Abby paused. "I didn't tell her the same thing had happened before."

"When?"

"I was a teen and I kissed a boy on the beach." Abby paused as if she were visualizing the past. "The EMT said it had to be lightning that time too."

"But you knew that wasn't the truth." Foster brushed Abby's cheek with her fingers.

"If it had been lightning, why wasn't I hurt…that's what I kept thinking. Deep down I had this feeling that it was my fault."

"You were just a kid—"

"A kid with the beginnings of strange powers she didn't understand."

"Hey, that was the past. You didn't hurt me." Foster stroked Abby's arm. "I'm holding you and kissing you and I'm totally fine."

"I know, and that scares me, because I have no idea what's going on."

Abby rolled away again, but she let Foster hold her. Foster kissed Abby's hair. She wasn't sure what was happening either, but for some reason, she wasn't afraid of it.

She held Abby as she transitioned to sleep. Abby's breathing was deep and even, her energy calm and restful. Foster felt it was her duty to keep a vigil until Abby drifted off. She listened to the sounds of the Pacific. The ebb and flow of the distant surf were soothing. Her libido eventually eased off the accelerator. The rhythmic crash of the waves against the rocky cliff and the warmth of Abby snuggled in her arms lulled her to sleep.

CHAPTER THIRTEEN

Abby directed Boots to the path along the cliff. The morning was pristine. The marine layer had chosen to sleep in and hovered at the horizon, hiding the curved edge of the earth from view. The sea was a dazzling azure blue, reflecting back the brilliance of the cloudless sky above.

How could her mood be so dark on a day such as this? She blamed the dream.

She sank her fingers into Boots's mane. Not simply to steady herself in the saddle, but to keep from floating away. The boundary between her body and the world seemed blurred, permeable. She was acutely aware of the scent of seaweed from the surf below, the call of the ravens in the tree behind her. She could even sense the movement of creatures beneath the ocean's surface. It was as if the entire world was seething with a fresh dynamism and her body was one big receptor. Moments earlier, she'd stepped away from herself, separated, and looked back at her body seated atop Boots.

Maybe she should have asked Foster to ride with her, but there was part of her that refused to believe what Evan had said. Whatever this was, whatever was happening, she was determined to control it. This…what had Evan called it? A transmutation? Well, she wasn't going to let it run her life.

A small patch of cowslip swayed in the breeze, moving the tall grass on either side. The wind had come from nowhere, a microburst.

Abby could have sworn that the gust had carried a sound, or more specifically, a word. The word was more feeling than speech, an insinuation, an agent of contagion. A threat? A chill traveled up her arm. Abruptly, she turned to look over her shoulder because it was as if some menacing presence had brushed past her, carried along by the wind.

Possibly sensing her sudden unease, Boots turned and trotted toward the barn. Abby rotated in the saddle, looking south and then north, but nothing followed them although she'd have sworn it had.

Evan stepped from the shadow of the barn's interior as they approached. It was weird that they had both unintentionally revealed things about themselves the previous night. Evan knew her now, in a way she hadn't before, and the opposite was also true. She was unsure what this new knowing would feel like. Evan held Boots's cheek strap as she dismounted. Only then was she able to give the feeling a name: awkward. She met Evan's gaze only for a moment before averting her eyes to the enclosure where Journey and Sasha moseyed about.

"How are you this morning?" Evan patted Boots's neck.

"Fine." Nothing was probably further from the truth.

"Are you sure?"

"No, I'm not sure." Abby had to shield her eyes from the sun with her hand when she looked up at Evan. "I had a horrible dream last night."

Abby never talked about her dreams. She wasn't sure why she was doing it now. Possibly because Evan had asked as if she really wanted to know.

"Tell me about it."

"I don't really remember it. It just left me with a sense of foreboding." That was as much detail as she felt like sharing at the moment.

"As you transition, your dreams will become more vivid, more like visions than dreams." Evan rubbed Boots's nose gently as she talked, not really making eye contact with Abby. "I'm happy to listen if you decide to share any of your visions."

Abby was surprised by Evan's statement, and her offer to listen. Dreams weren't real, were they? Although as soon as the thought formed in her mind, she remembered the taste of salt on her lips and the indentation of the amulet in her palm. She glanced toward the house, then back at Evan.

They were quiet for a moment. Abby turned toward the ocean. She could just glimpse the curve of it from the slight rise of the ground where they stood. Evan disappeared into the barn with Boots and Abby stood still and waited.

The tall, golden grass in the open acres between the barn and the cliffs swayed with the rippling breeze like undulating waves. But no more words came with the wind, only the cleansing scent of salt from the Pacific.

Foster squinted at the window. It seemed early, but the sun was relentlessly bright. It sliced across the room from the partially open drapes. She rubbed her eyes. Abby's side of the bed was empty. She fumbled around on the bedside table for her glasses. When she put them on, a thumbprint in the middle of the right lens blurred her vision. She polished the lens with the hem of her T-shirt and put them back on. Better. She fished in her discarded jeans pocket for her cell. The time on her phone told her it was still early and that she had a text from Rosalind.

How's it going on the Left Coast?

Hmm, how much should she say? Not much.

Great.

Foster added a little smiling emoji with nerd glasses and clicked off. That should be enough to hold Rosalind at bay for now. She had bigger things to think about than a memoir project.

She dangled her feet off the side of the bed and waited for her brain to wake up. They hadn't had any alcohol the previous night, but Foster felt seriously hung over. When her eyes adjusted to the half-light of the room she could see that the salt pentagram was still on the floor, right where they'd left it. Somewhere, in the recesses of her foggy brain, she'd hoped the entire episode from last night had been a weird dream. But the five-pointed star drawn with salt confirmed that it was real.

Other details started to emerge. Like how Abby had kissed her. Abby had kissed her and she'd kissed her back. And they slept next to each other, although, Foster wasn't sure how much sleep she actually got. During the night she'd been hyper aware of Abby's every movement, the lightest contact, the brush of Abby's fingers across her arm, had caused a cascading electrical storm through her entire nervous system. They had not done much more than kiss and hold each other, but if Abby had wanted more Foster would have been happy to offer it. From the first moment their lips touched, Foster's insides churned as if a thousand butterflies had taken up residence in her stomach.

What had Evan said? That she was supposed to be Abby's keeper, or something. What did that mean? If it meant that she was completely smitten to the point where Abby pretty much owned her, then yeah, she was in real trouble. Who was keeping whom, that was the question.

As it was, though, Foster couldn't deny the urgent need to lay eyes on Abby. She didn't simply want to see her, she *needed* to see her. And then she needed coffee. Abby first, coffee second. She'd been in California for two days, and her priorities were already completely upended.

Foster tugged jeans on over her boxer shorts and slipped her wingtips on without socks. She finger-combed her hair as she descended the staircase and headed toward the kitchen.

"Well, good morning." Cora's face brightened when she saw Foster.

"Good morning." Foster wasn't really one of those *talk first thing in the morning* sorts of people, but good Southern manners demanded that she make an effort.

"I see someone was hungry last night." Cora seemed pleased that almost all of her casserole had been eaten.

"Yeah…" Foster was about to say more when Abby walked into the room. Evan wasn't far behind.

Foster had served herself a cup of coffee and was leaning against the counter. She was about to take a sip, but Abby's smoldering gaze from across the room pinned her in place, with the cup midair. Abby crossed the room and invaded Foster's personal space as she reached past her for a mug. When Abby had the cup in hand, she didn't move away. Abby reached around on the other side for a teabag, stepped away to add hot water, then returned to add a little cream.

Abby was so close that Foster could feel the warmth from her skin, smell the light scent of sea air, and see the flecks of darker blue swimming in her irises. If Abby was aware anyone else was in the room she gave no indication of it. For a minute, Foster thought Abby might even kiss her in front of everyone. At one point, Abby was laser focused on Foster's lips and was a hair's breadth from making contact, but at the last second, she met Foster's gaze and abruptly left the room.

Everyone seemed dumbstruck, silently staring at Foster, and all Foster could do was follow Abby's retreat with wide eyes, speechless. Abby had practically undressed Foster with her eyes; her physical presence left a heat signature in the room that Foster was pretty sure everyone felt.

"Well, now, it's so nice to see you two have made friends." Cora was blushing. She cleared her throat. "Is anyone hungry for breakfast?"

Foster was definitely hungry, but she was fairly certain that eggs and toast weren't going to satisfy the craving Abby had just stoked. She set her cup on the counter, almost missing the edge altogether, with the intention of following Abby.

"You should eat first." It was as if Evan read her mind.

Foster blinked a few times and swallowed. Her throat was dry, her palms were sweaty, and her libido was humming. She nodded, took a deep breath, and sank to a nearby chair.

❖

Abby was burning up. She unzipped her jacket as she retreated to her room and dropped it over a chair. Her shirt was next. Everything she was wearing was suddenly too much, restrictive. Her skin tingled, prickled was more accurate. A soak in the tub was what she needed. Just now in the kitchen she'd been completely outside herself, unable to control the urge to be close to Foster. The entire encounter was so out of the norm for her that she didn't know what else to do but flee.

She sat on the edge of the tub to check the water temperature. She piled her undergarments in the hamper and sank into the steaming water. She pulled her hair aside. The curve at the back of the deep, clawfoot tub was cool against her neck. She dropped lower, so that her shoulders were submerged.

Her hormones were raging in a way she'd never experienced before. She took deep breaths and exhaled slowly. She wanted Foster so badly and she had no idea what to do about it. They barely knew each other, although they'd begun to share something that seemed fairly unexplainable. But did that shared experience translate to sex?

I hope so.

The internal thought surprised Abby. *Be serious.* She splashed water on her face and tried to focus on anything but Foster. She closed her eyes and concentrated on the liquid embrace of the water surrounding her. It caressed her flesh. Its warmth was above her and beneath her. *Foster's lips. Foster's hands.*

Her eyes flew open. She'd done it again. She seemed unable to truly redirect her thoughts. Was Foster feeling the same intense attraction? Abby gripped the side of the tub and pulled herself up to a seated position. The need, no, the urgent, desperate need, to find out how Foster was feeling made it impossible to relax. Abby reached for a towel, determined to avoid Foster at all cost until she could control her hormones.

CHAPTER FOURTEEN

Cora served food for Evan and Foster, then settled at the table with them for a cup of tea and some toast.

"Did you gals hear this morning's news?" Cora looked as if she would burst if she didn't get to share her gossip.

Foster's mouth was full of scrambled eggs. She shook her head.

"There was a UFO over the cemetery last night. And Edith Mills from the county office said it left a huge circular charred area in the grass." Cora paused for effect. "Just like one of those crop circles, only burned." She sipped her tea. "And then Iain noticed one outside the horse pen. Do you suppose we had extraterrestrial visitors in the night?"

The eggs she'd just choked down threatened to revolt. Foster took a big gulp of coffee and glanced sideways at Evan, who seemed as cool as cucumber salad.

"Maybe. I've always wanted to see a UFO. I must have slept through it if they were here." Evan calmly bit into her toast.

"Edith said that gravestones were toppled and there were tree limbs down everywhere at the cemetery...even a few dead birds."

"Hmm." Evan chewed slowly.

Foster looked at Cora. This was clearly not the response she had hoped for. She was disappointed that her story hadn't gotten a better, more excitable reception.

"Do you think your friend Edith would let me interview her? You know, for my research." Foster's appetite was gone. She pushed the last of her eggs around on her plate.

"Oh, yes, I'm sure she would." Cora's mood brightened. "I'll ring her later and ask just to make sure. She works at the county office next to the library."

The library was definitely on Foster's agenda for today, so that would work out nicely. Cora stood up and poured tea into a fresh mug.

"You two enjoy your breakfast. I'm just going to run this cup of tea out for Mr. Green. I want to see the spot by the fence row for myself." UFOs or not, Cora was still on a mission to win Iain over with daily installments of tea and baked goods.

The minute Cora closed the door some of the tension eased from Foster's shoulders. She slouched in her chair and waited for Evan to say something, anything, but Evan was annoyingly mute as she finished off her own plate of eggs.

"Well?" Foster couldn't stand it any longer.

"Well, what?"

"What are we going to do about this whole UFO thing?"

"Nothing."

"Nothing?"

"Yeah, a UFO sighting is a best-case scenario as far as I'm concerned. It completely throws everyone off Abby's trail."

"Seriously?"

"Yes, seriously." Evan took a sip of coffee and glared at Foster. "And by the way, you're not going to the library or anywhere else."

"Says who?" Foster crossed her arms in front of her chest and hoped she was giving Evan her best *not you* look.

"You can't be that far away from Abby...not right now." Evan studied Foster over the rim of her coffee cup. "I'm serious."

"Why?" Foster leaned forward, with her elbows at the edge of the table. "I mean, I have no idea what's going on with this... this...transmutation. I don't even know if that's even what's really happening. And even if it is, what am I supposed to do about it?" She was all for spending more time with Abby, but not because Evan was telling her to.

"As her keeper, you need to be here for her. She may not know it yet, but she needs you." Evan smiled slyly. "She may not know yet that she *needs* you, but if this morning's display was any indication I'd say she *wants* you."

Foster had just taken a swig of coffee and almost snorted it out her nose. A coughing fit ensued.

"If you'll excuse me, I need to make a phone call." Foster wasn't about to discuss her attraction for Abby with Evan or guess at Abby's feelings for her.

She checked her cell phone as she ambled down the hall. The signal strength switched back and forth from no service to one bar. There was a landline in the library. She'd noticed it the first night she'd arrived and borrowed the books. She'd make the call from there. The library was so quiet and charming. The thought of having a few days to do nothing but survey the collection and lounge around reading was heavenly. It didn't seem like her two-week research trip was going to allow for any significant down time, especially with everything that was going on with Abby.

The phone was on a small table near the chaise lounge. Foster lifted it off the table onto her lap and dialed.

"Hello?" It was nice to hear a familiar voice.

"Hi, Mom."

"Foster, are you still in California?"

"Yeah, I only just got here a day or so ago."

"Don't say *yeah* to me."

"Yes, ma'am."

"Is something wrong? You don't sound like yourself. Is California as strange as they say it is on FOX News?"

"No, Mom. It's actually beautiful here. The ocean, the redwoods…you'd like it. You should visit here sometime."

"If I didn't have to get on an airplane to do it, then maybe. You know how your father and I hate to fly."

It was true. The only family vacations she'd ever been on as a kid were in places within driving distance of home. Foster hadn't gotten to fly on a plane until she was seventeen and had flown with her classmates to New York City for a field trip.

"Mom, I wanted to ask you about Aunt Vera."

There was silence on the other end.

"Mom, are you still there?"

"Yes, yes, I'm still here. Why are you asking about Vera?"

Vera had been dead for several years. She was her mother's only sister and had practically been shunned by the family for her, as her grandmother put it, *queer ways.* Although, by queer she didn't mean gay; she just meant strange, or *touched,* pronounced "tetched" by southerners.

"Was she really crazy?" Foster had been formulating a theory, but she needed more information to sort it all out. "I mean, I've heard you say she was crazy...but was she? Really?"

"Well, Vera never learned to cook." According to her mother's rule book, a southern woman with a lack of culinary skill was an epic fail. But did that indicate insanity? Foster couldn't cook either and she felt fairly sane. "She always had her nose in some book. She read the entire *Encyclopedia Britania* through twice."

"You mean, *Britannica?*"

"Don't sass me, young lady."

"Sorry, Mama." Foster gave her mother a moment to regroup. "So, why do you think she did that much reading?"

Foster wondered why she'd never asked.

"She had trouble sleeping. She heard voices." Her mother took a deep breath. "Lord, she even ran the vacuum cleaner most of the day so that no one could listen in on her conversations. Heaven only knows who she was talking to...herself mostly."

A chill ran up Foster's arm from the receiver. Knowing what she now knew about what was happening with Abby, and what Foster was experiencing, she wondered if something similar might have been going on with Vera. If Vera had had some connection to witchcraft, given her family's staunch Baptist beliefs, Vera would have had to hide any hint of paganism.

"Are you sure she was talking to herself?"

"What sort of question is that?" Her mother sounded annoyed. "She was by herself."

"You didn't ever wonder if she saw ghosts or something?"

"She said she saw people, but I never put any stock in it."

It was always strange to Foster that people of faith, people who believed in an afterlife and heaven and hell, had such difficulty believing in spiritual manifestations.

"Your uncle knows more about it than me. I never had time for such nonsense, I had kids to raise." Vera couldn't cook and didn't have children. Foster was sure that was a sore spot for a family who prided themselves on both.

"You mean, Uncle Ed?"

"Yes, call Eddie. I'm sure he'd love to regale you with his most recent conspiracy theory too."

Ed was her mother's older brother. He lived in New Orleans and rarely made it home for family reunions. If Vera was the *queer* one, then Ed was certainly considered a Left Leaning Liberal. He'd learned the hard way that you couldn't mix politics and potlucks in the Deep South. That was eight years ago when he'd worn an Obama T-shirt to the family reunion. Foster hadn't really seen him much since.

"But you best make yourself a sandwich if you do call him, because you'll be on the phone for a while. That man loves to hear himself talk."

A thumping sound pulled Foster's attention to the ceiling, where the vintage chandelier jostled with each muted thump. Maybe this house was haunted after all.

"Mama, I've gotta go."

"Now don't you let any of those coastal elites sway you."

Foster almost laughed. Iain and Cora weren't exactly folks she'd describe as elite, maybe Abby, but certainly not Evan.

"Mama, don't believe everything you see on FOX News."

"Don't sass me—"

"Sorry, Mama, I gotta go." Foster cut her off before she got an earful. She knew better than to disparage her mother's sole source for news, but sometimes she just couldn't help herself.

There it was again, a dull thumping sound overhead. Foster's hand still rested on the receiver in its cradle. The sound hadn't moved. It seemed to be repeating in the same place overhead. Foster was anxious to call her uncle but decided to investigate the noise first.

It was still early. Didn't ghosts do most of their haunting at night? Foster crept up the grand staircase. Nothing. The passageway was completely clear. Then she heard the noise again and she followed the sound. At the far end of the hallway, past Abby's bedroom, was another set of narrow stairs. How had she missed the fact that this place had a third floor? The steep wooden stairs were definitely not meant to accommodate furniture, so she doubted there were more bedrooms upstairs, maybe just storage.

There was a door at the top, along a narrow landing. When she opened it, she could plainly see the ghost was no ghost at all. Abby leapt upward and landed on the floor. After a few seconds, she jumped again.

"For a minute, I thought this place was haunted."

Abby was startled by Foster. She closed her eyes for a few seconds, and placed her hand over her heart.

"You scared me."

She'd hoped Abby would be happy to see her, but she didn't seem to be. Her hair was damp and she'd changed into jeans and a cotton blouse. The blouse was fitted and accentuated her figure.

"Sorry. What are you doing?" The long, open room smelled dusty.

It was obvious this space didn't get much use. There were some cast-off wooden chairs with the woven seats frayed and missing, and a few boxes stacked along the wall, a bed frame, but no mattress. There was a window at each end of the simple room.

"I'm trying to pull down the attic stairs."

"Oh." It had been hard to discern the dangling cord in the dimly lit room.

Abby didn't really want to be around Foster, not feeling the way she was feeling. Just the sight of Foster sent her heart racing. But now Foster was here, and she was tall enough to reach the cord.

"Here, let me get that for you." Foster smiled as she stretched and pulled the section above them down, and then Abby moved as Foster unfolded the wooden steps, which were more like a ladder than actual stairs.

Foster stepped aside to allow Abby to go first. Abby wanted to ask Foster not to follow her, but that seemed rude, especially since Foster helped her lower the stairs.

The walls angled in, probably matching the slant of the roofline. The air in the attic space was thick and stale. It smelled like old paper and dusty fabric. It smelled like the past. A fine layer of powdery debris covered everything—the plank floor, small wooden boxes, a cracked leather suitcase, and at the farthest end of the long narrow room, a trunk. A tiny octagon-shaped window was set into the triangle of wall just above where the trunk rested. Light from the window dissected the angular room; particles floated in the brightly lit swath. She reached up and tugged the chain that illuminated a single, naked light bulb overhead and stared at the trunk. Abby felt the large brown trunk tug her forward, almost as if it was calling her name. She looked over at Foster, thumbing through some old *Life* magazines, the pages yellowed, brittle, and frayed. If something had called her name, Foster obviously hadn't heard it.

She knelt beside the case, which looked as if it hadn't been disturbed in decades. The clasp at the front was stiff, but with a little effort she was able to free it. She lifted the heavy lid until the hinges caught, keeping it aloft.

"What did you find?" Foster was leaning over her shoulder.

Abby didn't answer. She gently began to lift items, anxious to see for herself what was inside. When she was a child, the attic had always been off limits. Her mother's excuse was that the ladder was too dangerous and that she could easily get locked inside if it retracted unexpectedly. Now, after all these years, Abby couldn't help wondering if there was another reason her mother had discouraged exploration.

A white dress lay on top of everything. Folded so that the intricate embroidery at the collar was on top. It was a small garment, obviously for a girl, not a woman. She draped it across the edge of the trunk. The next layer revealed photos in frames and a wooden box. Underneath the photos was a leather-bound journal or book, definitely a well-used book of some sort. The cover was aged and cracked from time and use.

The first photo was of a young girl wearing the white dress, standing next to a bearded man. Abby angled it toward the light for a better look. She wiped the glass with the sleeve of her shirt. Her heart began to race again. She took a deep breath. This was the girl and the man she'd seen in her dream, her vision.

"What is it?" Foster must have sensed her surprise.

"Nothing." She wasn't ready to share.

Abby handed the photograph to Foster and leaned into the dark interior of the trunk to retrieve the wooden box. Her fingers trembled as she opened it. Only one thing resided in the box, cradled by a red velvet cloth. The amulet from her dream, the one with the braided gold rope along the edge of the stone, caught the light from the window. She could have sworn the instant light hit the aquamarine stone it vibrated, but surely, she only imagined it.

"Wow, that's beautiful."

She'd almost forgotten Foster was nearby, almost. It was as if her body knew of Foster's presence whether she wished it or not. Every time Foster was close, Abby's skin warmed, and the thin cushion of air that separated them crackled with electricity. Did she imagine that too? Was Foster experiencing the same strange connection?

"Aquamarine is one of my favorite stones. It always makes me think of water." The soft tone of Foster's words seemed to caress her ears.

Abby was still kneeling in front of the trunk. She looked up at Foster, standing behind her.

"I did some research about gemstones for one of my novels." Foster crossed her arms as she talked, not defensively, but self-consciously. "It's a symbol of youth, hope, health, and fidelity. Since this gemstone is the color of water and the sky, it's also said to embody eternal life."

Abby returned her attention to the amulet. With caution, she lifted it and held it up by the braided chain. Now she was sure of the vibration, like the low hum of electrical current. She felt a strong urge to wear it, so she did. She slipped the chain over her head and then pulled her hair free from the back of it. The stone fell at a perfect length, just inside the open collar of her shirt.

"Was that what you expected to find?"

"Why do you ask that?" Abby got to her feet. Her knees were beginning to stiffen from the hard floor.

"Because…well, you just seemed to know what it was."

Should she tell Foster the story? She hesitated.

"It's odd how sometimes I swear I know what you're thinking." Foster made a circular motion with her hand at the side of her head. "Like a whisper inside my head."

"I saw this amulet in a dream." Abby held the stone up in her hand and looked at it. "It was more of a vision than a dream. I really had no idea I'd find it, or even that it still existed, but something told me to look here."

"It seems like we're both getting whispered messages then." Foster swept her fingers through her hair.

"Those people were in my vision also." Abby pointed toward the photo perched on the corner of the old trunk.

Foster picked up the frame and studied the image for a moment, then flipped it over and looked at the back. She saw something and held the dark backing up to the light.

"There's a name here…" She turned to look at Abby with wide eyes.

"What?" Abby reached for the frame. "What does it say?"

"Mercy Howe, age twelve."

"Mercy… Her father called her by name in my dream."

"She's your great-great-great grandmother."

"How did you know that?" Abby was sure she hadn't shared any family history with Foster, and she hadn't remembered Mercy's name until she'd had the vision. She was sure she'd known it at some point but had forgotten.

"When I was doing research at the library about the ship wreck and the founding of Spencer's Cove, her name came up. She was the only survivor of the shipwreck."

Abby was reminded of why Foster was here. The memoir project had receded to the background of everything else that was going on.

"Do you mind if I take a look at that book?" Foster tipped her head toward the open trunk.

Abby shook her head. Maybe it was better for Foster to look first. She wasn't sure she was quite ready for other revelations. She covered the amulet with her palm and took some deep breaths. She walked a few feet away, putting a little space between them. When Foster was around she couldn't seem to think.

Foster bent to retrieve the book and gently opened the cover, then flipped the first few pages.

Foster squinted at the open page. "It's hard to make out the writing. I think I need more light because the ink is a bit faded."

"Let's get out of here." The tiny room with the sharply angled ceiling was beginning to close in on Abby.

Abby descended the first step down the ladder and looked back. Foster, reluctant to close the book, reached up to turn off the light, and then followed her.

CHAPTER FIFTEEN

Evan killed the engine. She circled to the back of the truck and considered reaching for the light-duty chainsaw. A rather large limb from one of the coastal live oaks had fallen across the fence at the back of the property.

She spotted a quail perched on part of the fallen limb, just above the ground. He had the teardrop plume of feathers poking out from his forehead. She'd only taken a few strides in the tall grass when he sounded the alarm. A female and probably a dozen chicks scurried under the fence. She held her breath as they rushed away into the high grass single file.

Quail had always fascinated her. A bird that, when it sensed danger, preferred to run instead of fly.

She looked up at the sky. As if to further prove her point, a red-tailed hawk flew overhead, no doubt on the hunt for something. She wondered if it was folly not to follow the quail's lead and flee—run or fly. Abby was certainly at risk from some predator. Whom, she wasn't sure yet. She had her suspicions and she hoped she was wrong.

Leath Dane was ambitious and ruthless, a bad combination. And she'd been denied what she believed was rightfully hers, Jacqueline's power. The handoff had been derailed by the platform's collapse and Jacqueline's sudden death. So, add angry to the list—ambitious, ruthless, and angry. A lethal cocktail that Abby was in no way prepared to combat.

Evan jerked the starter cord handle, once, twice. The saw came to life and she adjusted the throttle. The cutting chain made fast work of the smaller limbs. As they fell away, she tossed them to the side in a pile. She made an angled cut near where the limb rested on the top rail of the wooden fence. Her goal was to have the weight of the limb tilt the larger piece back over the fence so that it didn't land on the far side where she'd have to climb the fence to retrieve it.

Once she had the sections on the ground, she cut them into foot-long pieces that she could split for firewood. Thoughts crowded her head as she worked.

Why wasn't the Council communicating the plan, any plan, with her?

Abby's birthday was only two days away. That was only forty-eight hours, and Evan had heard nothing and no extraction team had arrived to transport Abby. She would head to town soon. Hopefully, her scheduled call with Lisel would offer some good news.

She stacked the small lengths of wood in the back of the truck and closed the tailgate. The horses grazed leisurely in the large enclosure near the barn. Abby had been slowly acclimating them to each other. It seemed they found comfort in one another. Horses were no different than people in some ways. Recovering from trauma only by sharing it with others. Maybe Evan should consider sharing some of hers. But that just made things messy, emotional, and she wasn't sure she was ready for that.

After stacking the wood in a covered alcove near the back of the manor, Evan knocked at the back door. There was no answer. After a second knock, she entered. The huge mansion was eerily quiet. Where was Abby? Losing track of Abby made Evan nervous.

Maybe Abby had gone into town with Cora and Foster was obviously with them. Yeah, that was probably it. She'd seen Cora leave earlier. She returned to her truck. Now was as good a time as any to make a call to the Council and then she'd wait for word from Lisel.

❖

The rental car was right where Foster left it. She wasn't sure what she'd expected. But leaving a vehicle unattended overnight in Atlanta sometimes meant you came back to find a window broken and any loose objects, including small change from the cup holder, missing. Cora angled her vintage Toyota up next to the rental, close enough for the cables to reach. Abby and Foster got out while Cora rummaged around in the trunk. Foster opened the driver's side door and checked the ignition. Nope, still dead. Abby was giving Foster an intense look through the windshield. The same sort of sizzling gaze Abby had given Foster in the kitchen earlier that morning, the kind of look that sent tendrils of arousal through Foster's entire body. Without breaking eye contact, Abby leaned against the car, placing her hand on the front quarter panel. Foster's finger was still on the ignition button, and the minute Abby rested her palm on the car sparks bounced off the hood and the car roared to life.

Cora's head popped up over the trunk of her car; she had a curious look on her face.

Abby stepped away from the car, hugging herself. The static discharge had obviously surprised her as much as it had Foster.

"I guess it wasn't dead after all." Foster quickly stood up, attempting to deflect attention away from what had just happened.

"All is well then." Cora closed the trunk and joined them beside Foster's car.

Someone in a pickup truck drove slowly past. Cora smiled and waved. Cora was so friendly Foster figured she knew everyone in town. Plus, she'd lived there for at least two decades, maybe longer.

"Thanks anyway. Sorry to cause all this trouble." Foster left the car running and stood in the open door.

"Well, Abby, shall we get back to the house then? I wanted to start some baking later this afternoon." Cora clasped her hands in front of her as if she were about to burst into applause.

"I should probably drive this around a bit just to make sure the battery is fully charged." Foster wasn't overly mechanically inclined, but she knew that much.

"I'll ride with you."

Abby's offer surprised her. Aside from the smoldering look that had just generated enough of a charge to jump start a dead battery, Abby had been giving clear signals all day that she didn't really want Foster around. At least that was Foster's interpretation of Abby's distance.

Abby had let Foster keep the book, although she hadn't gotten a chance to look through it. After the excursion to the attic, she'd showered and was about to take some time with the book when Cora mentioned she was driving to the grocery in town. Foster jumped at the chance to get her wheels back. She'd been taken off guard when Abby asked to ride with them and now she was offering to go for a drive. Foster couldn't quite navigate Abby's moods. Sweet one moment, remote the next, with intermittent bouts of scorching flirtation. Foster was beginning to get whiplash just trying to keep up.

"Are you sure?" Because Foster wasn't.

"Yes, I could show you around a little…if you like." Abby sounded as if she was already having second thoughts.

"Well, you girls have a nice drive. I have many errands and then I'll see you at the house later." Cora seemed tickled by this spontaneous plan and was making a quick exit before Abby had time to change her mind. She was in her car and gone in a quick second.

Foster turned to Abby and smiled.

"Where does the tour guide suggest we go?" Foster leaned against the top of the open door.

"Let's drive to the river. There's a good place at the overlook where we could have lunch."

"Which way is the river?" Hmm, a tour and a meal. Foster was feeling pretty happy about the whole dead battery excursion now.

"South." Abby got in the car.

Foster climbed in, checked traffic and did a U-turn.

"South it is." Lunch out with Abby sounded great. Maybe they could finally have a normal conversation. Although as soon as the thought materialized she realized nothing about her time with Abby had been *normal*. Why would normal start now?

CHAPTER SIXTEEN

Evan parked across the street. She checked in both directions before trotting to the pay phone. The coffee shop was in her peripheral vision, and for a second, she thought of making a quick detour to see if Jai was working.

Get your head in the game, Evan.

She dialed the number and waited for what seemed like forever.

"Identify."

A different woman answered. This didn't strike Evan as strange since normally she called much later in the day. Although this whole system of calling in was starting to feel like weird clandestine cloak-and-dagger spy stuff, and Evan was getting annoyed.

"Evan Bell…" She was about to launch into her list of questions about an extraction team, but the woman cut her off.

"We were ready to send a search team out for you. Why haven't you reported in? We haven't had a status update from you in more than two weeks." It sounded as if the woman was trying to sound neutral, but her words were edged with frustration.

Evan had called every day since she'd arrived. Who the hell had she been giving status updates to? Something was off, way off. Evan's gut told her to be evasive.

"I'm sorry, I've been ill. I only just arrived." Evan looked over her shoulder. She had a weird, creeping feeling of unease, and she wasn't sure of the source.

"You should have sent word. We'd have brought you in and sent a replacement."

"Well, I'm here now and I've identified the candidate. I'll report any signs of transmutation immediately."

"I'll inform the Council." The woman clicked off.

Fuck. Now what? She checked her watch. If things went as planned Lisel would ring this number in ten minutes. Until then she'd wait. Evan stepped away from the phone and leaned against the wall in an attempt to look casual. Her body was at rest while her mind raced.

When she'd left Salem for California, things had been unsettled. Jacqueline had died without passing her power to the second in line, leaving a power vacuum. The Council of Elders, made up of twelve women, was at times a fucked-up tangle of fractured discord, but Jacqueline had managed to keep the balance for decades. Without Jacqueline at the helm, Evan feared the worst. The coven would become a morass of ego and backbiting and power grabs. The second in line was Leath Dane. Leath had stepped into the leadership role with half the power Jacqueline had wielded. A weak leader was a threatened leader, and feeling threatened would only make Leath pettier and more insecure, a bad combination.

Jacqueline's power had been lost to the ether. A wave of regret and recrimination washed over Evan again.

Ever since the sixteenth century, witches had been seen as a deadly threat to society, but mostly to the patriarchy. There'd been hundreds of years of witch hunts, hangings, and worse. Now it seemed the Council was becoming its own enemy, wounding itself from within. With Leath in the leadership role that situation would only worsen.

The transcript of the last status report she'd made ran through her head. The woman had challenged her, questioned her hesitation. She should have made the call to Lisel sooner. She'd had a weird feeling about this assignment from the very beginning. Was she the one getting set up or was Abby?

She worried that by reporting any details about Abby she'd set something in motion that she had no control over. Who the fuck had intercepted those calls? Scrolling through an index of possibilities in her head offered nothing conclusive, although the idea that Leath could be behind the confusion was gaining traction.

The phone rang and Evan picked it up before the second ring.

"Evan?"

"Yes."

"Get out of there." Lisel sounded spooked. "Leath left Salem. Without an escort."

"Where are you?"

"With a candidate in Florida. But when I called yesterday to report, I could tell something was wrong. I made a call to Bridget and she filled me in." Bridget was another member of Evan's former security team. Bridget seemed solid, but the only person Evan trusted completely was Lisel.

"Fuck."

"Evan, talk to me."

"Are you on a secure line?"

"I called you from a public phone."

"I've been reporting in every day, but someone has been intercepting the calls." Evan paused. "Lisel, my candidate is the real deal. I've never seen signs this powerful before. There's something different about this one."

"You need to evacuate with your candidate. Do it now. And call me when you're somewhere safe."

"What are you going to do?" Evan wished Lisel was with her. She needed more backup than some nerdy mystery writer and an Irish cook.

"My contact in LA is reaching out to the West Coast Coven—"

"They'll report this directly to the Council…that's not going to help."

"No, he's back-channeling. Evan, trust me…help is on the way." Lisel paused. "I'm just sorry I can't get there…"

"I know." Evan wanted to reach through the phone and touch Lisel. At least the sound of her voice reminded Evan that she wasn't crazy. And she wasn't alone.

Evan climbed back in her truck and did a U-turn, heading back toward the Spencer estate. She'd have to figure out a way to handle things on her own until help arrived. She knew Lisel wouldn't let her down. And she wasn't about to turn Abby over to that pit of vipers, not until she could figure out what was really going on and who she could actually trust. Abby would be safer among people who cared about her. Right now, from her perspective, that was a short list of two—Cora and Foster. Three if she counted herself. No one else was going to be lost on her watch. She white-knuckled the steering wheel and hit the gas.

After a scenic twenty-minute drive, Abby and Foster pulled into a parking lot in front of a rustic looking spot called the Trinity Café.

"Before we go in you should see the view." Abby motioned for Foster to follow.

They wove between weathered Adirondack chairs and plank picnic tables to a cliffside overlook. A waist-high fence made of vertical slatted redwood, gray from the elements, was set back a few feet from the drop-off. The uneven, ragged board fence was more of a suggestion than a firm boundary providing safety. Foster suspected that if she leaned against it she'd topple the whole business into the sea.

The view was breathtaking. They were probably two hundred or three hundred feet above the waterway and the sea. The blue-green river flowed from the east and bumped up against a sandbar that blocked its entrance to the Pacific except for a narrow sluice.

"This is the West River." Abby had a far-off look. Loose strands of hair swirled around her face in the breeze.

"What's that down there?" Foster pointed toward some brown lumps on the sandy shore of the river near where it met the ocean.

"Seals."

"Really?"

"Yes, they sun in that spot quite often. It has good access to the river, but it's protected because it's hard for people to get close."

They stood quietly for a few minutes, enjoying the view, then turned back toward the café. It was warm enough so that after they ordered they chose one of the picnic tables outside. The air was light and crisp compared to the moist, dense air of the Deep South. If the wind picked up Foster would need a jacket, but for the moment she was enjoying wearing only shirtsleeves.

"You don't really want to do this memoir thing do you?" Foster had never been very accomplished at small talk, and she'd been dying to just come right out and ask Abby if she wanted to call the whole thing off.

Abby seemed a little taken aback by the direct question, but she rallied.

"You don't think there's a good story here?"

"Oh, there's definitely a story, but if you'd prefer, I could write it as fiction...I mean, if you didn't mind." Foster paused. "There's a shipwreck, a lone girl the survivor, a town built on an industry now long gone...all elements for the basis of a compelling narrative."

"Let me think about it." Abby sipped her water thoughtfully.

"Fair enough." Foster had a million questions queued up but was afraid she might overwhelm Abby with her curiosity. Sometimes as a writer, it was difficult not to transition from a conversation to what might feel like an interrogation without realizing it.

Abby turned from the view and pinned Foster with another one of her intense looks.

"Just go ahead and ask me."

As if she'd read her mind, Abby's words sounded almost like a dare. Foster laughed.

"Okay... Can I ask how your parents died?" She'd been curious since seeing their joint headstone in the graveyard.

"A plane crash when I was sixteen." Abby took another sip of water but didn't take her eyes off Foster. "My father was a pilot. It was a small plane. It went down during a night flight through the Sierras."

"And you weren't with them." It wasn't really a question, but she hoped it would prompt Abby to offer more details.

"I was…well, let's just say that I was a teenager and I didn't want to spend every weekend with my parents. So I stayed home with Cora to work on a project for school." Abby looked away, toward the open sea. "It's strange, thinking back, I knew the minute it happened." She turned to Foster. "Do you think that's possible?"

She wondered what Abby was really asking.

"Are you asking me if I believe all the stuff that Evan has been saying? That you're becoming a—"

A young waiter with long hair pulled into a man bun cut Foster off with food delivery. Foster smiled and waited for him to leave before continuing.

"What do *you* think is happening?" Foster opened the bag of chips and dumped them onto the plate with her sandwich.

"I'm not sure, but…I don't feel like myself." Abby looked down at her food, hands in her lap, as if lunch were some foreign concept. When she looked up at Foster, tears were pooling along her lashes. She looked away again and dabbed at them with her napkin. "I don't know why I'm feeling so emotional. It's like I can't control it."

Foster swallowed. She felt guilty about eating while Abby seemed so upset.

Instinctively, she reached across the table and covered Abby's hand with hers.

Abby looked down at Foster's hand. There it was again, that low-level current, a vibration, whenever they touched. It should frighten her, but instead it settled her. It soothed her. She took a deep breath and then the first bite of her sandwich.

"Better?"

She nodded. She couldn't explain it, but Foster did make her feel better.

"You've never suspected you had...powers?" Foster looked at her expectantly. There was no judgment in her expression.

Abby took a deep breath and tried to relax. She wanted to be honest with Foster. It felt good to talk about things openly.

"There were things that made me wonder. After the incident with Elissa I started to notice that electrical devices sometimes acted strangely when I held them." She pulled a bit of the crust from her sandwich and chewed thoughtfully. "Cell phones always seemed to malfunction. Which is why I rarely use mine, and if I do I can only use it for brief moments. That's the real reason we don't have Wi–Fi at the house. Whenever I was near the router it would stop working."

"Wow."

"Yeah." Abby rested her chin in her hand. She just wasn't hungry. Sitting across from Foster made her stomach unstable. "I knew that I was different in some way, but you don't assume you're anything special."

"Abby, trust me when I say you're special."

Abby's cheeks warmed and she had to look away for a few seconds.

"How is it you don't have a girlfriend?" Abby stole a chip from Foster's plate.

Foster had just taken a big swig of her Coke. She sputtered, and then coughed.

"Have you ever dated a writer?" Foster coughed again. "We're terrible girlfriends. We pretend to listen, but all the while we're thinking about the next scene we're going to write."

"You seem like a good listener to me."

"We keep odd hours too. We work in binges, all-nighters, and then the rest of the time whine about writer's block."

"I think you're a great writer."

"I aspired to greatness, and I'm pretty sure I ended up somewhere just south of average."

"I disagree."

Foster exuded the kind of solid decency and humility that made Abby want more time with her, not less. The stories Foster wrote were filled with both angst and kindness, filled with the sort of characters readers fell in love with. Characters in search of redemption, undiscovered heroes for the modern world. Foster's modesty only made her more adorable.

"If you're trying to convince me not to like you then you're too late."

She was pleased that her flirtatious comment made Foster blush. Abby had the sudden desire to drag Foster back to the car, climb into her lap, and make out. She unfastened another button and tugged the collar of her shirt open farther. Why was she so warm? She leaned forward, no doubt giving Foster a tempting view of cleavage. She didn't care. She wanted to fan Foster's desire and somehow, she knew just how to do that.

Foster cleared her throat and looked down at her plate as if her half-eaten sandwich was the most interesting thing around.

"Where did you go to college?" Foster was obviously trying to redirect the conversation back to get-to-know-you topics.

"Smith, but I'm not in the mood to talk about college."

Foster adjusted her glasses nervously and swallowed.

"Foster, I need…"

Before she could finish the request, Foster's plate began to levitate off the table. She grabbed it with both hands and forced it back to the table's surface. The water in Abby's glass began to bubble and boil.

"Abby?"

Abby rocked backward, gripping the edge of the table, which now also began to rise off the ground.

"Abby…" Foster reached over and grabbed Abby's hand. "Abby, stop."

"I'm not doing anything—"

"Look at me."

Foster entwined her fingers with Abby's. Abby focused on Foster's mouth as she said the words again *look at me*. Abby exhaled slowly, and the table sank back to the ground. Luckily, the legs had only risen six inches or so off the ground so hopefully no one noticed.

"Will you take me home?"

"Of course." Foster started to get up.

"Don't let go." She squeezed foster's hand.

"I won't let go. I promise."

Somehow, she had no doubt that Foster would do everything within her power never to break that promise.

CHAPTER SEVENTEEN

Evan drove from the barn to the house. There was still no sign of Abby, Cora, or Foster. She checked the back door. It was unlocked.

"Hello?" she called, but there was no reply.

She wrestled free of her muddy boots, left them by the back entry, and started to search the house. No one was around. That seemed odd. Cora sometimes ran into town for groceries or to run errands, but Abby rarely went with her. And Foster's rental car was still in town with a dead battery, so she should be around also. The tiny hairs at the back of Evan's neck prickled. She was descending the stairs from the second floor when she heard a knock at the door.

There was another rapid knock at the front door before Evan reached it. She swung the heavy door open. She blinked a couple of times to clear her vision, but Jai was still standing on the doorstep, with another older dark-haired woman.

"Jai?"

"We're here to help."

"Help who?"

"You and Abby. This is Dena Alvarez." Jai began introductions as if they'd been expected for afternoon tea. "Dena, this is Evan Bell."

Evan was simultaneously intrigued and annoyed. She didn't remember giving Jai her last name. In fact, she'd made a point not to.

"May we come in?"

"Why not?" Evan couldn't help the sarcasm and stepped aside to let them pass. She was sure they could tell she was annoyed, but she didn't care. *What the fuck?*

"I'm sorry if this bothers you, but we've been tracking the movement of some dark matter, and it seems to be traveling in this direction. And then we received a message from a contact in LA that you required assistance."

Lisel's back channel request. That had to be the reason Jai was here.

"This place is beautiful." Dena was looking around at her surroundings as if she wasn't really listening to what Jai had said. "Is it true that it's haunted?"

"Okay, just hold on a damn minute. Who are you?" Evan wanted some answers before she offered up anything.

Jai didn't respond right away. She looked at Dena, but Dena was too distracted by the décor.

"We're part of the western sisterhood," Jai finally answered.

"As in—" Dena cut Evan off.

"The Bay Area Coven, not to be confused with the LA branch, which is not completely in bed with a division of So Cal vampires, but they might as well be." Dena snorted and adjusted her glasses. "Hmph, LA…what more do I need to say."

"I'm an understudy. Dena is third chair on our board of elders."

Jai was an entry-level witch, why didn't that surprise her. Dena, on the other hand, seemed more like an angry librarian than a witch. She didn't look the part, well, except for the dated fashion from the eighties. That was usually more of a giveaway for vampires. When you lived forever it was sometimes hard to keep up with trends. Mostly, witches just kept things simple and wore black. Black was classic, always in style. Dena was the first elder witch she'd ever seen in plaid flannel and Crocs, but she was on the crunchy, granola Left Coast, so what did she expect?

"Wait a minute…what do you mean you're tracking some dark matter? How?"

"Look, Egor—"

"Evan."

"Sorry, Evan, the Bay Area Coven takes full advantage of the technological advances of our sisters in Silicon Valley. We are wired, new tech. We aren't living in the Dark Ages like—"

"I think I've heard enough from y—"

"Okay, okay, everyone just take a breath." Jai stepped between Dena and Evan. "Dena, remember how I told Evan we were here to help? Those sorts of comments aren't helping."

"You sound more like a therapist than an understudy." Evan was starting to get really pissed. If Jai hadn't stepped in she'd have shown Dena the door, with her boot. Elder or no elder.

"I have a degree in social work. Sometimes it comes in handy."

Was Jai making a joke? Either way, her intervention had lightened the mood. Dena was circling the entry now, checking out all the paintings and tapestries on the walls.

"Is Abby here?" Jai's fingers brushed Evan's exposed arm lightly.

Her arm tingled from Jai's touch. She focused on Jai's beautiful face, her lips, the dark pools of her eyes. For a moment, Evan wondered if Jai's powers were more advanced than she was letting on.

"She's not here." The words sounded far away, inside Evan's head.

"Snap out of it, Romeo." Dena pierced Evan's ear curtly.

Evan's temper launched like a rocket from zero to a hundred. She was about to say something she'd regret, but Dena spoke again.

"She shouldn't be allowed to leave the estate unprotected. Not right now."

"No shit." Evan wasn't bound in any way to Dena. She didn't have to make nice, and she certainly didn't have to take any direction from her. "It's not like I have her on a leash. Besides, she's with her keeper." At least Evan hoped that was the case.

"You mean Foster?" Did Jai know every secret Evan thought she'd been keeping?

"How do you know Foster?"

"We met briefly at the coffee shop. She's cute, in a nerdy, bookworm sort of way."

"Okay, rewind." Evan pinched the bridge of her nose. She was trying desperately to regain control and focus. "This dark matter... You need to fill me in."

"What dark matter?" Foster asked. She and Abby stood in the open doorway.

The only person who'd noticed their arrival was Dena. Abby had a look of wide-eyed surprise. Foster was openly holding Abby's hand as if her life depended on it. Evan shook her head. She needed to get back on point. She strode to the door and ushered Abby and Foster inside.

Foster was surprised to see Dena outside her natural habitat. Jai from the coffee shop was here too. It seemed that Abby hadn't expected company when they returned to the estate any more than she had. Cora didn't seem to be about. Abby squeezed her hand.

"What are you guys doing here? And why are we talking about dark matter?" Foster asked again.

"Dark matter accounts for about eighty percent of all the matter in the universe and about a quarter of the universe's total energy density." Dena stepped closer as she delivered one of her librarian info dumps. "Dark matter is composed of subatomic particles."

"I thought that was hypothetical." Foster looked at Evan for some clue about why they were getting a science lecture from Dena in the entry hall. Evan's expression was hard to read, but Foster was fairly certain Evan was annoyed.

"Nice to see someone has read the occasional science journal." Dena crossed her arms and quirked the side of her mouth up.

"I like to read."

"The established scientific community is slow to believe what we already know. Dark matter has not been directly observed by the nongifted, but its presence is impossible to deny. A variety of astrophysical observations, including gravitational effects that cannot be explained unless more matter is present than can be seen prove its existence. Dark matter is ubiquitous."

Everyone was quiet for a moment.

"Who's *we*?" Foster was a journalist at heart and she needed details, facts.

"Witches." Abby spoke for the first time. She released Foster's hand. "It's going to be okay." She touched Evan's arm and Evan visibly relaxed.

"Hello, Abby. It's good to finally meet you." Dena was suddenly transformed into a gracious guest. Her tone softened and she took Abby's hand between hers. "I'm Dena and this is Jaiden, Jai for short. I don't believe we've ever formally been introduced."

"And you're here for me?"

"We're here to help you...and Evan and Foster." Dena's demeanor had completely changed, suddenly sweet, almost maternal.

"Well, heavens above." Cora appeared out of nowhere, standing at the hallway on the other side of the grand staircase. She must have come from the back entrance by the kitchen. She held two brown paper bags, one balanced on each hip. "Something told me I should prepare a large evening meal, and I can see I was right. Can someone help me retrieve the rest of the groceries from the car?"

CHAPTER EIGHTEEN

Foster decided to go in search of Abby. She found Abby standing just inside one of the horse enclosures on the lower part of the property. It was late afternoon. A chilly breeze gusted from the west. Foster buttoned the front of the Levi's jacket Abby had given her. She tilted the fleece collar up against the wind. Abby turned and smiled as she drew close. It seemed since their lunch outing that Abby was no longer trying to keep Foster at arm's length. Abby was letting Foster in, little by little.

"How are you feeling?" She knew it was stressful for Abby to have a house full of people she didn't know very well.

Dena and Jai had been invited to stay for dinner. Evan had left them alone in the house with Cora while she brought in firewood and spread fresh hay in the barn stalls and probably a bunch of other daily tasks that had to be done regardless of how much dark matter was imminent. Besides, Evan had clearly needed to cool off. She'd been completely on edge since they'd returned to the house after lunch.

Abby walked back to the fence and leaned against the top rail, facing the horses. Foster leaned against the fence from the other side.

"I'm okay. Thanks for asking." Abby's hair was back, pulled into a ponytail that hung above the turned-up collar of her heavy cotton jacket.

"What gave you the idea to start rescuing horses?" Foster thought maybe talking about the horses would take Abby's mind off the stress of everything else.

"Hmm, I think ever since I was a little girl I wanted to rescue the world, but I decided to start with horses…and just rescue one small part of the world."

"What's her name?" Foster's chin rested on the back of her hand on the top rail as she watched the brown mare grazing about thirty feet away.

"That's Callie. She's ten."

"What's her story?" Foster knew she had one. All the horses seemed to, and she'd already met Boots and Journey.

"Her owner was a victim of the economic downturn. She could no longer afford her and, coupled with a foreclosure, well, Callie was going to be without a home. The owner contacted us through a good friend of Iain's."

"What would have happened if you hadn't taken her?"

"Callie would have ended up at an auction yard which is a one-way ticket to slaughter."

Foster let that terrible thought run through her head for a minute. That was probably a sad reality for many horses whose situation became upended.

"What about him?" Foster wanted to know everything about the things Abby cared about, and that certainly included the horses.

The stallion was pretty far across the pasture, but he raised his head and looked at them, as if he'd heard Abby call his name. He was dark in color, a rich, espresso brown, with a white blaze on his face.

"A woman discovered him starving, dehydrated, and neglected on private property near Hayward. After asking around, she finally discovered that someone had abandoned him on the property." Abby kept watching the horses as she talked. She wasn't looking at Foster. "The property owner wasn't willing to feed him so he was slowly dying from lack of food and water."

"Seriously?" That sort of cruelty and neglect was hard to imagine. What kind of person could stand by and watch an animal waste away from starvation?

"The woman negotiated his release and called our rescue because she knew nothing about how to take care of a starving horse."

"Jeezus."

"It's never easy to see the results of suffering. His extremely gaunt frame and physical weakness were quite a shock. I'd never seen anything like it." Abby faltered, as if she were reliving the moment. "It took everything I had to walk up the ramp into the trailer when he arrived."

"And look at him now. He looks terrific."

"Yes, he's really healthy now. He's the only other horse I ride besides Boots."

"He's lucky to be here…and lucky he met you."

"I call him Brother, because in this case, I am my brother's keeper."

Foster was touched by the story. Abby had such a good heart and such a gentle way. How could these wounded animals not fall madly in love with her. Foster wondered the same thing about herself.

"Is a horse scarred for life after something like that?"

"Initially, they're flawed, wounded in body and spirit." Abby rotated to face Foster, bracing an elbow on the railing. "But don't flaws make a thing more beautiful? A flaw creates something singularly unique and powerful."

"I suppose flaws do deepen the beauty and character of a thing sometimes." Foster thought of some of her favorite objects, family heirlooms, scratched and worn from use, cherished for their scuffs and scars, roadmaps of their journey.

"I believe the shape of each soul is crafted by small flaws and imperfections." Abby caressed Foster's arm. Foster was mesmerized, glimpsing a part of Abby she hadn't known before. "Flaws hold wisdom, life lessons…broken dreams."

She wasn't sure they were talking about horses any longer. Abby was sharing some deeper truth, some personal ethos, and Foster was swept away by it. She angled her face close to Abby's and kissed her.

CHAPTER NINETEEN

Abby sat in the chair next to Foster at the long, rectangular table in the kitchen. There was a formal dining room in the house, but Abby always preferred the coziness of the kitchen. Foster and Evan sat at opposite ends of the table, and there were five people seated for dinner, six if she counted herself.

How had she let this happen? A house full of people, dinner guests, some of them she knew only from extremely brief encounters in town. She'd interacted with Dena once at the library, but she'd never really spoken with her or Jai before, and now both of them were in her kitchen about to share a meal. The two of them could not seem more different from each other. As a matter of fact, this gathering couldn't be more eclectic—a mystery writer, an Irish cook, a surly groundskeeper, an angry librarian, a sexy barista, and...who was she becoming? Yet again, she had the sensation of being someone else, of existing outside herself. Her social anxiety should have kicked into high gear, but for some reason Abby felt oddly at ease.

"Now isn't this nice. I love cooking for a crowd." Cora was thrilled to host a dinner party.

Abby normally preferred solitude. She was sure this rare event was going to be the highlight of Cora's year. Abby wondered how long it would take for Cora to become curious about why this strange menagerie of visitors had convened. And then what? Abby felt an obligation to tell Cora the truth. Cora was like family. Plus, she was at risk of being swept along by whatever was coming. The shadow of dread, of some unwelcomed thing, hovered at the back of her mind. She knew that Evan sensed it too.

"What strategy have you made?" The question was for Evan. Dena wasn't one for ignoring the elephant in the room. It seemed that if Cora had any curiosity about this gathering she was about to find out what was really happening.

Evan leaned on the edge of the table and glared at Dena.

"What? You don't want to talk in front of Cora?" Dena served herself a second helping of green beans. "She needs to be informed so that she can help us."

Cora perked up, her eyes brightened, but she didn't say a word. She looked back and forth from Dena to Evan, waiting expectantly.

"Cora, tomorrow night, at nine p.m. on Abby's thirtieth birthday, she'll become a witch. It's gonna be a big, scary lightshow event that could go terribly wrong. Dena's a witch, Jai's a witch in training, I'm a member of the protectorate, and Foster is Abby's soul keeper. There, I think that catches you up on everything." Evan turned to Dena. "How was that?"

"Would anyone care for another biscuit?" Cora held the basket up.

"Cora, did you hear what I said?" Evan furrowed her brow.

"Yes, yes, dear…Abby's a witch. I've suspected it all along. I'm so happy you're finally coming out, dear. Biscuit?"

Abby couldn't help laughing. The entire scene was so utterly absurd. Her laughter was contagious. After a few seconds, everyone except for Dena and Evan was laughing. It felt so good to laugh in the face of the unknown. Laughter lightened the air all around them.

"Okay, settle down, everyone." Dena was all business. "We need to take this seriously. Evan, you didn't answer my question."

"I considered relocation."

"I don't think that's wise." Dena adjusted her glasses. "We're too close to the hour of ascension. If Abby were to shift while traveling that wouldn't be good. We need a safe space. Somewhere we can control and protect."

Evan knew in her gut that Dena was right, despite Lisel's urgent advice to flee. It would be hard to defend a position that was in motion.

"I think you might be right about staying put." Evan relaxed in her chair for the first time. Finally acknowledging that she needed help took some of the stiffness from her shoulders. "There's a completely subterranean wine cellar beneath the kitchen. I think that might be our most defensible space for the transmutation."

"Any windows?" Dena spoke around a mouthful of mashed potatoes.

"One...small."

"Not bad. That might work." Dena threaded her fingers and chewed thoughtfully, looking upward at nothing. "What about the ring of fire?"

"There's an earthen floor, and I've already been working on digging out the trench. I stopped working on it when I thought we might vacate, but it wouldn't take much to finish it."

"You mean there will literally be a ring of fire?" The question escaped before Abby could stop it.

"This is so exciting." Cora held her teacup in both hands as she sat on the edge of her seat. "It sounds just like a coronation... you know, except that those mostly happen above ground." Cora reached across the table and patted Abby's hand. "Your parents would be so proud."

"Would they?" Abby couldn't imagine it.

"I know your mother worried that this...gift...might be hard for you, because you'd be different from the other girls, but your father always knew you'd be able to handle this when the time came." Cora touched Abby's hand again. "Parents just want their children to be happy. That's all that really matters."

Abby had begun to wonder why her parents never gave her one clue about their family's link to witchcraft. And now it seemed Cora had some knowledge of it all along. Foster had uncovered a connection that began in Salem in the 1600s. Not merely a connection but a conviction that had resulted in Mercy Howe being hanged. Her parents must have known this. Surely her grandfather had known. She'd discovered the mentions of Mercy in his journal. She'd assumed at first that he meant mercy, as in grace, but now she knew he wasn't searching for clemency; he'd been in search of a long-lost lineage, a thread connecting Abby to the dark matter, the sacred calling. She'd have to read further in his journal to discover what he knew. There was also the book they'd found in the trunk in the attic. She'd let Foster read it first, but she wanted to examine that text as well. She felt for the amulet just inside her open collar. The stone was cool against her skin.

Abby had so many questions; most of them would have to wait it seemed.

"At some point, are you planning on filling the rest of us in on what's supposed to happen tomorrow night?" Foster looked at Evan and then Dena. "Oh, and can we circle back to the whole topic of dark matter so that you can explain how exactly you've been tracking it."

Evan had to give Foster points for paying attention. Just when Evan was in the mood to shout obscenities at her for being too cavalier about the entire situation, she'd show up with her head in the game.

"This is a tracker." Jai held up the rectangular electronic device with a case featuring a design of tiny pink skulls.

"That's a cell phone. Nice case, by the way." Foster leaned forward for a closer look.

"Thanks, but this isn't a cell phone. It just happens to be in a cell phone casing." Jai held her thumb over the touch key for a few seconds and the device came to life. Jai swiped up, and a grid appeared. Definitely not a cell phone. Evan got out of her chair and moved closer for a better look.

"This tracking software is designed to trace movement of dark matter." Jai zoomed in on the grid, and the outline of the California coast became obvious.

"How?" Foster asked the question, but Evan wanted to know too.

"It imports data readings of electromagnetic radiation, more specifically cosmic background radiation, the oldest radiation in the universe. Using an imbedded mapping tool, it cross-references calculations of slight variations in the gravitational field, giving us a point of origin, a path, and a projected terminus."

"I thought you said you majored in social work." The science Jai had just spouted was way over Evan's head.

"With a minor in physics." Jai smiled. "Listen, I can explain more about how this works later. What you really need to see is this." She punched in a sequence of numbers and then set the device on the table so the others could see it too.

A thin dark finger of blue stretched across the middle of the country and then continued west. From the eastern side of California, it moved farther west, and as the map refreshed, it zoomed in, once, twice, until the tip of the thin blue arc appeared to end at the outskirts of Spencer's Cove.

"Show them the rest." Dena had moved closer, standing behind Abby with her arms crossed. She wasn't looking at the tracking device.

"Yeah, this is where things get exciting." Jai held it up so she could enter another string of numbers.

When she set it down to let that search run, a second slender arc of blue appeared. It angled toward Spencer's Cove from the northeast. A third strand of blue was headed toward their location from the sea.

"That's all very interesting, but what does it mean?" Foster asked.

"I think it means we have not one, but three threats to worry about." Evan took an educated guess.

"Exactly." Dena looked at Abby. "When there is this much raw power at stake, there's always someone who wants to take it for their own purposes."

"Not all those who have the gift play for the good guys." That was as much as Evan wanted to say in front of Abby. She'd told Foster part of this.

"It's a bit more serious than that isn't it?" Foster glared at Evan.

"Save it for tomorrow, Foster." Evan wanted to shut this conversation down.

Abby was going to have enough anxiety dealing with the hormonal and energy shifts in the hours before her transition. Evan would carry the rest of this burden. She would be the one to worry about Abby's safety. Evan would be the one figuring out how to protect her.

"Well, now that we've seen Jai's magic cell phone at work, who's ready for dessert?" Cora held a pie aloft, warm from the oven.

CHAPTER TWENTY

F oster followed Abby to the library. She'd mentioned finding her grandfather's journal, and Foster was anxious to take a peek. Dinner had been a floor show, at times surreal, at other times hilariously morbid. The expressions on Evan's face were priceless. Foster had mostly just listened, committing the dialogue to memory for some later use. Authentic dialogue in fiction mostly had to be stolen from actual conversations. You could fake some of it, but there was no substitute for good old-fashioned eavesdropping.

Dena and Jai left after helping with the supper clean up. Everyone had exchanged phone numbers as if they were starting up a book club or planning for the lesbian national pastime, a potluck. They promised to return the next day. Dena was giving Evan a hard time about not having everything ready for the ceremony, which sounded a little scary. Abby didn't seem worried about it. She'd seen Abby transition already from the seriously shy girl she'd surprised in the kitchen the first night to a woman who seemed to be blooming into a confident woman. Sure, there'd been moments of uncertainty, but Abby's shyness was definitely receding.

The library was a welcomed oasis of calm. The soothing companionship of books was something Foster and Abby both appreciated.

There was a small room adjacent to the library. Abby disappeared into it for a moment and then returned with a leather-bound book in her hand. This volume wasn't nearly as old as the manuscript Foster had taken from the trunk, but it was obvious from the soft wear on the cover that it had seen some long years of use.

"I found it in my grandfather's desk." Abby handed it to Foster and then took a seat beside her on the chaise.

"Did you read any of it yet?" Foster turned the first few pages.

"Only a little. He was looking for Mercy. I only later realized what he meant by the reference."

Abby was sitting very close. She brushed a lock of short hair away from Foster's ear. Chills raced down Foster's arm. She was trying her best to focus on the words on each page, but Abby was making it hard to concentrate.

Abby scooted closer, resting her hand on Foster's thigh. Heat radiated down her leg. She cleared her throat and squinted at the book. Was the room suddenly warmer? She tugged at the neck of her T-shirt with her finger. She was wearing a white T-shirt under an oxford and was feeling that was two layers of clothing too many.

Abby's hand drifted up her leg, dangerously close to her crotch. She swallowed and tried to focus. She shifted away from Abby a few inches, but Abby scooted even closer. She almost jumped out of her skin when Abby traced the edge of Foster's ear with the tip of her tongue.

What book? Who cares? Forget the book.

"Abby?" Foster's throat was dry.

"Foster..."

"Yes?"

"Take me to bed," Abby whispered close to her ear.

She squeezed her eyes shut, but then felt Abby stroke the very sensitive inside of her thigh. She turned, and before she could say anything else, Abby kissed her. This was not a timid, first kiss, this was a deep, tongue dancing, passionate kiss. A kiss that lead to other things, a kiss that refused to be ignored.

Foster set the book on the side table without opening her eyes or breaking the kiss. She missed the table and heard the book flump to the floor. She didn't care. Abby was practically in her lap, kissing her, sinking her fingers in Foster's hair. Foster rested her hands on

Abby's waist. She teased the exposed skin at the hem of Abby's blouse.

Abby was tugging at the buttons of her oxford. She was trying to get past the T-shirt too. Abby moved into Foster's lap, straddling her waist. She was trying to go slow, but desire was ratcheting up in her system. Foster slid her palm up from the curve of Abby's waist until she cupped Abby's breast. She could feel the hard point of Abby's nipple through the thin material of her blouse.

Abby surprised her by unbuttoning her blouse and pulling her bra aside. She raised up, positioning her breast near Foster's mouth. Foster willingly obliged Abby's silent demand. Abby moaned softly as she teased Abby's nipple with her tongue.

Foster was lost in erotic exploration, every curve, every inch of hot exposed flesh. She wanted Abby in the worst way. But this angle was no good. Foster rotated Abby onto her back and began to work the button of her jeans free, then the zipper. Abby's hands were inside her shirt, her nails skimmed across Foster's lower back.

Somewhere in the recesses of her brain, Foster had the thought that maybe they should move to Abby's bedroom, but she was powerless to take her hands off Abby, even for a moment. She caressed Abby through her underwear, her arousal obvious despite the thin fabric barrier. Abby moaned against her mouth as Foster touched her. God, Abby was so wet. She spread her legs and Foster stroked as Abby arched against her palm.

Abby's hand was inside the back of Foster's jeans. She squeezed Foster's ass.

"I want you..." Abby's words were breathy against her neck.

"Abby, I've wanted you since the first night...and every night since then." She realized she'd only been there for a couple of days, but to her libido, two days in close proximity to Abby felt like eternity.

"I want to feel you against me." Abby was unfastening Foster's belt. She started to push Foster's jeans down over her hips.

Had they closed the door to the library when they came in? She couldn't remember, but in the haze of her raging libido, she swore she heard a door slam. A rushing sound circled. Her eyes were closed, so she assumed it was the sound of blood swarming, pounding in her ears.

She wanted desperately to be inside Abby. The friction between them was going to bring them both to orgasm, and they were still wearing way too many clothes. She could sense Abby's cresting arousal as if it were her own. Maybe it was her own. She was having a hard time telling the difference. Every sensation seemed swirled and amplified.

Abby kissed her, open-mouthed and desperate. The rushing sound was getting louder. Foster opened one eye, and something whooshed past where they were lying on the chaise. Foster broke the kiss and stared.

"What's wrong?" Abby still hadn't noticed what was happening around them.

"Abby…the books…"

Books, all shapes and all sizes, swirled around them. The entire collection was spinning around and above them as if every volume had been swept up by a tornado. Foster blinked a few times, but this was real. Her eyes weren't playing tricks on her.

Beneath her, Abby's skin glistened with a light sheen of perspiration, her cheeks were flushed and her eyes darted about the room.

"Abby, sweetheart…"

"Yes?"

"Are you doing this?"

The look on her face told Foster that Abby was equally surprised, but the swirling books had to be Abby's doing. That was the only believable explanation.

"I didn't mean to do that." There was uncertainty in Abby's voice, possibly a brief return of shyness.

"It's okay." She stroked Abby's cheek. "Everything is okay."

Abby smiled up at Foster. She pulled Foster down into a deep, languorous kiss, and out of the corner of her eye, Foster saw the swirling storm begin to slow, and one by one, books dropped softly to the carpeted floor.

❖

Evan followed the fence line to the barn. The horses were clustered together in the open grassy area of the largest paddock. Even with cozy, clean stalls available in the barn, sometimes even at night the horses preferred to be in the open.

Tonight, they seemed a little spooked, restless, on high alert. *I know just how you feel.*

Tomorrow, the eve of Abby's thirtieth birthday, would be the full moon, and dark matter was gathering. Why not just hold the ceremony in a graveyard while they were at it and throw a little more gasoline on the fire?

She hit the switch on the box just inside the door, and a glaring overhead light cast sharp shadows into the corners. After a few minutes of rummaging in the tool cabinet, she found what she was looking for, a pickax. She shouldered the axe and strode back toward the house. Only the lights in the library and the kitchen were visible. Cora left an hour earlier. Foster and Abby were somewhere in the house, and it didn't take a deductive genius to figure out what they were probably up to. The sexual tension between them was so thick you could cut it with a knife.

No one had thrown up a roadblock for her plan to utilize the wine cellar so she was proceeding. The narrow steep stairs led from the large pantry down to the cool, dimly lit subterranean room. Dusty bottles were nestled inside a honeycomb style rack along one wall. Tomorrow she should take some time and remove all the glass from the room, except for the small window, which she'd cover with plywood. Maybe Foster could help her move the wine bottles to a safe distance after breakfast.

The circular trench she'd started wasn't quite deep enough, and the dirt floor was so hard-packed that the axe had become necessary. The first couple of swings didn't find much purchase in the ancient, rigid soil. Each swing was bone jarring, but she kept at it. As she worked she started to heat up and stripped down to her tank undershirt. This felt good. Physical exertion was what she needed to lose some of the tension from the day, hell, this whole week, the entire month. She took a break for a moment and wiped her face with the shirt she'd tossed aside.

Evan had been on the verge of losing patience with Foster and her cavalier attitude, but during dinner she'd sensed a cognitive shift. Foster and Abby both were beginning to believe. Abby was surely having more symptoms than she was sharing. Maybe she was sharing with Foster. Evan hoped that was true. Abby had obviously crafted a solitary life for herself out on the edge of the world, but she was going to need help to get through this. Not just this part, but also the first days after the ascension.

She'd been annoyed by Dena at first, but the truth was they needed her, and Jai too. Evan let the axe rest on the ground as she stood and arced her back into a stretch. Jai was a fledgling witch. That had come as a surprise. No wonder she'd been drawn to Jai, aside from her looks. Damn, she was sexy as hell. But the fact that she'd been surprised by both of them bothered her. There had to have been signs of some kind, and she'd obviously missed them. Maybe she *was* slipping. Maybe she really was unfit to serve the Council after all. Fieldwork was all she was good for.

The axe struck with a hard and satisfying blow, kicking up debris on either edge of the trench. She knelt to check the depth. About ten inches. That was probably adequate.

She rocked on her heels and sat on the floor. She held the axe handle in both hands between her bent knees and rested it against her forehead. Angry tears rose and she couldn't stop them. Tears she hadn't shed for Jacqueline, tears she hadn't shed for herself. She buried her face against her arm and sobbed.

The sobs subsided as quickly as they'd come. She sniffed and pressed her wadded up discarded shirt to her face. This was her chance to make things right, and by God, she was going to do things perfectly this time, by the book. She would not let Abby down.

CHAPTER TWENTY-ONE

Abby tugged Foster by the hand. They wove between stacks of fallen, stacked books in the library and then up the staircase. Foster was holding her belt and jeans together with her one hand as Abby dragged her along. She felt like a teenager sneaking around with a secret lover. When they reached the guest room at the top of the stairs, she pulled Foster inside and closed the door. Foster was flushed and breathing hard. Her hair was adorably tousled and her unbuttoned oxford shirt all askew. Abby leaned against the door taking Foster in.

Being around Foster had evoked some deep yearning. Abby realized that she'd given up, closed herself off, locked away her heart, and then Foster had shown up, out of nowhere, with the key.

She advanced on Foster slowly, the way she would approach one of her startled horses. Foster's parted lips were a bit swollen from their kissing frenzy in the library. Abby brushed her lips across Foster's tenderly, then her cheek, kissing her way to Foster's ear where she whispered, "Let's get in bed."

Foster nodded mutely and released the top of her jeans. They drooped around her hipbones as she slowly took off her button-down shirt and then her T-shirt. Abby watched Foster undress as she opened the bottom few buttons of her blouse and then unfastened her bra and let it fall to the floor. Foster wasn't wearing a bra so once the undershirt was gone she was bare-chested too.

Abby pushed her pants over her hips and Foster mirrored her movements, letting her jeans pool around her ankles. She stepped out of them, and as Abby advanced she backed toward the bed in her Y-front briefs.

The drapes were open, bathing the room in moonlight. Foster crawled backward onto the bed and Abby followed on her knees. Her body was on fire; every nerve receptor vibrated, hummed with desire and need. She straddled Foster's waist, gently removed her glasses, and set them aside. Then Abby resumed her position, tossed her hair over her shoulder, and angled downward to kiss Foster. Her skin tingled everywhere Foster touched her. Foster finally rested her palms on Abby's thighs, squeezing with her fingers as if she felt the need to hang on as the kiss deepened.

Abby switched positions, curling up next to Foster. She trailed her fingertips down the center of Foster's chest and teased just below the waist of her briefs.

"I thought you said you'd never done this before." Foster caressed Abby's shoulder and swept her palm down Abby's arm.

"I haven't." Foster's hand covered hers, partway inside Foster's underwear.

She wasn't sure if this was a signal to slow down, but Abby didn't want to. She wanted to finish what they'd started in the library.

"How is that possible?" Foster brushed an errant strand of hair behind her ear. "You're so incredibly beautiful."

"It just never happened. I told you why." Abby wasn't really in the mood to talk about the past. She wanted the future and all the possibilities that the future held. She raised up on her elbow and kissed Foster. She whispered against Foster's lips. "Stop talking."

Foster laughed softly.

I don't really know what I'm doing.

"Yes, you do."

Abby was certain the thought had been just that, silent rather than voiced, but Foster answered. Foster rotated their positions so that she was on top.

"You seem to know exactly what to do to make me want to make love to you." Foster's gaze was intense, like a knife edge. She brushed the back of her fingers over Abby's cheek.

"Make love to me." Abby pushed Foster's briefs over her hips. She wanted nothing between them. She needed to feel all of Foster. Foster shoved the briefs down past her thighs, then farther with her foot until she could kick them off. She kissed her way down Abby's stomach until she reached the lowest part, just above the waist of her underwear. Foster kissed each inch of ultra-sensitive exposed skin as she eased the waistband down and over Abby's hips.

If Abby thought she was on fire before now she was in flames, a raging, uncontrolled burn. She writhed beneath Foster's mouth, arching into her, filling her fingers with Foster's hair. She squeezed her eyes shut and bit her lower lip. Foster's mouth was on her now. Her body began to convulse with each stroke of Foster's insistent tongue.

And then Foster stopped. Abby inhaled sharply from the painful loss of contact. She searched Foster's face. What was she doing?

Foster's mouth was on her breast now, and she felt Foster's fingers where Foster's mouth had been. She spread her legs and clung to Foster's shoulders as Foster's fingers slipped inside. Foster's movements were intoxicating, her mouth, her hands, her fingers thrusting slowly inside, deeper, deeper. Abby was coming undone. Foster was grinding her sex against Abby's thigh too. Abby became acutely aware of Foster's wet center riding her thigh. She put her hands on Foster's ass, applying pressure, increasing the friction between them.

She held Foster's face, pulling her upward against her mouth. Abby had the fiercest need to kiss Foster. The orgasm built to a crescendo and then exploded like the flash of so many stars against the black of night. Like an expanding supernova, her climax shattered every perception she'd held so tightly. All she could do was hold on to Foster as the orgasm claimed her, her senses rippled and broke apart like the surf against the ragged cliffs.

In her arms, Foster stiffened against her. They both convulsed until the tremors finally passed and they relaxed against each other. Foster collapsed against Abby's shoulder, and she caressed Foster's back.

She had the unfamiliar sense of weightlessness, of floating.

She opened her eyes to see that the bed had risen with her climax and was hovering several feet above the floor. Foster's eyes were still closed when Abby reached up and touched the decorative stucco pattern on the ceiling just above them.

She was not afraid.

Abby couldn't help but smile.

The sun streamed into the room with bothersome ferocity. Foster squinted and then shielded her eyes while she scanned nearby surfaces for her glasses. She put them on and then partially sat up in bed. Abby was asleep next to her. The sheet draped across Abby's waist as she lay on her side, facing away from Foster.

Abby was sleeping so soundly she decided not to wake her. The pink along the horizon suggested it was still early. There was a haphazard stack of books on the nightstand. One of them was the vintage book they'd taken from the attic. Foster opened the cover and flipped through a couple of pages. But who was she kidding? She was completely unable to relax and read. She was naked under the covers, and the warmth of Abby's body seeped in from the other side of the bed. She dropped the book and rolled on her side toward Abby, braced on her elbow.

The temptation of Abby's exposed shoulder was too great. The book completely forgotten, Foster spooned against Abby, moved her hair aside, and kissed her neck. Abby moaned softly.

Abby rotated in Foster's arms. Her breasts brushed teasingly against Foster's bare chest. Abby still hadn't opened her eyes when she kissed the sensitive spot just below Foster's ear.

"Good morning," Foster whispered. Abby was like a drowsy, beautiful angel, and Foster didn't want to startle her.

"Good morning." Abby squinted up at her. "What time is it?"

"Don't know and don't care." Foster smiled. She'd already decided she could just stay in bed with Abby all day.

"Last night was amazing." Abby smiled and stretched.

"I'm not sure amazing is the right word. I was thinking more like incredible, mind-blowing, intoxicating, dreamlike…"

"Yes, all of those." Abby's eyes sparkled in the cool, early morning light.

There was a brisk knock at the door.

"Foster?" Evan sounded annoyingly awake.

"Yeah?"

"Get up. We have a lot to do today." Her tone was brusque.

There was a pause and then Evan's tone softened. "Abby, I'm sorry if I woke you."

Foster's cheeks warmed, more for Abby than for herself. She turned sheepishly to Abby and shook her head to signal that Abby didn't have to respond if she didn't want to.

"It's okay, Evan. Thank you." Abby was always kind. Regardless of the circumstance, Foster had only seen kindness, even when Abby was suffering from one of her painful headaches she didn't want to burden anyone else.

She heard the thump of Evan's footfalls descend the stairs.

"What is she? The fun police?" Foster sank back into her pillow.

"I suppose she doesn't like playing that role any more than we like being on the receiving end of it." Abby swept her fingers through her hair to smooth it.

"If you say so." Foster wasn't so sure. From day one, Evan seemed to love playing the law-and-order role.

Abby climbed out from under the rumpled duvet and searched the floor for her clothes, giving Foster a lovely view during the process. Abby slipped into her pants and blouse without putting on her bra.

"I'm going to go shower and change. I'll see you later." Abby leaned over and kissed Foster. When Foster looked down she realized Abby had placed her discarded red silk underwear in Foster's hand.

Abby closed the door softly and Foster sank under the covers. She'd died and gone to heaven, she was sure of it.

Foster jolted awake. Shit. She'd fallen back asleep after Abby left her. What time was it? She fumbled around on the bedside table in search of her cell phone. It was dead. That was probably just as well. Gloria had such bad timing she'd no doubt have called or texted during the night with some mundane update about William Faulkner.

She rotated, draped her legs over the edge of the bed, and let her toes rest on the floor. She studied the dark screen for a moment before she got up and crossed the room to check the antique clock on the mantel. Shit, shit, shit. It was almost nine o'clock. Why had Abby let her sleep so long, or Evan for that matter?

There was a robe hanging in the wardrobe across the room. Foster slipped it on and then plugged her phone in to leave it to charge. She peeked into the hallway. No one was about. She scurried across to the bathroom to take a quick shower.

Twenty minutes later, she was dressed and briskly finger-combing her damp hair. She needed coffee, badly. She strolled to the kitchen feeling oddly lightened by her night with Abby. She heated the kettle and made herself a cup of pour-over coffee. She painstakingly let the hot water wash coffee grounds into the bottom of the filter from each side and then impatiently waited for it to drip into the mug. All the while, she craned to look out the kitchen window for signs of activity. Where was everyone?

There was a cast iron skillet on the stovetop covered with a well-worn blue plaid cloth. She peeked under the corner of it as she stirred cream into her coffee. Biscuits with ham in them. Bless Cora's sweet heart.

Foster took a bite, chewed, and then held the biscuit in her mouth to free up her hand. She reached for the knob of the back door. Just as she was about to make contact, the door opened. Abby was there, breathing hard, cheeks rosy from the chilly air. Abby tugged the knit cap off her head. Static made long strands fluff around her face. She smiled and Foster seriously thought that her smile was the most beautiful thing in the world, like a brilliant sunrise after days of rain.

"Hi."

"Hmph." Foster remembered the biscuit she was holding in her mouth. Somehow, the sight of Abby made her forget everything.

She took the biscuit out of her mouth and stepped aside to make room for Abby to come in. A draft of cool air swirled around them in the entry as Abby pulled the door closed.

"I was just about to go look for you." Foster sipped her coffee.

"And now you don't have to." Abby shucked out of her jacket and dropped her leather gloves on the bench just inside the door.

"The water is still hot in the kettle if you'd like some tea." Foster motioned toward the kitchen.

"That sounds perfect."

Abby was wearing her riding pants and boots. It surprised Foster a little that she'd obviously gone for a ride. But maybe it was good to treat today like every other normal day, even though tonight things might be different. Foster's stomach suddenly upended and sank. Was everything going to be different tomorrow?

What if this whole transmutation thing happens and Abby no longer had any interest in me?

"That's not going to happen." Abby kissed her on the cheek.

"You know what I was thinking just now?"

"Sorry, I can't help hearing your thoughts. I don't know how to turn it off." Abby poured water into a cup and then dropped a tea bag into it.

"Since when?" Foster was worried she'd thought things Abby wouldn't like or didn't need to know. Needless worries and fears.

"Since our lunch by the river…I think." Abby cocked her head as if she were thinking back. "Maybe hints and whispers after the graveyard…yes, I think that's when it started."

"So, what am I thinking now?"

Abby blushed and bit her lower lip. "Don't make me say it out loud."

"Wow…" Foster leaned against the edge of the counter opposite Abby.

"I know. I think there are other things too."

"Like what?"

"Can you feel this?"

Abby hadn't moved, but Foster had the distinct sensation of the warmth of Abby's touch inside her shirt. She swore she could feel Abby's fingertips trail across her stomach under her shirttail and then begin to descend lower. Abby's eyes were closed, her knuckles were white where she gripped the counter's edge. Foster braced her legs farther apart because she was afraid her knees were going to give way.

"Foster, where have you been?" Evan broke the connection.

Foster exhaled and cleared her throat. She tugged at the waist of her jeans, adjusting their position. She knew she was wet and Abby hadn't even touched her. Or had she? That was so strange.

Evan walked between them, crossing the kitchen to the refrigerator. She opened a soda and took a long drink. Her clothing was smudged with dirt, and she'd worn her boots into the kitchen, which seemed unlike her. She was sweating too, even though the temperature was cool.

"Hey, are you all right? You don't look so good." Foster set her coffee down.

"I'm fine…I just…I think…" Evan swayed on her feet and toppled backward. Foster managed to catch her head just before it struck the stone tiles.

"She's burning up." Abby's hand was on Evan's forehead.

"Call Dena." Evan's voice was raspy, as if she was moments from losing it completely.

"What?" Foster's hand still cradled Evan's head.

"Call Dena…it's a spell…"

Abby pressed her fingertips to Evan's neck. "Her pulse is too fast."

"My phone is upstairs charging. I'll get Dena's number."

Foster hustled upstairs only to discover that she hadn't actually plugged the phone in. Yes, she'd attached the charger to the phone, but the plug under the desk wasn't actually in the socket. Her brain had been so foggy earlier that she hadn't thought to check. The phone was completely dead. *Damn.*

Foster was breathless by the time she reached the kitchen. Evan looked worse if that was possible, pale and lifeless. Seeing someone so fit and strong collapse so suddenly freaked her out.

"My phone is completely dead. Did you get Dena's number?"

"No, I didn't think I needed to. You and Evan both had it."

"Where's Evan's phone?" Foster started searching Evan's pockets, nothing. It could be anywhere and she'd waste valuable time looking for it. "The library."

"What?"

"We could call the library from the landline."

Abby checked the clock on the stove. "It's only nine thirty. It's not open yet…but if you drive there you could reach Dena before they even open."

"Right. I'll be right back." She ran up the stairs again for a jacket and keys.

She stuck her head in the kitchen door before leaving.

"How is she?" Abby had placed a towel under Evan's head. The spilled soda pooled near the fridge where she'd dropped it.

"Not good. Hurry, Foster." Abby looked up from her kneeling position on the floor, worry evident on her face.

Foster hit the gas, throwing bits of debris from the stone driveway against the low undercarriage of her lame rental car. For a minute she wondered if getting out to push would make it go any faster.

The fifteen-minute drive into Spencer's cove seemed like it took forty-five. She angled into a parking spot beside the brick building. The car sputtered and died before she even got a chance to hit the ignition button. That seemed strange, but she had no time to sort it out now. She sprang from the car and trotted toward the side entrance. There was one other car in the parking lot. That must be Dena's. She cupped her hands so that she could see past the glare of the glass side door. She knocked on the glass. The library wasn't open for another fifteen minutes so the door was locked when she tried it. Regardless, she shook the handle a few times, rattling the whole business loudly.

Dammit, Dena, where are you?

She ran around to the front of the building and repeated her steps. It took another five minutes of banging to get Dena finally to the door.

"Didn't you hear me banging?" The minute Dena opened the door Foster launched into her.

"Well, hello to you too." Dena was as surly as usual.

"Evan's in trouble."

Dena's demeanor immediately shifted, suddenly she was alert and attentive.

"What happened?"

"I don't know." Foster shook her head. "She came in the kitchen to get a drink...she didn't look right...and then she just collapsed. She said for me to find you."

"Anything else?" Dena stepped through the door, leaving the *closed* sign in place, and locked it behind her.

"I think she said something about a spell. But I can't be sure."

"Go pick up Jai and meet me at the Spencer place." Dena started toward her car.

"Can't she just drive there herself?" Foster was anxious to get back to Abby. The thought that she was in the house, alone, and that Evan was incapacitated came crashing down. Her heart rate spiked. Evan had been very specific about the fact that Foster should stay with Abby.

"She doesn't drive...long story." Dena kept walking and Foster followed her. "We'll need things and she knows where they are at my house. I'll start the antivenom. We shouldn't delay. Trust me, this will be the quickest solution."

"Where is Jai?"

"Redwood Grove apartments just past the market. Number two three nine." Dena was in her car. It was in motion and she was shouting to Foster through the open window.

Foster didn't like this plan at all. She stood in the parking lot for a minute to catch her breath. She ran her fingers through her hair and slowly exhaled. Okay, be cool, just stay cool. Dena was on her way. Abby wouldn't be alone.

She got back in her car and hit the ignition button. The console lights came on, but the car wouldn't start. *What now? I hate this piece of shit.* She scanned the digital readouts on the dash, and then she saw it. Empty. The little gas pump was all lit up, but in her haste, she hadn't noticed that the car was out of gas.

"Car trouble?"

Foster almost jumped out of her skin. She looked up to see an elegant looking woman leaning against the car. Her arm was on the top of the car and she was bending down so that she could speak to Foster. The woman seemed harmless, but still Foster's stomach lurched.

"No, no trouble…just needs gas." Foster tried for her best, friendly Southerner routine to get the woman to go away.

"I could give you a ride to the service station. I bet they have a gas can they'd let you borrow."

Everything about this woman was wrong for this place. First off, she was wearing all black clothing in a town that seemed to go one of two ways, plaid flannel or tie-dyed. Second, her manner seemed too formal. This woman was not from Spencer's Cove.

But what were her choices?

Foster did some quick math in her head. The nearest gas station was probably five miles away, to the south. That would take too long on foot. She could hitchhike, but that might also take a while. This woman was offering. Even if she did trigger an orange caution flag inside Foster's head, this seemed like the only choice. Time was not on her side. She needed to get gas, pick up Jai, and get back to Abby and Evan as quickly as possible.

"Okay, if it's no trouble." The woman stepped back so Foster could open the door.

"It's no trouble." The woman smiled but the smile seemed disingenuous.

Okay, just suck it up and get this over with.

The woman seriously made her skin crawl. Her skin was too pale and too smooth, almost translucent. Foster was having a hard time guessing her age. Long, straight dark hair swirled around her head in the light breeze, but never once actually blew into her face, adding a surreal quality to her overall appearance. Every cautionary tale her mother had ever told her about accepting rides from strangers echoed loudly inside her head, but she ignored them.

"Um, where are you parked?" Foster had followed the willowy woman across the street and down a half block toward the pier.

Foster looked over her shoulder. How had this woman even seen her in the library parking lot from down here?

When she turned back, the woman had stopped in her path. She almost bumped into her. She smiled at Foster and grabbed her shoulder with some sort of Vulcan death grip.

"Hey! What the—" Her words died in her throat. Darkness invaded her senses until the entire world was night.

CHAPTER TWENTY-TWO

Abby heard someone approach the door. Without looking, she knew it was Dena. Evan's condition hadn't changed. Abby was at the door before Dena even knocked.

"Where is she?" Dena was all business.

"In the kitchen. We didn't move her." After Dena crossed the threshold Abby glanced out the door. "Where's Foster?"

"I sent her for Jai. They're right behind me." Dena rolled up the sleeves of her flannel shirt. "Let's get started. You can help me until they arrive with the other supplies I need."

"How do you know what you need without knowing what's wrong?"

"I don't…but Jai will know to bring my entire bag. So, we'll be covered." Dena patted Abby's shoulder. "Now, where is Evan?"

Dena followed her back to the kitchen where Evan lay on the floor, still as death.

"Is Cora here?"

"No, Thursdays she always drives down the coast to see her sister. She'll be back this evening."

"Too bad, we might need her. Three are always better than two." Dena studied the room. "Let's clear some space around her." Dena started moving chairs, and she and Abby worked together to slide the heavy table.

Abby started to suggest that Iain could assist, but then remembered that today was his day off too.

"I could call Iain. He helps with the horses."

"Better not to. The less regulars we involve the better."

"Regulars?"

"People outside the *family*, if you know what I mean."

Abby figured she didn't mean lesbian; she probably meant witch.

Dena knelt next to Evan. She touched the pulse point on the inside of her wrist. She held up Evan's palm and examined it, then Dena pressed her ear to Evan's chest. Dena opened Evan's eyelids. Her pupils were chalky white.

"Is she dead?" Nausea threatened to topple Abby. She was kneeling on the other side of Evan. She rocked back on her heels to steady herself against the cabinet.

"No, she's not dead. But this isn't good." Dena furrowed her brow and rubbed her chin. "Whoever did this...it was someone close to her."

"By close you mean, here? In the house?"

"No, I mean someone who knows her well enough to have access to her things. Probably access to personal items, like a toothbrush, hairbrush...something..." Dena didn't finish the thought.

She glanced up at the clock near the stove and then back to Abby.

"They should be here by now." Dena frowned.

Abby shivered. She hugged herself and looked at Dena.

"Why am I so cold all of a sudden?"

Cold, that was the first sensation Foster became aware of. She was cold and wet, but it was the sound of metal against metal that pulled her from unconsciousness, not the cold. Her head bobbed, and when it did, she got a mouth full of seawater. She sputtered and coughed and swung her arms, splashing about. Foster's foot slipped, but then found something to stand on. She wiped the salty water from her eyes and blinked. She was in some sort of cage, sunk up to her chest in the water. The bars of the cage were rough in places, slimy in others. She shook the bars, but they didn't give. Jostling around caused the chain holding the cage to slip, and it dropped with a jolt, sinking deeper. The water was up to her shirt collar, and when small waves came through the bars it splashed her face. Panic raced through her chest like a freight train.

"Help!" She tried to see what was above. The cage was in shadow. Was she under the pier? "Hey! Anybody up there!"

No response. Foster took a moment to examine the cage. There was a latch at the front with a padlock. How the hell did she end up here? Her last memory was following Cruella de Vil's twin sister down the street toward the pier. Who was that woman? Wait, she had a sneaking fear that she knew. *The trail of dark matter Jai was tracking. Those two things had to be connected.* The creepy woman must be a witch. She had to be. And not the Glinda-the-Good-Witch variety either. This woman reeked evil intent.

Why had she agreed to follow the woman?

Dumb, dumb, dumb. So stupid!

Foster shook the cage in frustration. The motion caused the unstable chain to give another few inches. The entire contraption dropped again. Now the water was up to her chin. She clung to the top of the cage in an attempt to get her face above water.

One thought crystallized for Foster—she was going to drown.

Death had always just been an idea, a notion that resided in a far-off place called the future. But here she was, in a vacuum of fear, all the unsaid things flashing through her mind. She closed her eyes and made a silent wish. *I want to live.* More than anything she wanted a chance to hold Abby in her arms again.

They'd had one night together. One fleeting night.

The wind gusted, and successive waves splashed over her face making it impossible for her to catch her breath. Disbelief and terror squeezed her lungs.

"I'm so cold." Abby rubbed her arms as she got to her feet. "It's Foster. Something's wrong." Abby looked at Dena. "She's afraid."

Dena fished her cell phone out of her pocket. "The service here sucks." She walked around the kitchen holding her phone out. "I'm getting one intermittent bar."

"There's a phone in the library, a landline."

"Who doesn't have a phone in the kitchen?" Dena frowned.

"Cora hates to be interrupted while she's cooking or during dinner, so we had it taken out."

"Show me the library then."

They practically jogged to the library where all the shelves were empty. She'd forgotten the tornado of books until they entered the room. Dena cocked an eyebrow and gave her a sideways look as they stepped in and around haphazard piles of books to reach the phone. Abby paced while Dena called Jai's cell number.

Something was terribly wrong. Abby could feel it as sure as she could see Dena standing in front of her.

"Jai, where are you?" Dena frowned. "What do you mean you're at your apartment? Didn't Foster pick you up?"

Panic bubbled up inside her chest. Abby swept her fingers through her hair.

"Tell Jai to go search for Foster now…right now."

Dena had just started to explain the situation with Evan. She stopped talking and looked up. "Hang on, Jai."

"Something has happened. She's trapped."

"How? What's happened?" Dena didn't seem to doubt Abby's intuition. "Jai needs to know where to look."

Abby squeezed her eyes shut. She visualized Foster, the warmth of her skin, the taste of her mouth, the dark pools of her eyes. And then her pupils morphed into an opening that she could enter. She moved through darkness until there was nothing. She stopped moving and used her arms to turn, as if she were treading water. She was cold, she tasted salt on her tongue. If she listened closely she could hear the lulling, dull sound of waves lapping against an unmoving object and the air smelled of dead fish.

Abby's eyes flew open.

"I think she's somewhere near the pier."

"Jai, did you hear that?" Dena was silent for a moment, listening to Jai on the other end. "We'll manage here. Go find Foster. Call us when you know something."

"I don't feel so good." Abby braced her arm against an empty shelf.

"Without my bag and my book, I'm going to have to take an educated guess about Evan's condition..." Dena was brainstorming out loud.

"I think I'm going to be sick."

"Save it." Dena brushed past her. "Help now, throw up later."

How could she help when she sensed that Foster was in imminent danger?

"Hey! Pull it together or we're going to lose both of them!" Dena must have sensed her silent question. She faced Abby, a fierce expression on her face.

"Okay." The word was almost choked by a sob. "Okay, I'll try. How can I help?" Abby tried by force of will to stabilize her stomach as she followed Dena back to the kitchen.

"I need a straight razor."

"There's one in my parents' room. It belonged to my father." Abby sprang up the steps to retrieve the blade.

CHAPTER TWENTY-THREE

Foster tried to hang onto the top bars of the cage, but her fingers were stiff and frozen from the chilled Pacific. Her teeth chattered making it hard not to swallow small splashes of salt water. The muscles in her arms trembled from fatigue and cold.

"Foster!"

She thought she'd imagined hearing her name. The moment she was above the water line and able, she'd called for help. She'd shouted until her throat was raspy, but no one had responded.

"Foster!"

There it was again. Was she dreaming?

"Here…" She tried to shout but ended up coughing instead. "Down here!" She slipped her fingers through the top of the cage in an attempt to signal her location.

A shadow figure breached the edge of the platform above Foster.

"Foster, hang on!"

Was that Jai? Foster was shivering uncontrollably now. Her head dropped below the surface. She sputtered and blinked against the salty water. Something banged loudly against the top of the cage.

"Foster, put the hook around the bars!"

Her fingers were so stiff it was hard to move, plus she had to stop and push against the top of the cage for air. After a few fumbled attempts, she pulled the hook through and against one of the bars near her head. She sensed it the moment the cable was taut and the cage lurched upward. As she breached the surface gravity worked against the Levi's jacket, soaked with seawater. Foster did her best to hold herself up, but cold, fatigue, and the sheer weight of her waterlogged clothing pinned her to the bottom of the cage.

The winch whined loudly as the cage kept rising, and then Jai grabbed the edges of her small cell and swung it over the solid surface of the pier. The box came to rest with the awful sound of metal scraping concrete. Foster slumped against the bars. She was vaguely aware of a loud clink as Jai used bolt clippers to sever the padlock's hold on the cage door.

"Foster, how long were you in the water?"

Jai struggled to tug her through the cage door. She was hardly any help. Her limbs were numb from the cold, stiff and clumsy. The wet clothing weighed down her already exhausted arms and legs. There was a wood railing along the edge of the pier and Foster slumped against it as soon as she was free from the trap, or whatever it was.

Jai knelt in front of her. She systematically checked Foster over, moving her arms, touching her legs, checking her pupils. Foster knew on some level that she'd survived, but she ached all over. Every single muscle contracted, and she began to shiver uncontrollably.

"Hey, stay with me." Jai grabbed the front of the soaked jacket. "Can you walk? We need to get you into dry clothes."

Foster nodded. With Jai's help she got to her feet and they walked away from the pier and up the hill. Foster stumbled twice, and she'd surely have done a face plant if Jai hadn't caught her.

Abby filled a large bowl with warm soapy water. Dena was kneeling beside Evan with the straight razor. Dena had drawn a rectangular pattern around Evan on the kitchen floor. Dena called the shape a rectangular pentagram. It looked different from the salt design on the floor in her bedroom. This shape had been drawn with chalk rather than salt, and as soon as Dena shaved Evan's head, Abby would place white candles from the pantry in a half circle around Evan's head and light them. This all seemed very bizarre, but in some odd way, it made sense at the same time.

Dena's phone rang and she fished it out of her pocket. "Hello? Hello? This connection is terrible. Text me." Dena clicked off but held the phone until a message popped up on the screen. She showed the screen to Abby.

Foster's okay. We will come to you.

Abby would have appreciated a bit more information, but she'd find out more when they arrived. Knowing Foster was safe would allow her to focus on Evan.

Abby held Evan's head off the floor as Dena cut as much of her hair away with scissors as she could, then she started to work slowly with the straight razor.

"Why are we doing this?" Abby hadn't asked and Dena hadn't offered an explanation. Dena barked directions and Abby had simply followed them.

"Usually for a spell like this someone uses the easiest source for the subject's DNA. And that's most commonly hair from a comb or brush." Dena lathered more soap onto Evan's scalp and slid the blade carefully up and around her ear. "We weaken the connection by removing the hair."

"And what if it wasn't a hair sample they used?"

"Then I hope Jai gets here with my supplies...because Evan is running out of time."

Evan was cool to the touch and her skin didn't look normal; it was ashy, almost gray in color. The hardest area to reach was the back of Evan's head. It took both of them to roll her onto her side so that Dena could gain access. As Dena wiped the remnants of hair and lather away with a towel, Abby could see that there was some intricate design on Evan's scalp, a tattoo under her hair.

"Well, well." Dena rocked back on her heels, a half-smile on her face.

"What is that?" Abby leaned in for a closer look.

"The Helm of Awe." Dena moved the razor and basin aside, clearing the space around the pentagram on the floor. "It was a symbol originally worn by Vikings for invincibility. See these?" Dena pointed toward the outer edge of the design which was made up of a circle, pierced by eight lines. Each line ended with three prongs, like a spear, crossed by three perpendicular shorter lines. "These are Z-runes…for protection and triumph over one's enemies."

"What does all that mean?"

"It means our friend Evan here is a regulation badass…that's what it means." Dena placed the candles in a semicircle. "Come on. Let's bring her back."

Dena lit the candles and held her hands out for Abby to clasp them above where Evan lay on the floor, deathly still.

"I'll start, then you say the words with me."

Abby nodded. A shiver ran up her spine.

"With faith there is strength, with strength there is power, with power there is light." Dena voiced the phrase once more before Abby joined her. Softly at first. "With faith there is strength, with strength there is power, with power there is light. With faith there is strength, with strength there is power, with power there is light… with light there is truth."

Dena squeezed her hand. While Abby repeated the same phrase, Dena added a separate plea.

"I call now upon the wellsprings of Hecate and ask that she lend her might to my spell." Dena nodded, a signal Abby interpreted as *continue*, so she did.

"With faith there is strength, with strength there is power, with power there is light. With light there is truth." And after a few refrains, Dena joined Abby in the chant.

"With faith there is strength, with strength there is power, with power there is light. With light there is truth."

Abby lost count of how many times they'd repeated the chant, when suddenly, the overhead light blew, raining glass down around them, and in the same instant, a gust of wind from nowhere extinguished the half circle of candles.

"Did it work?" Abby had covered Evan with her body to protect her from the broken glass. She plucked a few stray pieces from Evan's shirt.

"Give it a minute." Dena studied Evan's face.

A loud banging sound came from the front entry. It seemed odd that Foster would go to the front door, and if she did, why would she knock so loudly? Wait, that wasn't Foster. Abby got to her feet quickly and then helped Dena up. They'd been kneeling for too long on the stone tile.

As they approached the entry hall, Abby had the most unsettling sensation. Her skin tingled, and the air in the room seemed abnormally still, deadened, lifeless. She came to an abrupt stop when she saw the dark figure from her dream standing in the foyer, the ominous woman who'd said she was coming for Abby had been true to her word.

"Who are you?" Dena stepped protectively in front of Abby.

The woman oozed malicious intention. Abby instinctively took a step back.

"I told you I would come for you, and yet, you seem so surprised to see me. I'm crushed." The woman moved forward, her words dripping with sarcasm.

"Who are you?" Dena asked again.

"I am Leath Dane…what? Evan didn't tell you about me? She didn't tell you I was coming?"

Abby sensed a trap of some kind, and she had no idea how to avoid falling into it. She was drawn to Leath and repulsed by her at the same time. Leath was tall, willowy, elegant, but with an aura of cruelty. Abby was afraid.

"Back away." Dena wasn't giving up any ground. "Leave this house."

"I'm too powerful for some third chair, West Coast witch." Leath sneered.

Dena moved her hands as if she were forming an invisible snowball. Sparks leapt from her fingers. She hurled the electrically charged translucent sphere at Leath, who swung her arm, casting the missile aside as if it were nothing. The charged particles destroyed an armchair and a lamp along the far wall of the large entry hall.

It was as if they'd stepped into some green room where special effects were the norm. She'd never seen anything like what Dena had just done. Leath molded some darkly tinted sphere of her own and hurled it in their direction. Dena deflected it with raised arms and some sort of invisible force field like shield, but the strength of impact caused Dena to stagger backward. Abby caught her to keep her from toppling completely.

"Abby, come with me. Come now and no one else has to be hurt."

Abby's intuition told her that Leath was talking about Evan and Foster. At least she knew Foster was okay and with Jai. Evan's condition was still an unknown.

"Why are you here?" Abby tried to step in front of Dena, but Dena protectively blocked her.

"I'm here to celebrate your birthday." Leath stepped closer.

"That's far enough." Dena held a palm up.

"You have no idea how far I've come or how far I'm willing to go." Leath's expression darkened. Her pupils expanded so that her eyes went completely black.

Leath made a swift, sweeping arc with her left hand, as if she were brushing a veil aside. Maybe she was. Without making physical contact, Dena was thrown across the room. She thumped against the wall and dropped to the floor.

Abby held her ground as Leath came closer. She was close enough now that she could reach out and touch Abby if she wanted.

"I'm not coming with you."

"Is that your final answer?" Leath reached in the air in Dena's direction. When she closed her fingers into a fist, Dena cried out on the floor.

"Stop."

"Stop what?" Leath opened and closed her fingers into a fist again. Across the room, Dena curled into a fetal position.

"Why are you here? What do you really want?"

"I want you. All of you." Leath stroked a strand of Abby's hair between her fingers. She cocked her head and smiled, which made Abby even more unnerved.

"I don't know what that means." Abby considered turning and running, but where could she hide that Leath wouldn't find her?

"It means that in order for me to win, you must lose—your soul, your gift, your inheritance."

"I don't understand." Abby was trying frantically to buy some time for help to arrive.

"Poor Abby, she has no idea of the larger forces at work." Leath crossed her arms and sighed. "Evan knew you were special, different and yet she did nothing to protect you. She didn't protect Jacqueline and she won't protect you, I've seen to that."

One question answered. Leath was responsible for what had happened to Evan. If Abby could just keep Leath talking maybe she'd figure out what the hell was really going on. She didn't dare look in Dena's direction, but she hoped she was giving Dena time to regroup.

"Who is Jacqueline?"

"She was the eldest of our Council. She was to pass her power to me. It was my time to reign. I was second in line. But Evan fucked all of that up." Leath was becoming more agitated as she talked. "But it no longer matters because I'll have you, and your line is potent, ancient. You have no idea of the power you would have wielded if you'd been allowed to ascend."

Movement caught Abby's eye. Dena was on her feet, but Leath hadn't seen her get up.

"We're going to have a different sort of ritual tonight…"

"Get the fuck away from her, Yankee bitch."

Leath spun around.

Dena was defiant as they faced off. She kicked off her Crocs so that she was barefoot on the stone floor. A small electrical storm was building in front of Dena. She shifted quickly and hurled a large churning orb. Leath stopped the orb, holding it aloft with both hands. She divided it in two, and the roiling orbs doubled in size.

Dena assumed a defensive pose, but she was no match for the surge of power that detonated, first one and then the other, before she could recover.

Dena staggered backward as Leath pummeled her with a light show from her outstretched hands. Abby had to shield her eyes. She could no longer see Dena. She started to back slowly away. She needed to escape to get help. It was obvious that they were no match for Leath, and there was no way she'd risk Foster and Jai stumbling into this attack. She'd only made two or three steps when Leath turned and pinned her with a searing look. Her muscles refused to move, her arms pinned to her sides by some invisible binding. Her heart raced and her breath came in gasps. *Stay calm. Stay calm. Think.*

"Stop!" Abby shouted.

Leath dropped her hands and slowly turned. Abby could finally see beyond her to the scarred and blackened wall outside the library. Dena was on the floor, unmoving.

"Quite right. I've spent too much time here already. We should go." Leath was talking to Abby as if there was no doubt that Abby was leaving with her.

When Abby made no move to follow, Leath reached for her arm.

"Come."

"Please don't do this." Abby wasn't even sure what Leath planned to do, but every cell in her body told her she would not survive. Whatever this ritual was, it was her end.

"Don't plead. That is so tiresome."

"I'll give you whatever you want."

"Oh, I know you will." Leath's words were heavy with snarling contempt.

Abby shivered involuntarily.

"You will give me whatever I want before the night ends."

"You're not taking her anywhere." Evan leaned against the wall at the mouth of the hallway to the kitchen.

Abby's heart leapt to see Evan on her feet, but she could tell from across the room that Evan was a shadow of her former self.

Evan braced heavily against the wall as if letting go would mean falling. Evan would never be able to withstand what Leath had just done to Dena. Abby stepped in front of her, between them, to shield Evan.

"Hmm, interesting." Leath smiled thinly. "I thought you liked the writer. Your fondness for Evan is surprising."

Abby looked over her shoulder in Evan's direction. She wanted Evan to stay out of this, to stay safe.

"Abby, you don't need to protect me from this petulant, self-aggrandizing bitch."

Leath stiffened. If Evan was trying to make her angrier, then she was succeeding.

"She got what she deserved from Jacqueline...nothing." Evan practically spit the words.

Leath's hair swirled about her face as a static charge began to build.

"Please, don't—"

Abby's words were cut off by a bolt of electricity thrown at Evan. A black hole marked the spot where Evan had been standing. Somehow, she'd managed to move just in time. Leath and Evan seemed to have some serious history that Evan hadn't shared.

"Stop! I'll go with you."

"No, Abby! You—"

Whatever Evan was about to say was knocked from her as Leath used her powers to shove Evan against the wall. Evan dropped to her knees, gasping for breath. Leath pointed as if she were going to hit Evan again, but Abby stepped in front of her, blocking the strike.

"I said I would go with you." The strength of her own words surprised her.

Across the room, Evan groaned. If she was trying to say some final word to Abby, she was unable to discern what that was. Abby looked back one more time at Evan and then Dena as she allowed Leath to take her arm and steer her toward the door.

CHAPTER TWENTY-FOUR

Tremors shook Foster as she huddled in the large bath towel. She'd stripped out of her waterlogged clothing and was perched on the edge of Jai's bed as Jai searched for something that might fit Foster. Anything that actually fit Jai was not going to fit Foster, but all she needed was temporary cover. Reasonable cover to allow them to refuel the car and get back to Abby's house. *Abby.* The separation was making Foster anxious. Her gut told her to hurry. She was feeling more desperate by the minute.

"Here, I think these will work." Jai held up a zippered hoodie and some old-school sweatpants. "This is probably all I have that will even come close to fitting."

"Do you mind?" Foster gripped the towel with one hand and the sweats with the other. She was in a hurry, but not in the mood to give Jai a show.

"Oh, sorry, of course." Jai turned around to give Foster privacy to change.

Foster's hands still shook, making it hard to dress quickly. She wondered if she'd actually be able to drive.

"What happened, Foster?"

"I don't know."

"What do you mean you don't know?"

"You can turn around." Foster zipped the front of the sweatshirt and pulled the hood up over her damp hair for extra warmth. She wondered if she'd ever feel warm again. "I don't remember what happened."

Jai turned around with her arms across her chest. The look on her face told Foster she had doubts about Foster's selective amnesia.

"Dena told me to come get you...something happened to Evan..." She'd almost forgotten how the whole thing started. *Evan. Evan was sick.*

"Is Evan hurt?" The pitch of Jai's voice went up a little, a look of concern on her face.

"I'm not sure. She collapsed in the kitchen." Foster rubbed her eyes. She was trying to remember. "She said it was a spell and that we should get Dena...so that's what I did. I couldn't reach Dena by phone so I drove to the library...she left and that's when...that's when the woman came up to my car."

"Describe her."

"Tall, pale...too thin. She was wearing all black and she had dark hair...and her eyes...she had weird eyes." As Foster added that detail, she couldn't actually remember what the woman's eyes had looked like. She must have noticed their color, but for the life of her she couldn't visualize any specific details about the woman's facial features. That seemed odd.

"Listen, can we talk as we go. Something's not right. I have this terrible feeling." Foster covered her revolting stomach with her hand. For a minute she thought she might be sick. She focused on breathing, in and out, in and out.

"Yes, my neighbor does small engine repair. He always has a gas can in his truck." Jai grabbed a jacket and her keys. "I'm sure he'd let us have it for your car."

"I'd ask you to drive, but Dena says you don't drive." Foster followed Jai out the apartment door.

"I don't have a car, but I can certainly drive." She pulled the door closed behind them as she tugged on her jacket. "It's a long story."

Jai had been right about her neighbor. He wasn't around so Jai left ten dollars under a wrench where the gas can had been. In another few minutes they were refueled and on their way to the Spencer estate. Foster's hands were shaking so badly she had to press them against her thighs and hold on.

"Are you okay?" Jai glanced at her from the driver's seat.

"No." Might as well be honest. She wasn't okay. She was so far from okay that she'd probably never find it again. Something was wrong with Abby. Something had happened, and her skin was crawling from the not knowing.

When they turned into the driveway it was as if the Spencer house had been transformed into a haunted mansion. Low hanging fog swirled around the estate. Dense clouds blocked the sun over the property, despite the fact that the sun was blazing twelve miles away in Spencer's Cove. Ravens filled the trees along the drive like some eerie recreation of *The Birds*.

"What the hell?" Jai stopped the car before they reached the circular drive in front of the house.

Foster and Jai both leaned forward, craning to see through the windshield.

"Don't pull up to the house." Foster's bad feeling was getting worse.

They got out of the car and approached on foot. The sweat pants Jai had loaned her were several inches too short, a chilly draft seeped up each leg, past her exposed, sockless ankles. Her wingtips, still waterlogged, squeaked with each step. She looked down and considered taking them off, but the gravel underfoot would cut her soggy, cold feet to shreds, so she kept them on.

The front door was open, dark, like the entrance to a cave. Foster wanted to barge in, but Jai caught her arm to signal caution. Jai stepped in front of her and peered inside. The place was utterly silent. Jai crossed the threshold and Foster followed. It took a minute once inside the dimly lit entry hall to take in the scene. A skirmish of some kind had definitely gone down. Furniture was smashed and overturned, lamps and tables tossed about. The walls were marked with dark shapes that looked like detonations.

"There's Evan…but where is Dena?"

"And where is Abby?" Foster started across the room toward where Evan lay on the floor.

She heard a low moan from the other side of the room, coming from beneath a pile of charred furniture. Jai rushed in that direction.

"Dena is over here!" Jai tossed debris aside.

"Hey, easy." Foster knelt beside Evan and helped her sit up and then lean against the wall.

"Foster, she took Abby." Evan coughed and then gripped her side as if the cough had been painful.

"Who? Who took Abby?"

"Leath Dane."

The little hairs along Foster's arms stood at attention. She had to be the same woman who locked Foster in a cage so that she'd slowly drown. She rocked back on her heels so that she could put her head between her bent knees to keep from throwing up.

When she glanced up, Evan was watching her.

"Describe Leath Dane, because I'm pretty sure she's the one who just tried to send me to Davy Jones's locker."

"Tall, thin, long straight dark hair, dressed in black…epic bitch." Evan ran her hand across her scalp. She stopped mid stroke, as if she was surprised by some discovery.

"Yeah, someone shaved your head." Foster couldn't help noticing the tattoo now evident on Evan's scalp.

"Help me up." Evan reached for Foster, and she did her best to hoist Evan to a standing position.

Evan braced against her with an arm across her shoulders as they joined Jai on the other side of the room. Dena was alive, but she looked as if she'd been to hell and back. Both lenses of her glasses were cracked, her flannel shirt was torn and charred, her face was smudged with ash, and her Crocs were missing.

Jai was still kneeling beside Dena. She propped a singed cushion behind her head. Foster and Evan were standing, looking over Jai's shoulder. Dena pulled her glasses off to examine them and then tossed them onto the pile of broken furniture.

"Never really needed those anyway. Just for looks." Dena started to get up but grimaced and dropped back to the floor.

Jai gently probed along her left leg until she reached a spot just above her ankle that made Dena howl in pain. Jai lifted up the cuff of her jeans to examine the injury.

"It looks like it's broken, but the bone isn't through the skin." Jai calmly relayed the information and then looked up at Foster and Evan. "We need to get her to a doctor."

"No…no way." Dena's response was quick and stern. "You need to go after Abby. I'm perfectly capable of waiting here for an ambulance. I'll just—"

"Heaven's above!"

Everyone looked in Cora's direction. She was standing on the far side of the room, holding what looked like a birthday cake piled with flowers sculpted out of pink frosting. Cora took in the scene of disaster, wide-eyed, mouth ajar.

"I'll wait here for the ambulance." Dena started giving orders again. "You should go without me." She was looking at Evan.

"Go where?" Foster hated to state the obvious. She'd like nothing better than to run out the door and chase down this evil wench and get Abby back, but she had no idea where Leath had taken her.

The sensation of moving through space and time was an event like nothing Abby had ever experienced. The act of departure as much from self as place, a *real* event taking place in the realm of the invisible. She'd seen science fiction movies, she'd read even more books in the genre, and the closest description to what she'd just experienced was passing through a wormhole. Only this one was created by Leath, not some collapsing star. Although, Abby would certainly describe Leath's energy as something similar to a black hole, pulling in all light around it, including hers. Abby felt her essence retreat and weaken with every minute spent in close proximity to Leath. By the time the movement, the motion, stopped, she was drained and powerless.

The sound of the pounding surf was the first identifiable sound. The smell of salt and seaweed wafted in the damp air. Wherever they were, it was very close to the ocean. She tried to sit up and struggled to do so. Wet, black rock above and on three sides. Leath had brought her to a sunken chamber at sea level. The space was almost a cave, a concave chamber carved from the rock by millions of years of surf and wind.

She didn't recognize the place.

"Welcome to the party." Leath was near, but Abby couldn't see her.

Abby was sitting on a flat platform that rose up from the bedrock about three or four feet, like some sort of natural stone altar. Surely when the tide came in the platform would be cut off by water at the base, possibly submerged completely. She shivered and hugged herself. She hadn't taken time to grab a jacket. Between the salt spray and the wind, she was chilled. She brushed damp strands of hair away from her face and studied Leath.

"Why are you doing this?"

"You still don't know, do you?" She recoiled as Leath reached out and brushed her fingertips across Abby's cheek. There was no tenderness in the touch. "Poor Abby…orphaned so young by her parents. Left in the dark about her own destiny…until now."

Abby hated the truth of Leath's words. Why hadn't her parents told her about Mercy, about the ties to witchcraft? Why hadn't she been more curious about her own heredity? She'd had clues that she was different, but she'd tamped them down, buried them to protect others, and ultimately herself. She'd never wanted to be different. She just wanted to be normal. As she got older, she'd begun to see that there was no normal. Normal was a construct, completely subjective. Her act of denial had been an epic miscalculation, a huge mistake. Frantically, she tried to conjure a plan of escape so she could get back to Foster and see for herself that Foster was unhurt.

"Whatever it is you want, I'll give it to you."

"You will give me nothing. What I want has to be taken…at your expense, I'm afraid."

"What did you do to Foster?"

"Was that her name, your little butch bookworm girlfriend?" Leath smirked. "She's cute. I have to agree with you about that."

"Please don't hurt her."

"Let's see…" Leath looked at her arm as if she were checking the time, but she wore no watch. She was mocking Abby. "Given the time and the approach of high tide, I'm afraid it might be too late."

Abby's throat closed around a knot in her throat. She choked off the sob, refusing to cry in front of Leath. She looked away, toward the churning sea. The sky was dark with heavy cloud cover. Abby took a deep breath and closed her eyes. She thought of Foster. The warmth of her skin, the soothing calm of her presence, the touch of her fingers, and somewhere, deep inside, Abby knew that Foster was okay. Her senses confirmed it. She turned back to Leath, not revealing what she knew.

A strange pain began to build in her stomach. It felt like a cramp, but sharper. She bit her lip and pressed her fingers into the spot where the pain seemed worst. Leath cocked her head with a curious expression. Then a second pain, much worse than the first, caused Abby to curl up on her side, bringing her knees to her chest.

"The pain will get worse." Leath leaned over. Her voice barely audible over the rushing surf. "The transmutation has begun. It won't be long now…just a few hours."

Abby looked up. There was no mercy in Leath's eyes, only emptiness.

"Where are we?"

"We are where we will not be disturbed." Leath placed both palms on the stone platform and leaned uncomfortably into Abby's personal space.

Foster felt a pain so sharp in her stomach that she doubled over. She'd thought for a moment she was going to be ill. Then a second pain, more searing than the first, dropped her to her knees. She had to brace one hand on the floor to keep from toppling.

Cora was the first to notice.

"Foster, what's the matter?" Cora put her hand on Foster's shoulder.

"I don't know."

"What's wrong?" Evan bent over so that she could see Foster's face.

"I felt sharp pains in my stomach, like cramps."

"It's started." Evan's strength had been gradually returning over the past twenty minutes. She almost seemed back to her former self, except with a lot less hair. Foster hadn't gotten a chance to ask about that yet.

"What's started?" Foster got to her feet with Cora's help.

"The transmutation." Evan checked her phone. "We only have a few hours. We have to figure out where they are." She turned to Dena. "Any ideas? Did Leath say anything? It wouldn't be unlike her to gloat and drop some hints without realizing it."

"Nothing…she didn't say anything." Dena was propped against a cushion with ice on her leg. "She just came in here and started blowing things up."

"I think Cora and I should take Dena to the urgent care place in Hamden. Her leg is starting to swell." Jai held the ice bag up for a better look.

Evan agreed with Jai, but she needed Dena's help. If Foster could identify a location, then Dena was their best hope for recognizing the description. Dena knew the area better than they did. She was the local know-it-all librarian after all. Evan needed Dena to bring the knowledge. She ignored Jai's comment for the moment.

"Foster, this is all on you." Evan was getting her strength back. She was feeling stronger by the minute.

"What do you mean it's all on me?"

"You'll know where Abby is."

"How?"

"You're her keeper. You'll know. Those cramps mean the connection is strong. You're feeling at least some of what Abby is feeling." Evan faced Foster, with a hand on each shoulder. "Focus. Focus every cell in your body on Abby. Close your eyes. Focus."

Foster scowled at her but did as Evan asked. She knew Foster was worried, that heightened emotion would aid in the search. Foster and Abby had only gotten a few days of time together. Evan wasn't sure how close they'd gotten in that short amount of time. The binding in the graveyard would help, but that probably hadn't completely matured in terms of telepathy or other factors. Evan prayed their connection was strong enough to find Abby.

"She's afraid." Foster opened her eyes.

"Don't focus on that right now. Focus on environmental details."

Foster clenched her jaw and squeezed her eyes shut. She took a deep breath. Several minutes passed. No one spoke. Foster's demeanor shifted. The air around her vibrated with charged particles. The connection was working. Evan stepped away, giving Foster room.

"She is near the ocean, in a cave…no, three walls of dark rock facing the open sea. They are below a cliff. Offshore, I see two rocks jutting up from the surf, like sentinels." Foster paused and tilted her head as if she was trying to figure something out. "Abby is cold. She's lying on a raised stone platform, and the waves are splashing against the rock. She's—" Foster stumbled backward and almost fell. She turned to Evan with a wide-eyed expression.

"What? What just happened?" Evan caught Foster's arm to stabilize her.

"Abby saw me. She pushed me and told me not to come." She swiped at a tear on her cheek with her sleeve. "Evan, she's so afraid. We have to go. I don't care what she said."

"Don't worry. We're going." She squeezed Foster's shoulder. "We're not going to let anything happen to Abby."

"Devil's Basin." Dena spoke from across the room.

Evan spun around. "What did you say?"

"The place Foster just described sounds like Devil's Basin." Dena shifted so that she was sitting up. "It's a partial cave carved out by the ocean. It's north of here along the coast. It's only accessible on foot or on horseback." Dena looked at Cora. "Doesn't this mansion have a library?"

"Yes, yes, of course." Cora nodded.

"Then will someone please go find me a map?"

Cora scurried away.

Evan turned to Foster. "We have time. Leath won't harm her in any way before nine o'clock. We have plenty of time."

The look of worry on Foster's face said she wasn't so sure.

"If I only had my damn spell book." Dena scowled.

"I have one. I mean, I think we found one in the attic." Foster crossed her arms in front of her chest.

"Well, don't just stand there, go get it!" Dena was wounded and unable to move, but she had no qualms about barking orders from her throne of cushions.

Cora returned with a few large, rolled up maps that she handed off to Jai just as Foster trotted up the stairs.

Evan was feeling optimistic. There was no way she could have imagined this menagerie might be able to pull together into a team, but she now realized that among the five of them they might have all the skills they needed, even, in Cora's case, a cook and an ambulance driver.

"How are you feeling?"

Evan didn't realize immediately that Dena was talking to her.

"Better." She revised her answer. "Good."

"I bought you some time by shaving your head, but we should see about getting that spell monkey off your back." Dena held out her hand as Foster returned with the ancient book. "And you...you should put on some real clothes. You look like you're about ready to hop out of a clown car."

Foster looked down at her mismatched sweats, the pants and sleeves two sizes too short. Foster didn't answer; she just nodded and then headed back up the stairs.

"Hey, Foster." Foster stopped midway up the staircase and looked back at Dena. "How did you know this was a spell book?"

"I remembered seeing that same design…" She made a circle with her finger over her head. "You know, Evan's tattoo."

"Hmph, that's some good deducing there, Nerd. It's not like this book is in English."

Foster frowned and then half-smiled and continued up the stairs. Evan swept her palm over her bare head. She'd forgotten what it felt like. She'd kept her head shaved before, before the accident. During the depression that followed she'd just let it grow. Typical of Leath to seek out a weakness and exploit it. Her grief over losing Jacqueline had given Leath the opening.

Dena was intently focused on the book, thumbing through the pages slowly.

"Cora, you and Jai spread that map out while I sort out this weakness spell. I might be infirmed, but I'm still a librarian, and this librarian is about to kick some ass."

Evan couldn't help laughing. Dena was a bossy pain in the rear, but she was seriously starting to like her.

A half hour later, Jai and Evan had carried Dena out to Cora's car.

"I wish I could help more." The expression on Jai's face said that she wanted to go with them.

"You're not ready for this, Jai." Dena spoke to her from inside the car. "Your time will come, but it's not now."

Jai nodded reluctantly and got in the car. Foster bent down to speak to her through the window.

"Listen, Jai, I'm not sure I properly thanked you for saving my life." Foster shoved her hands in her pockets. "I mean, I'm sure this qualifies as one of those bequeath of first born moments, you know, if I had any plans to have kids."

Jai smiled. "A simple thank you is sufficient."

Foster nodded.

Evan and Foster stood for only a few seconds as the car sped out of the long driveway before they headed to the barn. Foster stood by as Evan saddled two of the horses—Brother and Boots. Evan was a little concerned about Foster's riding abilities, but she was counting on Boots to be gentle enough for an inexperienced rider.

She handed the reins for Boots to Foster, who looked a little spooked by the entire notion that they were going to ride horses at breakneck speed up the coastline. It was getting late. They needed to get to Abby before dark.

Cora, ever the caretaker, had packed them each a sandwich while Dena removed the weakness spell Leath had placed on Evan. Fucking Leath. Evan couldn't wait to get a shot at her. She'd never liked Leath, but back East, on Council grounds, she'd had to play nice and defer to Leath's second seat in the circle of elders. Not any longer. As far as Evan was concerned, Leath forfeited any respect or standing the minute she took Abby by force. The gloves were off now.

Evan was in the saddle before she realized Foster was still standing on the ground holding the reins as if she wasn't sure what to do with them.

"What's wrong?" Evan didn't have time for hand holding. Brother sidestepped and snorted, shaking his mane.

"I'm a writer, not a warrior."

"I thought your people were good with guns?" Evan prodded Foster. If she could make her angry, maybe Foster would find some courage.

"Do we have guns?" Foster prodded her back, the question edged with sarcasm.

"No." Guns wouldn't do them any good in this fight.

"Just so we're clear, it's a cultural myth about the South. Some of us prefer books to shotguns, despite the fact that they get handed down like family heirlooms."

"Foster, get on the damn horse." Evan adjusted her seat.

"Give me a minute."

Evan exhaled loudly, then she softened her words. "You can't sit this one out. As much as I hate to admit—and believe me when I say I hate this—I need you."

Foster watched Evan from her tall perch, all full of cockiness and badassery. What did she truly have to offer to this fight? She was more afraid that she'd do something supremely stupid and get Abby killed, like getting trapped in a submerged cage. She looked away, toward the tall, swaying brown grass between the barn and the cliff's edge, then closed her eyes and sighed.

With eyes still closed, she rested her forehead against Boots's cheek and sent him a silent plea for assistance. *Abby needs you, Boots. She needs both of us. And I haven't ridden a horse since church summer camp when I was twelve, and that was just a pony walking inside a round fence.* Boots bounced his head up and down almost as if he'd understood her. *Be gentle with me. And please, please, please, don't let me fall off.* She opened her eyes and gazed into the dark orb of his. She saw herself reflected there and his stoic presence gave her courage. *Okay, we're in this together.*

Foster placed one soggy wingtip in the stirrup and launched herself up. She nodded to let Evan know she was ready.

"Okay, then…let's ride like Abby's life depends on it." Evan zipped her jacket against the sinking temperature.

Evan took the lead, galloping at a fast clip. Foster followed. She leaned forward a little in the saddle trying to come to grips with how high her center of gravity was. Beneath her, Boots was sure-footed and steady. She focused her energy on staying in the saddle. Boots was following Brother, so she gave him his lead.

They were in it now, following the edge of old growth trees that bordered the grassy hills along the cliffs. The lost coast was remote, rugged, and beautiful. According to the map she'd seen over Evan's shoulder, this region of the coast was just south of Klamath tribal lands, a huge swath of mostly undeveloped land populated by some of the largest redwoods Foster had ever seen.

As they rode farther she caught glimpses, shapes of the Klamath Mountains, through the trees. Facts rose to the surface, tidbits from the small amount of research and reading she'd been able to do about the shipwreck of the *Equus* and the geology of the bay and the surrounding terrain. The rocks of the Klamath Mountains originated as island arcs and continental fragments in the Pacific Ocean. Some of that rock was five hundred million years old. Not that she'd always believed in the power of stones or gems, but with that sort of time on your hands there must be some seriously stored up energy. The perfect place to perform a ritual using the rocky cliffs between the mountains and the sea like a divining rod.

Foster filled her fingers with Boots's mane and tried to visualize Abby. When she'd hesitated to climb into the saddle it hadn't been because she was afraid of getting hurt herself, it was more that she was afraid she'd do something to hinder Evan. Her inexperience at this sort of conflict weighed heavy on her shoulders.

As her focus had turned to Abby, she'd fallen behind. When she caught up, Evan had pulled Brother to a stop. She waited for Foster to get closer and then dismounted.

"Let's take a break and eat something." Evan fished in the saddlebag for the food that Cora had packed. "We need our strength, and the horses could use a breather."

Foster tried to dismount but dropped back to the saddle. Her thighs ached. The second time, she was successful. When she stood up, her legs trembled from the fatigue of hanging on. Horseback riding used a different set of muscles than typing on a keyboard, as in, all of them.

"How are you holding up?" Evan held two sandwiches. She handed one to Foster.

Foster was mid-stretch, arching her back. "I'm fine." She accepted the food and found a spot to sit. She leaned against a large conifer while Boots grazed on the understory nearby.

It was getting late, and Foster wondered how close they were to Devil's Basin. That sounded like a name made up by some B-movie scriptwriter, not an actual place. But she'd seen the name on the map with her own eyes. As if responding to her silent question, Evan unfolded the section of the map she'd brought with her. She smoothed it onto the dry ground in front of her and studied it as she chewed.

"How close are we?" Foster strained to see the details on the map.

"If I'm figuring this right, based on how long it took us to get this far, we have probably another hour. That's a guess…maybe a little less, maybe a little more." Evan refolded the map and stowed it inside her jacket.

"What's the plan when we get there?" As far as Foster knew there wasn't a plan. Or if there was, no one had shared it with her.

"The plan is, I take care of Leath. You get Abby off that altar and away from the water." Evan finished the last bite of her sandwich and wiped her fingers on her jeans.

"Why away from the water? What does water have to do with anything? You know, aside from the fact that if someone locks you in a box you can drown in it." Foster couldn't help the embellishment. Evan hadn't asked what had happened and she hadn't offered it up.

"Water is a conduit. We don't want to give Leath more of an advantage than she already has." Evan stood up and scanned the tree line. "I'm going to go visit Mother Nature."

Evan rattled off details as if Foster should know all the inside lingo of *witchdom*, which she did not. She hated being in the dark, but apparently Evan wasn't quite ready to toss her a flashlight. What did she mean by conduit? She watched Evan disappear into the woods. After a few minutes, she returned.

"Would it kill you to explain things to me?" Foster wasn't stupid. If Evan would share just a little more information, then maybe Foster could be of more help.

"What do you want to know?"

"Explain what you said about the water."

"Water acts as an instrument. It channels and amplifies power."

"Thank you, now was that so hard?"

They were quiet for a moment as Foster finished her food.

Foster watched Evan. She was all business. Checking on the horses and taking a long draw from her canteen. It was getting darker. A thin ribbon of light gray stretched across the horizon beneath the clouds, the last remnant of the longest day ever. It was almost impossible to believe that it was only the previous night she'd been with Abby. Really been with her in a capital "I" intimacy sort of way. The thought of Abby's body entwined with hers caused her stomach to nose dive. She closed her eyes and swallowed. *Abby, we're coming.*

"You should take a minute to relieve yourself before we start again." Evan held Brother's reins in one hand and shoved her other hand into her jacket pocket. The evening air was cool and breezy.

"Yes, Mother." Foster wasn't in the mood to be bossed around.

"Suit yourself." Evan put her boot in the stirrup and effortlessly swung her leg over the saddle.

Jocks. They were so annoyingly good at everything. Except communication.

"Before we go charging into whatever this is, can you tell me something about Leath?" Any intel would surely be helpful, especially if they somehow became separated. Foster knew what Leath looked like and that one should never ask her for a ride, but that was about all.

"Leath Dane is a psychopath with paranormal powers." Evan's tone was icy. There was definitely some history here that Evan wasn't sharing. "She has no regard for the rights of others, especially anyone without powers. She's gifted at figuring out weak spots and exploiting them. She's callous, unemotional, and completely lacks either conscience or empathy."

"Jesus." The thought of sweet, gentle Abby in the custody of Leath made Foster ill. She took a deep breath and focused on getting her stomach to settle.

"Yeah, if you know him you should send up a prayer for sure." Evan tugged at Brother's reins, pointing him north. "He and I haven't spoken in a while, so I'm not sure he'd pick up if I called."

Brother was already trotting away by the time Foster climbed into the saddle. Once again, she fell in behind. *Hold on, Abby. We're coming.*

CHAPTER TWENTY-FIVE

A bby drifted in and out of consciousness. The pain had mostly subsided, but chills wracked her body, and her head throbbed. The headache was coming and there was no way to stop it, and no way to escape the noise inside her head. Leath hadn't touched her, but Abby sensed Leath's presence as if she had.

Darkness was coming too.

The dense cloud cover and intermittent fog hid any glimpse of sunset, but the waning light told Abby it was near. The low hum of voices inside her head competed with the rhythmic crashing of the waves against the rock. The tide was rising, and with each successive wave, Abby was closer to the ocean's surface, its slippery grasp trying to claim her. But she couldn't think of that now. The headache was pulling her down into another place. She was losing the world, or rather her connection to it, and she was afraid if she lost the world she'd lose herself. Without Foster to call her back, to anchor her, she was scared.

This space, this void, seemed different from before. She heard the murmur of a multitude of voices, but she saw no moving shapes. She was alone. There was no up, there was no down, there was no horizon.

Was this death? Was there no white light to guide her home to the heavens? This was not how she expected the end. She closed her eyes against the nothingness. The loneliness of this place was painful. Her breathing slowed, as did her heart. If she simply stopped breathing that would be the ending of everything distressing, so easy, so painless just to let go. No more days of watching the world decline, no more hours spent avoiding how hurtful humanity could be to its own kind, no more abuse of the creatures that roamed the earth, no more.

"Abby."

She heard someone speak her name softly. A woman she didn't recognize.

"Abby, hold on, they are coming."

"Who?" she asked without opening her eyes for fear the presence would leave her.

"Foster and Evan."

"Who are you?"

"I am Jacqueline Hughes." Her voice was so soothing, so comforting. "You can open your eyes, Abby. I will not leave you."

Abby opened her eyes. Jacqueline stood before her. She was beautiful, luminous. Jacqueline was taller than Abby, slender, with willowy limbs, and long wavy silver hair. It was hard to guess her age, but the lines around her eyes suggested an advanced number of years. Her blue eyes studied Abby in a way that made Abby feel truly seen, known.

"Why are you here?" No longer alone, Abby began to feel the smallest glimmer of hope.

"That's it. Hope is returning. Hope is the first step toward strength."

Had Abby lost hope? That something indiscernible could vanish and cause the collapse of everything was an idea she hadn't considered until now.

"Why are you here?" Abby asked the question again.

"I am here for you." Jacqueline reached out and took Abby's hand. "My earthly body had departed. I refused to bequeath my power to Leath. I had chosen you as my vessel."

"What? But how…?"

"Yours is an ancient line. Mercy was not the first, but to assure that the right person would receive her legacy, her gift, the line has remained dormant...until now." Jacqueline smiled, a genuine, sweet smile that warmed Abby's heart. "You are the one who can merge the ancient lines into one powerful force for good. You know this, but I think it's been hard for you to see this in yourself."

"But Leath...the ritual that Evan said killed you...she thinks it was all her fault."

"Dear Evan could not know of my plan to block Leath's ascension. Evan would have been honor bound to intercede."

"She loves you. She would have chosen you over anything else."

"I know." Jacqueline's eyes softened with gathered tears. "I could not let her act against her oath. She'd have been exiled, or worse. This was my choice and my decision to defy the Council for their own good."

"And for the greater good of the world." Abby was starting to understand.

"Yes. Leath's vicious tendencies would only have expanded if she'd inherited my power. She would have spread her own chaotic, violent world view."

"But I'm not part of the Council." Abby wasn't sure how an outsider could change things.

"Even better. The Council's ways no longer serve humanity. The Council has become elitist, insular, detached, and it was never supposed to be that way." Jacqueline released her hand and clasped her hands in front of her as she continued to talk. "When our sisters first arrived on this continent we had such high ideals. A new world, a new beginning. But some wanted more, and sects began to form and sisters turned against sisters. Those first nights of flight through the virgin forest became a hideous spectacle of accusations and death as jealousy outed some of the more gifted among our ranks."

"The witch trials."

"Yes. And Mercy Howe, part of your direct line, was one of the most gifted of all. Losing her was a blow we struggled to recover from for centuries." Jacqueline paced slowly back and forth, her demeanor dulled, as if she were remembering difficult things.

"Mercy's powers were lost to us because of the way she died. There was no chance to perform the necessary ritual before she was taken. Only much later did her powers return from the ether to her direct descendant, the much younger Mercy." She turned to look at Abby and smiled. "The girl from your vision."

Another figure began to materialize at the edge of nothing. Shadowy, undulating at first, then clearer as the woman drew closer. Abby recognized her right away.

"Mercy?" Abby could see the likeness of the young girl, despite her age.

"Hello, Abby. It's so good to finally meet you." She smiled and when she did, her eyes sparkled. She could have been an elder aunt, or her father's sister, their familial resemblance was obvious. Mercy looked like a more mature version of Abby, as if she was getting a glimpse of herself in her seventies.

"I can't believe you are here." And then Abby remembered the stone altar, and Leath, and the darkness approaching. "But it's too late."

"No, my dear, everything is happening as it should now." Mercy reached for her hand.

"The power of three, the triple braided cord is not so easily broken." Jacqueline reached for her other hand. Then she also took Mercy's hand.

Abby was not alone. Abby was no longer afraid.

CHAPTER TWENTY-SIX

Evan dismounted and tied Brother to a small sapling nearby. They were above the spot Dena had marked on the map, but even if she didn't have the map she'd have known this was the spot. Churning purplish gray-green clouds swirled overhead like some otherworldly tornado was about to drop down from the sky. The wind gusted and the ocean itself seemed angry. She approached the edge of the drop-off looking for a way down.

"How did they get down there?" Foster was beside her peering over the ledge.

"They flew. Witches fly."

"Okay, how are we getting down there? Did you forget to mention that you can fly too?"

"We'll repel." Evan reached for a length of rope attached to the saddle.

"Repel?"

"I think that's our only option." Evan started to tie a series of slipknots at the end of the rope.

"Did I mention I've never rock climbed?" Foster frowned.

"Hey, Foster, I know I've been hard on you."

Foster regarded her with surprise.

"I think you're okay. And I think Abby is lucky to have you on her side."

"Um...thanks." For the first time since they'd met, Foster seemed at a loss for words. "Just promise me we're going to get her home safely, okay?"

"I promise." She put her hand on Foster's shoulder.

Evan had decided to ease up on Foster. It wasn't like she asked to be part of any of this. She'd showed up in California expecting to write a memoir and now here she was about to go over a cliff, literally.

"You go first so I can monitor your descent."

She helped Foster adjust the rope around the top of her thighs, just under her butt, like a makeshift seat. Foster tentatively dropped over the edge. The other end of the rope was anchored to a tree. Evan let the rope slide slowly between her hands, keeping a bit of tension in the lead. She was thankful she'd remembered her leather work gloves.

Once Foster was on the ground Evan tugged the rope back up and fastened it around her thighs as she'd helped Foster do. As she stepped over the edge, Evan couldn't help thinking of Jacqueline. She hoped she could keep her promise to Foster. She'd do everything within her power to save Abby, even if that meant sacrificing herself.

They'd dropped to a slim strip of coarse wet sand. The incoming tide lapped at their feet. High tide was going to hit right around nine o'clock. Everything was converging, which meant they were almost out of time.

"Foster, you wait until I make contact with Leath. Once she's fully engaged and distracted, you get Abby to safety. Don't wait for me."

"That sounds ominous." Foster cleaned her glasses on a bit of shirttail exposed at the bottom of her sweater.

"Things are going to get ugly. Don't expect to understand everything that's about to happen and don't take time to try to figure it out." Evan needed Foster to understand. "You have one task—get Abby and leave."

Foster nodded.

"Listen, before we do this, I need to know your real name."

"What?" Evan looked at Foster. Was she serious?

"We're about to go to war here. I want to know your real name."

"What makes you think it isn't Evan?"

"Just a hunch."

Evan exhaled and frowned.

"My real name is Evangeline Bell."

Foster's eyes widened.

"And if we live through this, you're taking that to your grave. You hear me?" Evan jabbed a finger in Foster's direction. "Okay, spill. What's your real name?"

"Foster."

"Figures." Evan shook her head. "Okay, Foster for real, are you ready?"

Foster nodded, her expression suddenly serious and focused.

Evan took the lead as they worked their way down the beach toward the enormous dark shape of the Devil's Basin. It was aptly named. Evan crouched behind a large rock, its rough surface wet from the surf. She could see Leath's pale face, contrasted against the dark yaw of the basin, which looked like the gaping opening of some sinister cave. Evan was sure Leath was expecting them. Leath had to know that unless Evan was dead and in the ground, she'd show up.

"Foster, ease your way down to those rocks. Stay low. And remember, stay out of sight, wait for me to engage."

Foster nodded and then scuttled ahead, staying close to the cliff.

Evan waited until Foster was in position and then she was up and striding in Leath's direction with clenched fists, laser focused on her target. Abby was lying nearby. She seemed out of it. She didn't move or acknowledge that she saw them. She seemed deathly still. They were definitely running out of time.

"I thought you'd never arrive." A slow smile spread across Leath's face. "Hello, lover."

"Fuck you."

"I offered, but you declined. Are you regretting that now?"

Evan ignored the question.

"Leath, I'm not letting you take Abby's power." Evan squared her shoulders and braced for Leath's response.

"This fight will only make my victory sweeter."

Leath hurled a supercharged orb at Evan. She darted just at the last instant. When the second throw came, she braced her forearms together, matching the two sides of the tattoo into one image of the trinity. The action created a force field. The energy pulse discharged with a lightshow. Sparks bounced off the damp stone cliff above her head.

A wave crashed at Evan's feet causing her to lose her footing on the slick rock. The field created by the joined tattoo faltered, giving Leath's third strike an opening. At the last second, Evan braced her arms together and blocked the pulse. Sparks cascaded across the surface of the water as the surf ebbed.

She was in it now, blocking Leath's attack while slowly advancing on her position. Evan's mission was not defeating Leath, because she knew she couldn't. Her sole focus was giving Foster time to save Abby. Evan simply needed to abort the ritual to keep Abby alive. What came after? Evan had no idea.

CHAPTER TWENTY-SEVEN

Foster was in water up to her waist. There'd been no route by which to reach Abby undetected without getting in the tumultuous surf. She wasn't anxious to be in the ocean again, but there was no other way.

She'd been intently watching Abby as she edged closer, but Abby hadn't stirred. Foster's stomach was churning. She was terrified that they were too late. As she got closer she could see that Abby's hands were tied, and a rope stretched across the bottom and top of the naturally formed stone altar kept her arms and legs stretched out.

Explosions distracted her for a moment. Evan was engaged with Leath. Foster paused for a second to watch. She'd never seen anything like this surreal light show, except in the movies. She pushed off a submerged rock and swam toward Abby. The base of the altar was bedrock but was underwater. It took her a few missteps to find her footing. Foster tentatively stretched upward and touched Abby's hand. Her skin was cool, too cool. How long had she been tied like this, exposed to the elements?

She waited until Leath's back was turned, and she was fully distracted with Evan to hoist herself up onto the edge of the stone platform. She was able to get one knee over the edge, then she was all the way up. Foster carefully climbed over Abby and crouched low beside her so that she could work to free her from the ropes. Why hadn't she thought to bring a knife? Her chilled fingers struggled to loosen the knots.

Abby was unconscious. Foster touched her face, but Abby still didn't move. She put her cheek close. Good, she was still breathing, barely. Everything about Abby seemed in hibernation, her breathing, her pulse, even the color of her skin. Abby's clothing was soaked from the splashing surf. Foster dropped back into the water and gently eased Abby over the edge and into her arms.

Now what? She couldn't swim back the way they'd come. Foster hesitated for a moment. The only way to escape notice was to swim out into deeper water and then around the cliff's edge out of sight. On the back side of this huge rock formation they'd have cover. She could get Abby to shore and work on reviving her.

Foster swam with one arm, kicking as hard as she could against the incoming waves. Water splashed against her glasses making it hard to see. The sun was gone and the sky was becoming as murky as the sea. She tried to keep Abby's face above water, but it was almost impossible as they fought the surf. Out of nowhere, a huge wave rolled in. It crashed down with thunderous force. The undertow caught Foster, dragging her downward. She couldn't swim out of it with only one arm. Fatigued, she cradled Abby tightly against her body as they were sucked out to sea.

"The time has come, Abby." Jacqueline still held Abby's hand.

"Yes, it is time," Mercy said.

"Time for what?" Abby was still unsure.

"We are bequeathing our collective power to you, my dear." Jacqueline smiled warmly.

"Why me?"

"Because you have a pure soul. Only a pure soul can wield such power." Jacqueline paused. "The soul is the real vessel of a person's life; the soul surrounds and suffuses the body. The purest soul is never afraid."

Were they underwater now? It seemed as if they were. Abby's hair swirled about her face as if she were submerged.

"What will it feel like?"

"Sacrifice." Mercy squeezed her hand. "You are sacrificing what you are for what you can become."

"Where does the power come from?" Abby worried that this would be her only chance to ask.

"From the creator and ruler of the universe, the source of all moral authority, the supreme being. HaShem, the giver of life." Jacqueline looked at Abby, and Abby was warmed by the love in Jacqueline's expression. "Are you ready?"

Abby nodded.

Jacqueline and Mercy began to chant, eyes closed, as they held her hands.

"I am sought of them that asked not for me; I am found of them that sought me not. A nation that was not given a name."

The space around them began to glow with an ever-brightening white light, and Abby had the sensation of rising.

"I am sought of them that asked not for me; I am found of them that sought me not. A nation that was not given a name.

"I am sought of them that asked not for me; I am found of them that sought me not. A nation that was not given a name."

Now she was no longer sure if they were speaking or if she was only hearing the words inside her head. Something real was taking place in the realm of the invisible.

The light was too bright now, and Abby had to close her eyes to block it out.

With the light came the knowing.

Time was a circle, completed by this one embrace.

The power of three.

The act of abandon was becoming a ritual of presence.

Abby knew herself.

CHAPTER TWENTY-EIGHT

Evan saw the glowing orb first. She stumbled backward, bracing herself against the rock. Leath still hadn't noticed what was happening behind her, and Evan wanted to keep it that way. She needed to buy Abby just a little more time.

Exhaustion threatened to capsize her, but she rallied, bracing herself, planting her feet farther apart in a defensive pose. Abby must be alive. The water was amplifying the energy field of the transmutation. That had to be the only explanation.

"It's not too late to change your mind, Evan." Leath was breathing hard.

Surely expending this much energy was draining her reserve. But still, she was stronger than Evan remembered.

"Change my mind about what?" Evan was willing to keep her talking for a minute to give Abby more time. Plus, she was feeling winded herself.

"Come back with me. We would be good together." Leath's eyes flashed green momentarily.

"Are you seriously trying to use seduction flairs on me after you just tried to blast me into oblivion?" Evan would have laughed if the situation wasn't so dire.

"Lovers' quarrel?" Leath shrugged.

"Fuck you, Leath."

"You missed your chance for that." Leath advanced. "And now I'll rob you of any future you had with the coven. You're unfit to be a guardian of the Council, unfit and unworthy."

That stung, but Evan used her anger to regroup, recharge.

"I don't want any part of a Council you hold sway over."

"Jacqueline was weak, emotional…your incompetence at the ceremony was a symptom of her sentimentality and an act of defiance."

"It was an accident." Evan spoke softly, almost to herself.

It was at that moment that Leath finally noticed Abby's absence from where she'd been tethered to the stone. She'd turned to dismiss Evan, no doubt to return to her task, only to discover her sacrificial lamb was missing.

"That's right," Evan shouted. "She's gone. It's over, Leath. You've lost."

That did it. The fuse was lit.

Leath's eyes glowed red and her entire countenance went dark. Time to pull out the big guns. Evan braced her forearms together, and this time, dipped her head so that the Helm of Awe faced Leath. She threaded her fingers over the symbol, forearms together. When Leath hammered the charge at Evan, the blast was amplified. A deafening boom echoed off the cave walls, and the shock wave threw both of them to the ground.

Foster couldn't fight the undercurrent any longer. Her limbs were heavy, sluggish; the cold water was seeping into her bones. The light from the surface dimmed as they sank. She'd failed. Foster held Abby close.

I'm so sorry, Abby. I never got the chance to say…I love you.

This was it. Death was coming, quietly, insistently. She'd always read that drowning was the most painless way to die. Was that really true? Was any death painless? The loss of the future, any future, the end of everything you might have been or imagined you could be. Forever nothing.

Then something began to happen.

The amulet around Abby's neck began to glow, dimly at first, and then brightly. Abby opened her eyes and smiled at Foster. The darkness of their underwater tomb had been pushed back and away. Foster inhaled sharply. She could breathe; there was air. She took a few deep breaths. And they were floating, but on what, in what?

"How—"

"I love you too, Foster."

Color was returning to Abby's cheeks. She seemed so…happy. Abby practically glowed. No, wait, she was glowing.

"Thank you for saving me." Abby kissed her lightly, sweetly.

"Abby, I'm never letting you go."

"Then let's finish this, shall we?"

Foster didn't know what Abby meant by *finish this*, but she nodded anyway. At this point, she'd follow Abby to the absolute end of the earth. Whatever it took for them to be together, she was ready to give it all she had.

Abby placed her hands at Foster's waist and looked upward. They were ascending together toward the surface. When they broke through, the light stayed with them. They floated just above the white caps, gliding toward the raised stone altar.

Abby gently set Foster down and turned toward Leath, who spun to face her. Off to the side of where Leath stood, ankle deep in seawater, Evan braced for another attack. Abby was unsure how much time had passed or exactly what had transpired while she was with Jacqueline and Mercy. In a way, they were still with her. She could sense their shared experiences like memories that were her own.

"You should leave now." Abby was oddly no longer angry or afraid of Leath. All she felt was pity.

"I'm not leaving until I get what I came for."

"Leath Dane, I cast you out." Abby rose a few inches above the stone and glided across the space between them. She stopped several feet from Leath, hovering just above the water's surface. She could feel Leath's fear as if it were her own. "Your desolate soul is deadened with anger and hate. Let the dead dwell with the dead, let them dwell with you in the dust of your exile. I shut the door to thee. The sisterhood will weep, but you are lost to us."

Leath's expression changed, from fear to rage and then back to fear. She looked down at her hands, turning them over as if they were foreign to her, as if she could no longer feel them.

"Power corrupts the corruptible," Abby continued. "No life is without its broken, empty spaces, but you have chosen to fill those spaces with hatred and greed for power that was never destined to be yours." Abby paused for a moment. She raised her arms, palms up, in Leath's direction. "Leath Dane, I cast you out. This is good-bye."

A surge of power flowed from her fingers. Acting as a conduit for such voltage made the muscles of her arms and legs twitch and tingle. She felt lightheaded and had to blink and breathe deeply through the intoxicating waves that pulsed through her arms. She and Leath were enveloped now in light, blinding, explosive light. For a moment, an instant, time stopped. Recognition dawned on Leath's face, and Abby sensed her acceptance. Leath looked at Abby as if she were seeing her for the first time, as if she were witnessing the birth of new life, the birth of a star, some celestial being.

The luminosity spiked for a split second and then was gone.

Abby remained in the darkness of the cave facing no one. The light had taken Leath with it to a place where the wounded stood outside time and space. Abby knew this because Jacqueline knew it, and Jacqueline knew it because others before her had known it, and so on and so on into infinity.

"Thank you." Abby spoke to Evan for the first time. Evan looked as if she were in shock.

She turned back to Foster, who hugged herself, as she sat in a shivering heap in the center of the stone altar.

"Let's get you somewhere warm."

The surf swirled beneath her feet, and from it she sensed its collective life force, and the movement of the earth, and its place around the sun, and the wind. She closed her eyes and faced it—the winds of change.

CHAPTER TWENTY-NINE

Foster's body began to warm the moment she took Abby's hand. She was on one side and Evan was on the other. Abby closed her eyes, and they rose from the edge of the surf to the top of the cliff where they'd left the horses. Foster's arm tingled, like when your foot goes to sleep, but she held on tightly.

When they crested the cliff, she could see that Boots and Brother were not alone. Callie, Sasha, and Journey had come. All five horses formed a semicircle facing the cliff, as if they were sentinels, standing guard. Abby gently lowered Foster and Evan to the ground and walked toward the horses. They closed around her, nuzzling her and making small sounds. If they'd been cats, Foster would have sworn they were purring. She watched the touching scene as Abby whispered and caressed each of them.

It was very late, the wee hours of the morning, when they returned to the estate. She figured Abby could have flown them back, but they rode the horses instead, and even that seemed to take half the time as before. Her clothes were dry by the time they'd risen from the water, no doubt thanks to Abby's touch. Otherwise she'd have been freezing on the ride back. Even still, she was exhausted and emotionally raw.

Cora came rushing downstairs when she heard them, fussing over Evan's cuts and bruises like a mother hen. Everyone assured Cora that what they each needed most was rest. Once Evan was settled into the spare room, everyone retreated to their own spaces.

Foster mutely followed Abby to her room. She hadn't been invited to do so, but after what she'd just experienced, there was no way she was letting Abby out of her sight.

She closed the door behind her, and when she did, Abby turned and smiled as if she'd forgotten Foster was with her and was pleasantly surprised by the discovery. Abby stepped close and cradled Foster's face. Abby kissed Foster tenderly, her lips were warm and soft.

"How do you feel?" Foster couldn't put her finger on it exactly, but Abby seemed different. She had to be, right? Abby was different now, but what did that mean?

"Alive." Abby smiled broadly and her eyes sparkled.

"What were you before?"

"Asleep." Abby kissed her again, this time more deeply.

Abby tugged at the buttons of Foster's shirt and then pushed it off her shoulders. They undressed each other as they moved to the bed. Five minutes ago, she'd been too tired to stand but Abby's touch was bringing her back to life. She wanted Abby in the worst way.

They tumbled into bed, and Abby pulled the comforter up. Foster slipped her leg between Abby's and pulled her close. She needed to feel the warmth of Abby's body, firm, real, unharmed. *I was so scared. I thought I'd lost you.* She pressed her lips to Abby's forehead.

"You could never lose me," Abby whispered.

Foster hovered above Abby, studying her face. She wanted to make love to Abby, but fatigue was seeping into every muscle.

"Rest and let me hold you." Abby settled Foster's head on her shoulder. "We have all the time in the world now."

CHAPTER THIRTY

Foster poured herself a second cup of coffee. She could write about everything she'd seen, heard, and witnessed. Anyone who read it would assume it was pure fiction. Only the entire crazy tale would be true. She'd lived it and she almost didn't believe it herself. She'd been weak and utterly exhausted when Abby had taken her to bed the previous night. They'd slept curled against each other in the sweetest embrace. This morning she felt renewed.

Evan reached around her for a mug and poured herself a cup also. Foster stepped aside. She leaned against the counter's edge and took a few sips.

"I'm thinking of writing a new story."

"You don't say." Evan gave Foster a sideways glance as she stirred her coffee.

There were bruises on Evan's arms and a nasty cut on her cheek held together with several butterfly bandages. Foster was still getting used to Evan's shaved head. With the tattoo on her scalp, she did a good imitation of a Viking warrior. As if suddenly self-conscious about it, Evan tugged her well-worn baseball cap from her back pocket and pulled it on.

"Yeah, it's about a jock groundskeeper who starts out being an asshole and ends up being a hero." Foster sipped her coffee loudly for effect. "I think it's gonna be a best seller."

Evan turned toward Foster, smiling broadly.

"I'm pretty sure I'm not the hero of this story."

Evan winked at Foster just as Abby entered the kitchen.

"What are you two conspiring about?" Abby leaned into Foster and kissed her on the cheek.

"Hero worship." Foster pressed her lips to Abby's.

"Hmm, I'm on board with that." Abby nuzzled Foster's neck.

"And that's my cue to drive into town and check on Jai and Dena." Evan downed her coffee and made tracks for the door.

"Tell them we said hello," Abby called after Evan. "And tell them to come to the house for dinner tonight. Cora's cooking her famous lasagna."

Evan acknowledged the invite with a wave and she grabbed her jacket. The door closed and Abby returned her attention to Foster. Everything was different now. There was a lightness around Abby, and it was infectious.

"Hey, give me a minute." Abby kissed her lightly. "There's something I need to tell Evan."

Foster watched Abby leave with curiosity. What did she need to tell Evan that she couldn't say in front of Foster? She rotated toward the window and watched Abby cross the lawn toward Evan's truck while she sipped her coffee.

Abby saw Evan shifting some things in the back of her truck. The marine layer was thick this morning. She pulled the front of her shawl-neck cardigan together and hugged herself.

"Did you need something?" Evan looked up and stopped what she was doing.

"There was something I didn't get to tell you last night."

Evan walked around the truck within a few feet of Abby.

"Last night, before everything happened, Jacqueline was there."

"What do you mean?" Evan looked as if she'd just seen a ghost.

"Truthfully, I don't know exactly how to explain it, but Jacqueline was there and so was Mercy. They gave me their power. That's how I was able to so easily defeat Leath."

Evan looked stunned. And then she looked away, as if she were trying not to cry. Abby stepped closer and placed her hand on Evan's arm.

"Hey, it wasn't your fault."

"What?" Evan's voice was full of emotion.

"Jacqueline staged the collapse. She made it happen to keep Leath from receiving her power. Jacqueline planned and executed the collapse without telling you."

"She...why?"

"She knew you were honor bound, bound by oath to the Council, and she didn't want you to be put in a position to break that oath because of her. I also think she wanted to keep you safe." She caressed Evan's arm. "She loves you, Evan."

Evan couldn't stop the tears now. She covered her face and sobbed silently.

"Let it go." Abby wrapped her arms around Evan. Holding her.

"Is everything okay out here?" Foster was standing a few feet away, hands in her pockets.

"Yes, everything is okay." Abby smiled as she turned in Foster's direction. She still held Evan in a partial embrace.

Evan swiped at tears with her hand. Then she smiled too. She extended an arm in Foster's direction.

"Bring it in, Nerd." Evan motioned for Foster to come closer.

"What...we have to group hug now?" Foster joked as she stepped closer.

"Yeah, we're gonna group hug and you're gonna like it." Evan drew Foster close.

With one arm around Abby and one around Foster, they all held each other. Two were stronger than one, three were stronger than two.

Abby couldn't stop smiling. She snuggled against her guardian and her lover, her keeper, the keeper of her soul.

EPILOGUE

It was late when they finally got to the house. Weather delays in Atlanta had stalled their departure from San Francisco. Foster unlocked the door and ushered Abby past the laundry area and into the living room. Her house seemed quaint and small compared to the Spencer estate. She wondered what Abby would think of her life in Atlanta. She wondered if Abby had imagined a writer's life to be more glamorous than a sagging hand-me-down sofa and a twenty-pound cat.

William Faulkner screamed at her the minute she crossed the threshold. She was convinced if he could figure out the electric can opener he'd lock her out of the house for good. But as things stood, with no opposable thumbs, he still needed her.

"Don't mind William Faulkner. That's his 'I'm hungry' scream, even though I'm sure Gloria was just here last night. If he goes six hours without hearing the whine of the can opener he loses his feline mind." Foster dropped her shoulder bag at the end of the sofa in search of cat food.

"Don't feel bad if he ignores you," Foster yelled from the kitchen. After a minute, she headed back toward the living room. "He hates everyone, including me."

Foster stopped dead in her tracks, the open can of tuna and whitefish dinner in her hand. Abby had taken a seat in the leather armchair by the fireplace, and William Faulkner was curled up in her lap, rubbing his orange striped head under her chin as if she was cat nip incarnate, purring like a buzz saw.

Abby looked up at her and smiled. Abby did have a special way about her, and Foster didn't blame William Faulkner one bit. In fact, he was right where she wanted to be.

She fed William Faulkner, gave Abby a tour of the place, which took all of five minutes, then got fresh towels for Abby. Foster took a few minutes to spruce up the linens on the bed while Abby took a quick shower. By the time Foster showered, Abby was snuggled under the covers waiting for her.

Foster felt a little jolt from her heart to her stomach at the sight of Abby in her bed. She'd pulled on a clean T-shirt and boxers. With only ambient light seeping in from the bathroom, it wasn't until she was under the covers that she realized Abby wasn't wearing anything to bed.

Foster smiled and sat up to shrug out of her T-shirt, knocking her glasses askew in the process. She set them on the nightstand and tossed her T-shirt onto a chair across the room. She sank back to the pillow and Abby nestled into the hollow space of her shoulder. They entwined their fingers on top of the covers. Damn, this felt good.

"Can I ask you something?" Foster kissed the back of Abby's fingers.

Foster was still trying to figure everything out, and she wasn't sure why she hadn't asked before. In truth, the week since *the event*, as they'd begun to call it, had been a blur of activity. Abby's transmutation set many things in motion. The recognition of her ascension as elder supreme, which meant she held sway over all the covens on this continent, would be ratified by joint councils when they flew to Boston in a few days. Dena would be there along with Evan and Jai.

Abby would be required to travel more, so she'd made arrangements with Iain for the horses' care, and Cora would manage the household while she was away. Gertie had taken the news in stride, snapping into action to assure Abby's assets were separate and protected, whatever that meant. It seemed setting up an ironclad trust was Gertie's superpower. Hell, even Foster's mortgage had been paid off. She owned the house now free and clear, Abby had insisted.

"What do you want to ask me?" Abby asked sweetly.

The thought of falling to sleep and Abby being the last thing she heard made her smile.

"Why are you smiling?"

"No reason." But she couldn't stop. She kissed Abby's hair.

"So, what was your question?"

"It's about dark matter. I mean, I get that certain people have a gift for controlling it…that it's a thing that no one can see…that it holds everything together and keeps the universe from spinning apart…but what is it, exactly?"

"Don't you know?"

"No, not really."

"It's magic."

"Dark matter is magic." Foster repeated the words thoughtfully.

"Like this…like us… Magic." Abby squeezed Foster's hand.

Abby shifted beside her, leaning on her elbow. She placed her palm in the center of Foster's chest. Warmth spread through Foster's entire body from Abby's touch. She closed her eyes and swallowed.

"Think of all the things that are unseen but still have power." Foster's eyes were still closed. Abby whispered close to her ear. "Love, faith, forgiveness, kindness…all these things are magic, life-altering. Miracles to be witnessed and shared."

"Abby Spencer, you are all the magic I need." Foster rolled Abby onto her back and kissed her.

"Foster?"

"Yes?" Foster had moved from Abby's lips to nuzzling her neck.

"That night, under the water, I heard what you said." Abby sounded a little timid, self-conscious perhaps.

Foster raised up to look at Abby, reminded of the shy woman she'd met that first night in the kitchen, haloed by the light of the open refrigerator.

"Did you mean it?" Abby gazed up at Foster.

"Yes, I meant it." Foster brushed the back of her fingers gently across Abby's cheek. "I love you, Abby. Mind, body, and soul."

She kissed Abby, deeply, tenderly, with longing in her heart.

"I love you, Foster. Thank you for saving me."

"I'm not sure who exactly saved whom…I'm just happy to be here with you. You are the only place I want to be." Foster rolled onto her side and drew Abby close.

"Tell me a story."

Foster laughed at Abby's innocent request.

"Okay, I've got a good one… Once upon a time, there was a mystery writer who traveled to California in search of a beautiful witch."

"Did they live happily ever after?"

Foster smiled.

"Even better, they lived happily in love, forever."

The End

About the Author

Missouri Vaun spent a large part of her childhood in southern Mississippi, before attending high school in North Carolina and college in Tennessee. Strong connections to her roots in the rural south have been a grounding force throughout her life. Vaun spent twelve years finding her voice working as a journalist in places as disparate as Chicago, Atlanta, and Jackson, Miss., all along filing away characters and their stories. Her novels are heartfelt, earthy, and speak of loyalty and our responsibility to others. She and her wife currently live in northern California.

Books Available from Bold Strokes Books

A Chapter on Love by Laney Webber. When Jannika and Lee reunite, their instant connection feels like a gift, but neither is ready for a second chance at love. Will they finally get on the same page when it comes to love? (978-1-63555-366-6)

Drawing Down the Mist by Sheri Lewis Wohl. Everyone thinks Grand Duchess Maria Romanova died in 1918. They were almost right. (978-1-63555-341-3)

Listen by Kris Bryant. Lily Croft is inexplicably drawn to Hope D'Marco but will she have the courage to confront the consequences of her past and present colliding? (978-1-63555-318-5)

Perfect Partners by Maggie Cummings. Elite police dog trainer Sara Wright has no intention of falling in love with a coworker, until Isabel Marquez arrives at Homeland Security's Northeast Regional Training facility and Sara's good intentions start to falter. (978-1-63555-363-5)

Shut Up and Kiss Me by Julie Cannon. What better way to spend two weeks of hell in paradise than in the company of a hot, sexy woman? (978-1-63555-343-7)

Spencer's Cove by Missouri Vaun. When Foster Owen and Abigail Spencer meet they uncover a story of lives adrift, loves lost, and true love found. (978-1-63555-171-6)

Without Pretense by TJ Thomas. After living for decades hiding from the truth, can Ava learn to trust Bianca with her secrets and her heart? (978-1-63555-173-0)

Unexpected Lightning by Cass Sellars. Lightning strikes once more when Sydney and Parker fight a dangerous stranger who threatens the peace they both desperately want. (978-1-163555-276-8)

Emily's Art and Soul by Joy Argento. When Emily meets Andi Marino she thinks she's found a new best friend but Emily doesn't know that Andi is fast falling in love with her. Caught up in exploring her sexuality, will Emily see the only woman she needs is right in front of her? (978-1-63555-355-0)

Escape to Pleasure: Lesbian Travel Erotica edited by Sandy Lowe and Victoria Villasenor. Join these award-winning authors as they explore the sensual side of erotic lesbian travel. (978-1-63555-339-0)

Music City Dreamers by Robyn Nyx. Music can bring lovers together. In Music City, it can tear them apart. (978-1-63555-207-2)

Ordinary is Perfect by D. Jackson Leigh. Atlanta marketing superstar Autumn Swan's life derails when she inherits a country home, a child, and a very interesting neighbor. (978-1-63555-280-5)

Royal Court by Jenny Frame. When royal dresser Holly Weaver's passionate personality begins to melt Royal Marine Captain Quincy's icy heart, will Holly be ready for what she exposes beneath? (978-1-63555-290-4)

Strings Attached by Holly Stratimore. Success. Riches. Music. Passion. It's a life most can only dream of, but stardom comes at a cost. (978-1-63555-347-5)

The Ashford Place by Jean Copeland. When Isabelle Ashford inherits an old house in small-town Connecticut, family secrets, a shocking discovery, and an unexpected romance complicate her plan for a fast profit and a temporary stay. (978-1-63555-316-1)

Treason by Gun Brooke. Zoem Malderyn's existence is a deadly threat to everyone on Gemocon and Commander Neenja KahSandra must find a way to save the woman she loves from having to commit the ultimate sacrifice. (978-1-63555-244-7)

A Wish Upon a Star by Jeannie Levig. Erica Cooper has learned to depend on only herself, but when her new neighbor, Leslie Raymond, befriends Erica's special needs daughter, the walls protecting her heart threaten to crumble. (978-1-63555-274-4)

Answering the Call by Ali Vali. Detective Sept Savoie returns to the streets of New Orleans, as do the dead bodies from ritualistic killings, and she does everything in her power to bring them to justice while trying to keep her partner, Keegan Blanchard, safe. (978-1-63555-050-4)

Breaking Down Her Walls by Erin Zak. Could a love worth staying for be the key to breaking down Julia Finch's walls? (978-1-63555-369-7)

Exit Plans for Teenage Freaks by 'Nathan Burgoine. Cole always has a plan—especially for escaping his small-town reputation as "that kid who was kidnapped when he was four"—but when he teleports to a museum, it's time to face facts: it's possible he's a total freak after all. (978-1-63555-098-6)

Friends Without Benefits by Dena Blake. When Dex Putman gets the woman she thought she always wanted, she soon wonders if it's really love after all. (978-1-63555-349-9)

Invalid Evidence by Stevie Mikayne. Private Investigator Jil Kidd is called away to investigate a possible killer whale, just when her partner Jess needs her most. (978-1-63555-307-9)

Pursuit of Happiness by Carsen Taite. When attorney Stevie Palmer's client reveals a scandal that could derail Senator Meredith Mitchell's presidential bid, their chance at love may be collateral damage. (978-1-63555-044-3)

Seascape by Karis Walsh. Marine biologist Tess Hansen returns to Washington's isolated northern coast where she struggles to adjust to small-town living while courting an endowment for her orca research center from Brittany James. (978-1-63555-079-5)

Second in Command by VK Powell. Jazz Perry's life is disrupted and her career jeopardized when she becomes personally involved with the case of an abandoned child and the child's competent but strict social worker, Emory Blake. (978-1-63555-185-3)

Taking Chances by Erin McKenzie. When Valerie Cruz and Paige Wellington clash over what's in the best interest of the children in Valerie's care, the children may be the ones who teach them it's worth taking chances for love. (978-1-63555-209-6)

All of Me by Emily Smith. When chief surgical resident Galen Burgess meets her new intern, Rowan Duncan, she may finally discover that doing what you've always done will only give you what you've always had. (978-1-63555-321-5)

As the Crow Flies by Karen F. Williams. Romance seems to be blooming all around, but problems arise when a restless ghost emerges from the ether to roam the dark corners of this haunting tale. (978-1-63555-285-0)

Both Ways by Ileandra Young. SPEAR agent Danika Karson races to protect the city from a supernatural threat and must rely on the woman she's trained to despise: Rayne, an achingly beautiful vampire. (978-1-63555-298-0)

Calendar Girl by Georgia Beers. Forced to work together, Addison Fairchild and Kate Cooper discover that opposites really do attract. (978-1-63555-333-8)

Lovebirds by Lisa Moreau. Two women from different worlds collide in a small California mountain town, each with a mission that doesn't include falling in love. (978-1-63555-213-3)

Media Darling by Fiona Riley. Can Hollywood bad girl Emerson and reluctant celebrity gossip reporter Hayley work together to make each other's dreams come true? Or will Emerson's secrets ruin not one career, but two? (978-1-63555-278-2)

Stroke of Fate by Renee Roman. Can Sean Moore live up to her reputation and save Jade Rivers from the stalker determined to end Jade's career and, ultimately, her life? (978-1-63555-62-4)

The Rise of the Resistance by Jackie D. The soul of America has been lost for almost a century. A few people may be the difference between a phoenix rising to save the masses or permanent destruction. (978-1-63555-259-1)

The Sex Therapist Next Door by Meghan O'Brien. At the intersection of sex and intimacy, anything is possible. Even love. (978-1-63555-296-6)

Unforgettable by Elle Spencer. When one night changes a lifetime... Two romance novellas from best-selling author Elle Spencer. (978-1-63555-429-8)

Against All Odds by Kris Bryant, Maggie Cummings, M. Ullrich. Peyton and Tory escaped death once, but will they survive when Bradley's determined to make his kill rate one hundred percent? (978-1-63555-193-8)

Autumn's Light by Aurora Rey. Casual hookups aren't supposed to include romantic dinners and meeting the family. Can Mat Pero see beyond the heartbreak that led her to keep her worlds so separate, and will Graham Connor be waiting if she does? (978-1-63555-272-0)

Breaking the Rules by Larkin Rose. When Virginia and Carmen are thrown together by an embarrassing mistake they find out their stubborn determination isn't so heroic after all. (978-1-63555-261-4)

Broad Awakening by Mickey Brent. In the sequel to *Underwater Vibes*, Hélène and Sylvie find ruts in their road to eternal bliss. (978-1-63555-270-6)

Broken Vows by MJ Williamz. Sister Mary Margaret must reconcile her divided heart or risk losing a love that just might be heaven sent. (978-1-63555-022-1)

Flesh and Gold by Ann Aptaker. Havana, 1952, where art thief and smuggler Cantor Gold dodges gangland bullets and mobsters' schemes while she searches Havana's steamy Red Light district for her kidnapped love. (978-1-63555-153-2)

Isle of Broken Years by Jane Fletcher. Spanish noblewoman Catalina de Valasco is in peril, even before the pirates holding her for ransom sail into seas destined to become known as the Bermuda Triangle. (978-1-63555-175-4)

Love Like This by Melissa Brayden. Hadley Cooper and Spencer Adair set out to take the fashion world by storm. If only they knew their hearts were about to be taken. (978-1-63555-018-4)

Secrets On the Clock by Nicole Disney. Jenna and Danielle love their jobs helping endangered children, but that might not be enough to stop them from breaking the rules by falling in love. (978-1-63555-292-8)

Unexpected Partners by Michelle Larkin. Dr. Chloe Maddox tries desperately to deny her attraction for Detective Dana Blake as they flee from a serial killer who's hunting them both. (978-1-63555-203-4)